15 Minutes of Flame

A Nantucket Candle Maker Mystery

Christin Brecher

KENSINGTON BOOKS

www.kensingtonbooks.com

KENSINGTON BOOKS are published by

Kensington Publishing Corp.
119 West 40th Street
New York, NY 10018

All Kensington titles, imprints, and distributed lines are available at special quantity discounts for bulk purchases for sales promotion, premiums, fund-raising, educational, or institutional use.

Special book excerpts or customized printings can also be created to fit specific needs. For details, write or phone the office of the Kensington Sales Manager: Attn.: Sales Department. Kensington Publishing Corp., 119 West 40th Street, New York, NY 10018. Phone: 1-800-221-2647.

Kensington and the K logo Reg. U.S. Pat. & TM Off.

First Printing: September 2020
ISBN-13: 978-1-4967-2143-3
ISBN-10: 1-4967-2143-8

ISBN-13: 978-1-4967-2144-0 (ebook)
ISBN-10: 1-4967-2144-6 (ebook)

10 9 8 7 6 5 4 3 2 1

Printed in the United States of America

To Bandit and his best friend, Steve

Chapter 1

Saturday morning, I was lounging in my backyard and enjoying a little sun. My chaise for such luxury was a fold-out chair, the kind with plastic straps across a metal frame where one or two bands always seem to be missing in crucial places. Even though my rear end sank a little lower to the ground than I'd prefer, I was deeply engaged with the clouds rolling above me on this late October day. Thick, fluffy, bright white, and moving fast along an otherwise clear blue sky. As one remarkably beautiful apparition whisked by me, I remembered a game I used to play as a kid. My friends and I would study a cloud, and then we'd compare the images we saw. Mickey Mouse, a choo-choo train, a duck. It was amazing how often we saw different pictures in the same floating cloud.

You'd think I'd have learned from our game that there are a thousand ways to see the world, but it took me until I was almost thirty years old to really grasp the concept. Less than six months ago, I was grappling with the fact that my small candle business, the Wick & Flame, would not make it through another year on Nantucket Island. My dream of making candles and selling them in a store I owned, in my hometown, with the good fortune of being with family and friends, could have vanished like the flicker of a flame when it's snuffed out. But then solving a murder, of all things, helped me see the world differently. Puzzling out a crime and restoring justice was as fascinating to me as studying the ways a wick might last longer or a flame might burn brighter. I'd jumped in to help before I'd even thought about it, and never looked back. After I solved the case, my business grew like a wildfire, and, most surprisingly, I fell in love with Peter Bailey, the town's newest reporter for the local *Inquirer & Mirror*.

To my surprise, it was my fate to find murder one more time, less than two weeks ago. Unlike my first foray into the world of crime, no one knew I was even on a murder case except for my mom, who'd been home for a short while. Andy Southerland, the town's best police officer and one of my oldest friends, caught on too. It's a good story—spies and national security abound—but that's a whole other kettle of clues.

This morning, my thoughts drifted to something much lighter: Halloween, which was only six days away. This year, I'd volunteered to assist the Girl Scouts' Halloween Haunts fund-raiser for the island's neediest. I'd helped them over the last week build papier-mâché cauldrons, bats, and spider décor. We'd carved pumpkins. We'd planned activities for all ages, ranging from crafts and apple bobbing to a scary, ghostly maze. Today my sales assistant, Cherry, was covering for me at the Wick & Flame, and I planned to use my free time to drop by the girls' weekend meeting.

I raised one leg in the air and pulled it toward my forehead as a cloud that looked like a gun—I'm not kidding—rolled by. For one moment, I had the witchy feeling that I was too complacent. As its shadow passed, I caught my breath, wondering if the peaceful afternoon, the healthy stock in my store, and the warmth of my relationship with Peter was no more than the calm before another storm. I shook it off. The flip side of having solved two murders is the danger of getting a little paranoid.

Also, I was in close proximity to two boys, all of eight and ten years old. They were the sons of my cousin Chris, with whom I was sharing my patch of lawn. My home is the apartment over Chris's garage. My bucket list includes owning my own place one day, something with room for a studio and a garden out back, but for now, the company of Chris and his family is wonderful, and the modest rent is ideal for my entrepreneurial ambitions. The boys had inched closer and closer to my personal space over the last half hour, however, so I chalked up my unease to their questionable skill set when it comes to a ball and mitt.

Chris appeared at his kitchen window as their last pitch zoomed over my chair.

"Dudes! Don't bug Stella," he said.

"Hi!" I waved to him as the boys retrieved their ball and continued their game.

"Do you want some oatmeal? I'm on breakfast duty," Chris called out to me.

"That's very tempting, but I can't," I answered. "I'm heading over to the Morton house in about ten minutes."

The Morton house was home to Halloween Haunts. It was owned by John Pierre Morton, whom I'd met during my last case, when he'd come to our island to check out his inheritance of the musty, forgotten home. Although I'd briefly considered John Pierre a murder suspect, we'd left on good terms when he returned to Canada.

There's something about the house that has a spell on me. It is inviting in spite of, or perhaps because of, its walls' crooked lines. The Girl Scouts' troop leader, Shelly, had the same reaction while shopping at my store one day when she heard me talking to Cherry about the creaky old place. On the spot, Shelly decided it would be the perfect location for her troop's event. At her request, I gave John Pierre a call, and he graciously agreed to allow the scouts to use his house.

"That place is haunted," said Chris's youngest, rubbing his ball into his mitt.

I smiled, knowing the source of his fears. In an effort to drum up business, the troop had circulated a few rumors that the house was actually haunted. Given Nantucket's foggy nights and seafaring past, filled with shipwrecks and whales' tales, the town has no shortage of ghost stories. It wasn't hard for the girls' propaganda to take off.

"Things aren't haunted in real life," I said.

"Yes, they are," he said, pulling his arm back for a throw.

"Mwah-ha-ha," I said with my campiest vampire-slash-ghost voice, my arms held high in zombie fashion to play along.

"Boys!" said Chris.

It was then that I realized how sharp a parents' instincts can be. My arms still raised, I looked up to a new vision of white streaking across the sky. Not a cloud. Nay, it was the white leather of a baseball that flew from the hand of Chris's youngest with the greatest speed and farthest distance of the day. Right toward the closed kitchen window of my apartment. Unable to interrupt its trajectory, the four of us watched, our jaws hanging, as the ball hurtled toward my window and crashed unapologetically through the glass.

The boys took a step back, and then froze, torn between the primordial instincts of fight or flight.

I managed to stifle an "Oh, no!" in spite of my shock. The boys would have enough to answer for without me. The window's glass hadn't even hit the ground before Chris's back door shot open.

"What the—?" he said, storming across the law. "Get inside!"

"It wasn't my fault," each boy said in his own fashion as they both scrambled, defiantly but obediently, toward the main house.

"Sorry, Stella," said Chris, not pausing to stop.

I grasped at the unbroken chair straps beneath me and hopped up as Chris opened my unlocked door and stormed up the stairs to my apartment. Following him, I saw my cat, Tinker, who was on the top step. His whiskers peeked over his paws in a way that suggested a combination of empathy for and disappointment in his humans. Indeed, there were glass shards on my countertop and in the sink. The window would need to be replaced.

Chris, a contractor, immediately dialed his window-repair guy on the Cape, so I grabbed a broom and got to work. I looked at the window as I heard him complain to his colleague about how long the delivery might take. I knew he was concerned about being a good landlord, but I figured with a trash bag and some heavy tape from under my kitchen sink, I could probably cover the hole well enough until a new window arrived.

"I got this," Chris said to me, his hand over the receiver. "Really. Scoot."

Chris went right back to his phone call without waiting for me to answer. Realizing my garbage-bag proposal might only serve to add to his frustration with the boys' shenanigans, I tactfully traded my broom for my keys and wallet. I silently waved to Chris. He responded with a shooing motion toward my stairs, so I headed down with Tinker behind me. My pet refuses to limit his role to house cat. Sometimes I think he sees himself as another human, or maybe a faithful dog. I didn't mind. Aside from saving me the worry of having one of his paws land on a shard of glass in my absence, I knew the girls would get a kick out of seeing him.

The two of us jumped in my red Beetle and headed to the Morton house. Having left the chaos of the boys' game of catch, I was delighted when Tinker and I stepped out of the car to hear a happy chorus of voices coming from inside.

As I was heading up the stairs to the front door,

ready to give Shelly a break, I was surprised to hear another sound. It was of a heavy creak from behind the house, followed by a shriek that sang of pure mischief. Fool me once, as they say. My radar for middle-school high jinx was on red alert, thanks to my own family. I headed around the back to investigate.

The backyard was empty, but I wasn't ready to concede that I was alone. I headed across the half acre of dead grass which was shrouded in fallen leaves, toward a dilapidated stone structure behind the main house that had once been a smokehouse. The girls affectionately called it The Shack. Homes built in the early nineteenth century sometimes had additional buildings behind them that served as workshops. By now, most of these structures have been razed for garages or more yard space, but the Morton house still had one. It was so run-down, however, that no one particularly relished it as history.

The scouts were strictly forbidden to enter The Shack, partly because a chain, which usually secured the front door, screamed tetanus shot. From the squeal I'd heard and the now-opened door, however, I concluded that some of our scouts had decided to break a few rules today. I didn't blame them. I'd have likely done the same at their age. The question, now, was whether they'd scrambled back into the house or were still exploring. When I reached the front door of The Shack, I heard nothing from within, but I lifted Tinker into my arms.

"Ready?" I said into his soft, pink ear.

With a Cheshire smile, Tinker answered me by jumping from my arms into the small building with one big yowl, which can be deafening when he's in the mood. His cry, however, was followed by a disappointed sniff. I gathered that his performance had been for nothing. The girls had not waited around to see what was inside.

I, however, decided to finish what they'd started. I was more than a little intrigued as I slipped around the thick, rotting door, standing ajar, and into the one-room building. After I brushed aside some cobwebs, I found myself in a space that smelled of dried dirt and a few autumn leaves. Although the main house was old and musty due to years of neglect by its last owner, it was thoroughly modernized compared to The Shack. Some daylight crept through the door, but the only other source of light was a small window, across which several weeds had taken root. The floor was made of wide wooden planks, which were warped from damp and neglect. The walls were exposed stones, round and about the size of the cobblestones on Main Street. It was a pleasant day outside, but the room was noticeably cold.

As I took a step forward, my phone rang, and my boyfriend's name scrolled across my screen. My ring tone is an old-fashioned one, but it sounded loud and alien in those hollow surroundings.

"Hello, handsome," I said.

"Hello, beautiful," said Peter. "Are you interested in joining me at Crab City later? Low tide is in two hours."

Peter was working on a story that had lately consumed him about the island's hermit crabs. He was having the time of his life studying the thousands of crabs that emerge at low tide off the shore of the Nantucket Field Station, which is managed by the

University of Massachusetts's environmental studies department. I'd been competing with the crabs for his time lately, but I was glad that he had taken such an interest in the ocean life that surrounded us. I was still figuring out how I might share his latest passion. Fortunately, I'd come up with an idea this morning.

"Sure," I said. "I've been wondering if it's possible to develop a marine-life scent that's appealing for a summer candle."

"Sounds like an impossible challenge, but I'm sure you will figure it out if anyone can," he said.

"I'm at the Morton house," I said, appreciating the compliment. "I can meet you when I'm done."

"I'm happy to carve pumpkins or whatever you need until low tide," he said.

"Your skills with a staple gun and your eye for boyishly creepy things might be of use," I said.

"You had me at staple gun," he said. "See you."

I smiled, and figured I had about twenty minutes before he arrived, so I walked toward the most notable feature of The Shack, a hearth at the back of the dimly lit room. I passed a few odds and ends from the last owner. A rusty bike wheel. A spade. A roll of chicken-coop wire. Tinker sprang to my shoulder as a field mouse scrambled along the base of one of the walls.

"You're a cat," I said, in case he'd forgotten. "You're supposed to chase mice."

He put a paw on my forehead for balance, however, and did not budge.

Like many old fireplaces, the one I approached was huge, at least seven feet wide and maybe three feet tall, with a cooking hook on the left and space to

build a large fire. In their day, these household features had served as heaters, lights, stoves, dryers, and
more. The mantel of the hearth was made of the
same stones as the walls, and cantilevered over the
firepit for protection.

As my eyes adjusted, I noticed a sign hanging
above the hearth. It was the length of the mantel and
about two feet high. Holding up my phone for extra
light, I made out the words: COOPER'S CANDLES. The
letters were painted in pale blue, were faded and
cracked in some places, but were still clear.

"No way," I said, as much to myself as to Tinker,
who whisked his tail and jumped to the ground to investigate.

I realized, with much delight, that I was in a chandlery. The Shack was, in fact, Cooper's Candles. I
couldn't believe I had accepted Shelly's explanation
that the building had been used for smoking meats
when, in fact, the fireproof stone structure with its
large chimney was once a place where candles had
been made, stored, and, it seemed, sold. The discovery caught me completely by surprise, although the
business of Cooper's Candles would not have been
an unusual one for Nantucket during the period the
Morton house had been built. Around that time,
about a third of the island's economy came from candle making. Nantucket's candles were known to have
the brightest and whitest light due to the islanders'
access to spermaceti oil from sperm whales.

I couldn't help it, but I envisioned a young me, sitting by the flames in this room, melting wax and
pouring candles that the neighbors might buy. I
touched the name on the sign and wondered who

Cooper had been. It was likely a family surname, as was the custom back then. My sign over the Wick & Flame is a shiny black quarter board, framed in silver with expertly carved, silver block letters announcing the name. Cooper's sign was homier. I imagined its architect with a brush in one hand and a paint can in the other.

I took a poorly lit photo and sent it to John Pierre Morton in Canada. A moment later, he responded with words to brighten a candle maker's day.

Amazing! He wrote. *Take it for your apartment. It was meant for you.*

I'd lost a window but gained a treasure. I sent back a thank-you, and a heart.

Then I got to work.

First, I tugged at the oversized board, gently, so as not to break it. The wood was thick and still strong in spite of years of neglect and the island's sea air. When I realized it wouldn't budge, I searched the items strewn about the floor and picked up the spade. Carefully, I used it as a lever to pry the wood ever so slowly from the wall. Before I knew it, I was building up a sweat, but I didn't mind. At one point, my phone pinged. I knew it was probably Shelly, wondering where I was, but I'll admit I couldn't stop. Although we'd steered clear of The Shack, I was seduced by it now that I was inside. I felt like I had crossed from one world and back into another.

Finally, the wood came free. I slowly lowered it to the floor. I'm respectably strong, but the sign was long and wobbled in my arms like a seesaw. Once I'd laid it on the ground, I needed to stand up to make sure my limbs were still intact. It was a good thing I did because a stone fell from the newly exposed wall, missing my head by a couple of inches. Another followed. Then another. I looked above the mantel and caught another. They loosened like dominos. I removed a couple more before they could fly into the room on their own.

"Psssssst," said Tinker, coming to my heels.

I pulled three or four more stones from the wall. As I did, I was sure I felt the room became icy cold. Then, behind us, I heard the door move, and with it, a ray of light crossed the floor.

"Stella?" said Peter, peeking through the door frame, first at me and then at the mantel behind me. He straightened at the sight. "Wow. I thought the decorations would be spooky in the house, but that's overkill. Get it?"

"It's not a decoration," I said, staring back at the hole in the wall. "John Pierre said I could have a candle sign I found. When I took it down, this is what I found."

The two of us faced the mantel, and the human skeleton I'd uncovered, nestled into a carved-out space in the wall.

Chapter 2

"Is that a real skeleton?" said Peter.

"Looks like it," I said, staring at a skull that seemed to look right back at me.

Peter switched on his phone's flashlight and joined me. I wouldn't say I was afraid of my discovery, but it's not every day you plan to carve a pumpkin and end up finding a skeleton. It was nice to have his warm body beside me at that moment.

"Are you sure the scouts didn't pull a prank on you?" he said, lowering the phone under his chin for a spooky effect.

"Not a chance," I said. "This is the real deal."

I explained how I'd found the body behind the mantel's large stones, which had been covered by the heavy, wooden sign.

We both shuddered.

"I wonder how long it's been here," he said.

I'd been wondering the same thing. I closed my eyes and inhaled deeply, deconstructing the odors in the room as I did so. I smelled the autumn leaves, the dirt, the rusted wheel, gate, and spade. I also picked up the scent of turkey and swiss, with a dash of mustard, that wafted from Peter's knapsack, and a little of his Old Spice. I did not, however, smell any rotting flesh. Granted, my experience with the smell of body decomposition was limited to a squirrel that had died in my wall last year, but that odor was filed away in my highly sensitive olfactory files, honed after years of mixing and matching candle scents for customers.

"I think this guy's been here a long while," I said, opening my eyes.

"I can't believe you found a skeleton," he said, absently touching a pencil he keeps behind his ear, ready for any story. "You're like a tomb raider."

I had to agree I'd stumbled on an unbelievable find. I picked up my phone, which I'd left lying on the floor, and turned its flashlight toward my skeleton. Moving another stone aside with my free hand, I realized the body was clothed.

My beam of light joined Peter's on a pair of boots with two bones extending from them. They were black leather, with decent soles and tightly bound laces, still tied into a bow. The shoes were sturdy, but the stitching looked as if it had been made by hand and not by a machine.

"They're so tiny," Peter said.

Tracing the light up the body, we realized that the skeleton was enrobed in a dress and matching bonnet, both in a somber gray and black.

This was no guy.

"She looks like a Quaker," I said. "When I worked at the Whaling Museum in high school, I sometimes gave tours of the decorative arts rooms. I remember this kind of attire was from around the early to mid-eighteen hundreds."

"I didn't know you were a museum docent," said Peter with a smile. Even in front of a dead body, I was suddenly very aware of his dirty-blond hair, which always flops over his left eye when he's excited, and the blue plaid shirt he was wearing today. I love that one. It brightens his baby blues to an irresistible shade.

"The teen docent program didn't last long," I said. "Some of us had too much fun making up stories."

"Too bad you didn't have this one to tell." Peter's light hovered over the woman's bodice and stopped at the hands, which were folded over what had probably once been her heart.

"Check out her shirt," said Peter. He pointed to a pattern on the woman's blouse.

I peered more closely. I'd never been up close to a skeleton, and I felt like I was intruding and also like she might reach out and grab me at the same time.

"That's not a design," I said. "It's a bloodstain."

"Maybe she died in an accident," he said.

"And they buried her in the same bloody clothes? Above the mantel?"

I couldn't believe that the cantilevered mantel had been chosen as a grave, but someone had gone to great lengths to remove pieces of the hearth's thick wall to bury the blood-soaked woman there. I looked around the room in search of the stones that had originally been removed to make space for the small corpse. There was no sign of them. All I saw were the ones that had fallen when I'd moved the sign and those I'd cleared away. Given the condition of the corpse and the way the grave had been boarded up, it was clear to me that the woman had been hidden there.

There was only one conclusion to make.

"I think she was murdered," I said.

"This is definitely an eerie set up, but murder?" said Peter. He pulled a small notepad from the pocket of his pants. "Either way, your find is a great local interest story, especially leading up to Halloween."

I ignored the doubt in his voice about my murder theory. I had no misgiving that the woman I was looking at had been murdered, and not because I had some experience in the matter. I didn't have evidence, but I had common sense. For one, although I knew it was a custom for Quakers to be buried in unmarked tombs, I'd never heard of home burials like this one. Otherwise, dozens of historic houses on the island would have produced a cemetery's worth of remains over the decades.

Also, I had been the one to discover the body. I had seen the building's stones fall from the wall. They hadn't been carefully sealed into place, as one would have done in a thoughtful, premeditated burial. Instead, they had practically sprung from the wall after years of compression behind the large and heavy sign that had covered the body.

It felt as if we were far from civilization, but outside The Shack, I heard the back door to the Morton house open, along with the sound of young girls. I wasn't exactly standing in a crime scene, given that the murder had probably been committed over a hundred years ago, but I knew enough to keep the girls at bay. I wasn't sure whom to call about a century-old skeleton, so I hit Officer Andy Southerland's number on speed dial before I was halfway out the door, waving my hands like an air-traffic controller to stop the girls from approaching.

Shelly came up behind them and gave me a look that said, *Where have you been?* and *What's inside that I don't want to know about?* (aka, better you than me), and *I was hoping to let the girls run around back here for a few minutes.* Three emotions rolled into one piercing stare, which ended with a mutual nod of sympathy from each of us.

As the girls headed back into the house, equally disappointed that their free play had been canceled, Tinker joined them. His ears twitched with excitement at the prospect of a dozen scouts lavishing affection on him. I hoped he could provide enough entertainment so that Shelly could have her break. While I explained to Andy our need for his services, I heard the girls already making up stories about what was inside The Shack. In this instance, I suspected that even their wildest imaginings would not match my find.

After the back door shut behind them, the reality of my discovery hit me. Outside, the sun was still shining, the clouds were still rolling, but in the building behind me lay the bones of mystery. An irresistible puzzle. I wanted to know who the woman buried behind the Cooper's Candles sign had been. I also wanted to know who had killed her and why. The combination of the dead woman's carefully crossed arms over her bloodstained shirt in an old candle shop made me curious. What had happened?

There was no electricity in the building, but I wanted a better view of everything inside. Fortunately, I'm the kind of person who always has at least one box of candles stashed in the back of her car, which I now retrieved. While Peter phoned the *Inky Mirror*, the islanders' nickname for the newspaper, to tell them he had a breaking story, I went back into the old chandlery and placed my candles around the perimeter of the room. When Peter finished his call, I handed him a pack of matches, and we lit the wicks.

"I can't decide if this is romantic or the beginning of a horror movie," he said when we'd finished and found ourselves surrounded by candlelight in the small, historic room.

"It's authentic," I said.

No disrespect to the dead, but I would have done anything to set up a Wick & Flame holiday-themed pop-up shop right there. I felt like my candles had brought Cooper's Candles back to life.

"I wonder if the murder weapon is still here," I said.

"Assuming she was murdered," said Peter. "My editor is excited about the discovery, either way, so thank you for handing me an exclusive. I'll be cooking up my cheese spaghetti to celebrate. I'm sending in a story on my way to Crab City. Can I get a quote from you?"

"Here's my quote: I'm sure there's more to this story. Aren't you?"

"Maybe," Peter said, "but I like to print facts, not speculation."

"Ok," I said.

I knew a weapon could have been tossed into the

ocean over a hundred years ago, but it was worth a look around. I started with the item I knew best, the sign.

"Hold this, please," I said to Peter, handing him my phone and kneeling on the ground before the sign.

There were no traces of blood on the front or back of the heavy wood plank, so I studied the nails that had secured the sign to the wall. There were eight of them, and none of the nail heads were the same size, nor were the shafts of equal length. I lifted one that had fallen free, and I could feel the iron pin's irregularities. I decided they were handmade. Old. That meant that the woman had been there a long time too. Based on the absence of dried blood, I decided that the sign had not been used as a murder weapon. Its function was to seal the tomb with the aid of a few hammered nails.

My eyes wandered up to the oversized hearth. I wondered if the murderer had hidden incriminating evidence there.

"Excuse me," I said to Peter. I slid around him, still on my hands and knees, and began to explore the stones inside the hearth, which were thankfully free of mice. Before I knew it, my head and shoulders were entombed in the lowest part of the wide-based chimney. I was impressed with how well the structure had stood the test of time. A few of the stones were wobbly, but they were all still in place.

"Who was the guy who owned the house? I wonder if he buried the woman here," said Peter as I felt around the dark, enclosed space.

"John Pierre's great uncle, Fritz Hepenheimer," I

said to him as I continued to feel around. "He was a captain for the US Coast Guard. He died two years ago at one hundred years old."

I wiped my hand on my leggings as my hand had touched something slimy and entirely gross.

"John Pierre told me that Uncle Fritz served in the nineteen forties at the island's Coast Guard base. He bought the house in hopes of marrying a Nantucket girl, but she turned him down, so he hightailed it off the island and rarely returned."

"Maybe she didn't turn him down," said Peter. "Maybe they married, and she died, and he had some fetish about Quaker garb, and he buried her here."

"Nope," I said. "You have a twisted imagination, but legend has it that he left after she dumped him. Between the Quaker dress on our skeleton and the period nails from the sign, I think it's safe to assume that John Pierre's uncle wasn't a murderer. One suspect down, who knows how many more to go."

At that moment, I heard the front door budge against the warped floor. I looked down from my post in the chimney and saw Andy's black, police-issue shoes arrive at the edge of the hearth and face mine.

"So you found a human skeleton," said Andy.

"Yup," said Peter.

"I found her," I said, ducking out of the chimney and into the room. "She was hidden behind this sign."

Andy gave me a smile, one of the warm "hey how're ya doing?" smiles he's known for, but he also folded his arms and studied my excavation. I was about to return his greeting, but he held up his hand.

"I hate to break it to you, but according to sections five and six of Title Six, chapter thirty-eight of the Massachusetts General Laws, the medical examiner or, subsequently, an archaeologist if the body is more than one hundred years old, are the only individuals who can be touching the body right now," he said.

As he spoke, he led us outside of The Shack before we quite realized what he was doing. I turned to reenter the building, but Andy stood between me and the door, his solid frame blocking my path.

"Slow down, Stella," he said to me. "You will be happy to know that I called the medical examiner on my way here. He was leaving for his Saturday round of golf, but he's on his way. Meanwhile, I have a job for you."

Good thinking on his part. He had to follow protocol, but since I'd found the body, I wasn't going anywhere, and he knew it.

"Bring it on," I said, folding my arms in the same way he had only moments ago.

Peter nodded supportively, but Andy laughed as if he still couldn't believe I had a newfound interest in tackling a good mystery. It really is sort of crazy that we've known each other all our lives but had only recently realized we shared a similar tenacity when faced with solving a good puzzle.

"You're friends with the guy who owns the house, right?" said Andy.

I nodded.

"Can you call him?" he said.

"I can," I said, dialing John Pierre, but sure we could come up with something more for me to do.

"Find any more candle artifacts?" John Pierre said to me after a couple of rings. I heard the sound of a bird in the background, on his end of the line. John Pierre owns a Christmas tree farm, so I imagined he was reviewing the stock for his upcoming season.

I put him on speaker, thanked him again for the sign, and let Andy give him the details of my discovery while I watched the ME arrive with a bag of tools and gadgets I'd have loved to explore.

"This is an incredible find," said John Pierre when Andy finished.

"We'll have to figure out what to do with her, but I can keep you updated on our options by phone," said Andy

"Was there ever any sort of legend in your family, or clue that there might be a body on the premises?" I said to John Pierre after Andy handed me the phone.

The tiniest little shift in Andy's jaw let me know that he was trying to decide a few things: how the case would need to be handled, how interested I was going to be in the case, and which of those two issues would be harder to manage.

"I never heard about a body," said John Pierre. "But my great uncle kept to himself."

"When you were visiting the island, did you spend time at the house?" said Andy.

I was happy to see that although he was following protocol, his natural curiosity was as high as mine.

"I didn't spend much time out back," said John

Pierre. "I meant to peek in The Shack, but it wasn't high on my list."

"Southerland!" With that exclamation, the chief of police now made his appearance and crossed the yard.

"Sir," said Andy, his attention shifting to his boss.

"What do we have?" said the chief.

The chief directed his question to Andy, but the medical examiner must have heard him from inside the building because he emerged too. As he exited, he pushed a pair of goggles to his forehead and peeled off a pair of latex gloves.

"I've given the skeletal remains and clothing a preliminary look. Judging from the bone structure, it's a woman," said the ME. "From her attire and the level of decay, I'd say she's been deceased for over one hundred years. The body has suffered trauma. Cause of death could have been foul play, could have been an accident. This is more of an archaeological and historical site than a police matter. Maybe historians can ascertain more about her identity, or at least develop a composite description of who she might have been."

Behind me, I now heard cars pulling up to the Morton house. From the moment Andy had arrived, my discovery of the hidden world of Cooper's Candles had begun to feel like a three-ring circus. As the scouts began to open and close the car doors for their rides home, I picked up the chatter of parents calling out to each other from one vehicle to another. Their conversations focused on their concerns about what was happening in The Shack and were underscored by excited but also frightened chatter of the girls.

"Samantha is too afraid to come back," said a mom's voice.

"I think we should cancel," said a worried dad. "This isn't worth Cindy having nightmares."

"And who knows what sort of toxins they've just let loose?" said another voice. "I googled it. Decomposing bodies emit chemicals that are harmful to the girls' health. And there will be guests coming on Friday night too. We don't need a lawsuit."

"We'll see what we can do," I heard Shelly say.

"I think Jane will have to bow out moving forward," said a dad.

I waited for an argument from Jane, the most boisterous of the scouts. I'd be willing to bet she was one of the imps who'd thought to take a peek at The Shack. To my surprise, I heard no protest.

Andy had his list of concerns; I now had my own. The first was the medical examiner's suggestion that this was at most a project for historians. I had a vision of well-meaning professor types, taking their time to brush off dirt and catalog bones over months and months of tedious work, only to conclude what we already knew: that our skeleton had been a Quaker woman who had suffered trauma and had been mysteriously buried in an unmarked and unusual grave. The house would become a tourist attraction, and ridiculous stories would abound. I knew that even by the end of today, rumors and fantastically tall tales would begin to make the rounds. But I, for one, wanted the real scoop on what had happened in this small candle workshop.

I was also entirely disappointed that the Girl Scouts had fallen for their own propaganda about ghosts and goblins. I didn't mind a few scary stories floating around, but fear of a skeleton, an historic discovery no less, was unacceptable. We were not going to let a few old bones keep us from raising money for the island's neediest, and having a great event in the process. We needed a dose of girl power to show everyone that there was nothing to fear.

I was still holding up my phone, and John Pierre was still on the line.

"John Pierre? It's Stella," I said. "What would you think about letting me stay in the main house? I'd like to show the girls that there's nothing here to be afraid of."

Andy, ever on alert for my extracurricular interests, raised an eyebrow, but I was prepared for that.

"As it turns out, my kitchen window broke this morning, and I'd love a place to stay while it's being fixed."

It was Peter's turn to look surprised. And a little concerned.

"What happened to your window? Also, this place is really old and drafty," he said. "You should stay with me."

"I love the house," I said, truthfully. "When else will I be able to enjoy it? Tinker's already made himself at home inside."

We looked at the back window, where Tinker, in fact, could be seen happily curled in a ball and taking a nap on the sill. Peter shoved his hands into his pockets, knowing not to fight me.

"You know we'll lock up the door at night and

keep everyone—that means you—away from the skeleton until an archaeologist takes a look," said Andy.

I nodded, seriously. As if a lock would stop me.

"Sure, you can stay," said John Pierre. "It would give me some peace of mind, actually."

With that much decided, John Pierre and I worked out the details of my stay while the officers considered the next step of calling in an anthropologist.

"If you don't need us," Peter said to the group when I hung up, "we're heading out to Crab City for low tide."

Andy smiled with something of a victorious look.

"I'm working on a seaside scent," I said.

Did I sound defensive? Perhaps. Nonetheless, Peter and I left the action and walked to the sidewalk in front of the Morton house.

"You want to work on the skeleton, don't you?" Peter said when we reached my car door.

"Do you blame me?"

"Nope," he said with a kiss on my forehead for good measure.

"Say hi to the crabs for me?"

He pulled out his pad and untucked his pencil.

"Say-hi-to-crabs," he said, writing in his pad. Then he gave me a smile and headed to his car.

I followed behind Peter's car for a couple of streets, knowing exactly where to start. Nantucket is a small town with a big history. Fortunately, it's been well documented. The Research Library on Fair Street holds thousands of pictures, periodicals, and documents related to the island's history, many from the time that the Coopers had run their chandlery. If there was any information to be found about my skeleton, the library would have it.

I liked the plan, but it came with one immediate problem. Extended periods of time amid the quiet, peaceful air of a library have resulted time and again with me falling into a cozy nap, my head on a table or against a chair, until my arm drops or my foot falls asleep. It's a curse. In high school, Andy and my best friend, Emily Gardner, even drew a mustache on me once while I soundly slept. And I'd been working on college applications at the time. Skeleton or not, I knew myself, so when I reached the road to Main Street, I decided to make a pit stop at my favorite coffee place in town, The Bean.

Chapter 3

Parking in town, I walked down Centre Street and passed my store, the Wick & Flame. I waved through the window at my assistant, Cherry Waddle, who was covering for me this weekend. She waved back, busy with a customer, and I paused momentarily to study my window display, which was filled with orange and black candles I'd made every night over the last week. For fun, I'd come up with some unique scents for the holiday, like Eyeball of Newt and Spider Soup for those who were really into the spirit of the season. As you might imagine, Halloween is one of the highlights of the year at the Wick & Flame. I light many candles to turn up the spooky vibe, albeit one that includes jack-o'-lantern candles scented with pumpkin spice and glow-in-the-dark ghost candles. This year, I'd added the Tinker Special to my product line. It was a black cat, inspired by my feline friend, Tinker, wearing a jaunty orange witch's hat from which the wick extends.

It's hard to pass my store without stopping in, but I had no idea how things would unfold back at the Morton House, so I forged ahead to my caffeine fix and trip to the library. When I rounded the corner and reached the entrance to The Bean, I stood aside as a woman exited the cafe.

"Hello!" I said, realizing I'd come face-to-face with Brenda Worthington.

Over the last decade, Brenda has become a sort of fixture on the island. She runs Nantucket Legends and Lore, one of the best ghost tours in town, and we have a lot of ghost tours. Brenda's tours are unique for two reasons. The first is that she is a walking encyclopedia about the island's history. Not textbook stories, but legends handed down from generation to generation. My family, the Wrights, can be found in every nook and cranny on the island, and it was a proud day for us when Brenda added the tale of how my great-grandma once chained herself to a flagpole on Centre Street, in front of where my store is now, to advocate for women's right to vote.

The second of Brenda's specialties is her claim that she can speak with the dead. As a result, Brenda was not the kind of person that the police or historians would solicit for help. I, however, wondered if she might have an angle on my discovery that others would not. It was worth a shot.

"Greetings, friend," she said.

There's something about Brenda that feels otherworldly. For example, although she was wearing sweats and a windbreaker, today her prematurely graying hair was in an old-fashioned bun, and she was carrying a basket of produce from a local farm's truck stand in town. The basket looked like something my Quaker skeleton would have owned.

"I have news for you," I said. "I think you'll soon have a new addition to your ghost tour."

"Not a ghost tour," said Brenda with an ethereal wave of her hand. "A history tour that includes visits to the ghosts of Nantucket's past."

"My mistake," I said, fearing she'd try to explain the theoretical difference between the two. Emily, who is an event planner, had made the error once when planning a party, and had been an hour late for a movie night we'd planned, so I kept talking. "You know the house that the Girl Scouts are using for Halloween Haunts?"

"A wonderful house, although a little worse for wear," she said. "You know, the building out back used to be an old smokehouse."

I smiled and realized who Shelly's source was. I also made a note that all of Brenda's facts weren't necessarily true. I understood why the experts didn't pay her much attention.

"I found a skeleton buried above the mantel," I said.

For a moment, I thought that Brenda might drop her basket. She looked like a Girl Scout who had sold her five-hundredth box of cookies and won the big prize.

"The police are there now, but I'm staying at the main house," I said. "Feel free to stop by tomorrow."

"I will," said Brenda, her hazel eyes dancing with excitement.

"By the way," I said, "have you ever heard of a candle maker named Cooper from the eighteen hundreds?"

"No," she said, "but there were many candle makers back then. They were as common on Nantucket then as tourists are now."

"Have you ever heard of Quakers burying the dead at home?" I asked, trying another angle.

"Oh, no," she said. "This is very mysterious. I'd like to see if the woman's aura is still in the room."

"It's worth a shot," I said, hoping I hadn't made a mistake by reaching out to her.

"Did you say Cooper?" Brenda asked, furrowing her brow.

I nodded.

"Does the name ring a bell?" I said.

She shook her head, but I had a feeling she was searching through her encyclopedic mind.

"I spoke to the ghost of Mary Coffin the other day," she said instead.

"Get out," I said.

Brenda's eyes widened.

"OK," she said, and headed down the street.

"I didn't mean 'leave,' " I said, calling after her. "It's an expression."

But Brenda continued along her way. I let another patron pass me out of The Bean and entered to the rich aroma of their brews.

My coffee stop was uneventful after that. My favorite barista, Clemmie, gave me a sympathetic smile after seeing Brenda bolt from me down the street. I downed a shot of espresso and continued on to the library. When I pulled up to the building, it looked empty, but I got out to make sure. The library is fittingly an extension behind the old Quaker Meeting House. The front door was closed, but I knocked and tried to listen for noise inside. When none was forthcoming, I knocked again. I was about to leave when the door opened.

"I heard the wind is going to pick up this afternoon, so I closed the door," said a friendly, familiar face.

"I didn't know you worked here," I said to Agnes Hussey, whose laugh lines framed her fading hazel eyes and whose gray hair looked something like a halo. Agnes is a sometimes member of my candle-making classes. She is a gem. She had joined my current workshop, and had arrived for the first class with delicious, freshly baked scones.

"I volunteer here," she said, welcoming me inside. "Since my family and I have been on Nantucket for as long as I can remember, I decided to do my part. I'm helping an historian today. Jameson Bellows. He's been working at the Historical Association for the last six months, preparing for an exhibit at the Whaling Museum. I hear they're planning to hire him full-time if all goes well. He's certainly hungry for the job. I can't remember the last time we opened up on a Saturday for someone."

"Well, I'm in luck because of it," I said. "I'm here to research a few old stories, but I don't know where to start."

"Then you need to come upstairs," said Agnes, leading the way inside.

I followed her up a flight of stairs and to a light-filled reading room on the second floor, which was empty aside from one gentleman who had his head buried in a large tome with yellowed pages. The aroma of old books wafted through my delighted nose; it's a scent that is hard to describe but is familiar to everyone who loves books.

"Here you go," Agnes said, motioning to a computer terminal. "This will connect you to our research database. If you find a manuscript or a photo or a map you like, I can pull it out for you to peruse further."

"Perfect," I said, taking a seat.

When Agnes left me, the man across the room looked up as if noticing me for the first time. He wore a corduroy jacket whose elbow patches seemed to have been added for necessity rather than style. His forehead was a little shiny, and his hair was a bit matted. I surmised that the fashion statement of his jacket was important to him since he wore it in spite of his growing perspiration.

I smiled. He nodded and went back to his tome, so I typed in the first word that came to mind in the search box on my screen.

MURDER

I was surprised to find twenty-five hits, most of which were dated from the nineteenth century. I clicked on each return, and realized that much of the information came from private journals. These dozens of journals—all owned by different individuals—included pasted-in newspaper clippings, handwritten notes about local news and family issues, accounting lists, and some drawings, doodles, and creative writings.

I felt I'd come to the right place when the name Cooper jumped out halfway down my search results with a listing from a diary from the 1860s. I clicked on the header, but when the summary of information found in the diary popped onto my screen, I knew I'd have more work ahead of me. The entry mentioned the confession of one Phoebe Cooper about the murder of one Phoebe Fuller. Unfortunately, there was no missing body in Phoebe's confession. Also, Miss Cooper was described as a servant. It was therefore unlikely that she was a member of the Cooper family that had lived in my friend Jean Pierre's good-sized house and had owned Cooper's Candles. I was disappointed, but honestly not surprised I hadn't found a good lead right away.

I continued to scroll down the page.

In his letter book, William Coffin, a well-known Nantucketer, noted the murder of Barnard Grayham by Jaiz Cushman. Two men. Not my story.

Eduard Stackpole mentioned "the trial of two Indians held for murder" in the 1730s, which was too early to be connected to my skeleton if I was to believe the medical examiner, which I did.

There were also notes about murders on board ships from the right time period that were interesting, but not helpful.

Putting aside the hope that I'd find a story about the Cooper murder I was seeking, I typed my next query:

COOPER'S CANDLES

The return was disappointing: NO RECORDS FOUND BY LATEST QUERY.

I typed in HOME BURIAL.

NO RECORDS FOUND BY LATEST QUERY.

I typed in MISSING WOMAN.

This time, I was happy when NO RECORDS FOUND BY LATEST QUERY popped onto my screen again. If I wasn't going to learn more about my skeleton with this search, I didn't want to find anything.

After a few other dead ends, I typed in COOPER, on its own, to see if anything other than the Phoebe Fuller murder might come up.

Sometimes the simplest route is the best. I was in luck. Two pages of listings hit my screen. The Cooper murder I'd already read about was featured, but to my surprise, another story was listed that had nothing to do with murder. Instead, the listing referenced COOPER THIEVES.

Thieves and murder felt like a potential marriage, so I scanned these listings. The database information was limited, but one entry jumped out at me from the diary of one Mary Backus: COOPER THIEVES ROBBERY OF PETTICOAT ROW FUNDS.

At the mention of Petticoat Row, I froze. I already felt a personal connection to the woman and the chandlery I'd found, but here was another tie. About the time my skeleton was alive, Centre Street, where my store is located, was familiarly called Petticoat Row because the establishments that lined the road were all run by women. They were power babes who used their business endeavors to support their families while their husbands were away. They were also able to build nest eggs in case of an unsuccessful voyage or, sadly, in case a husband was lost at sea. Most of the women who worked on Petticoat Row were dressmakers, dry goods retailers, and the like. I was as much a kindred spirit to the Petticoat Row ladies as I was to my candle maker.

Wondering if there could be a connection between the Cooper Thieves and Cooper's Candles, I decided to look at Mary Backus's diary. I printed out the screen result and took the page down to Agnes. She was busy studying a crossword puzzle when I arrived at her post.

"Can you think of a seven-letter word for 'tiramisu part?' " she said.

"Espresso?" I said.

"That's eight. I'll think of it," she said, absently taking the sheet from me and heading to the back room.

While I waited for her to return, I stretched a bit. I was reaching down to my toes, enjoying the fact that this was my first library visit that had not ended with me falling asleep, when a phone began to ring from the center of the building, which rose to a loft-like opening to the second floor. I looked above me to the source of the sound.

"Bellows speaking," the guest curator said in a voice that suited his name.

I'd always thought that talking on the phone in a library was a no-no, but apparently not.

"Uh-huh," Bellows said.

"Uh-huh," he said again.

Sounded like business.

There was a nice spindle-back chair reproduction across from Agnes's reception desk, so I took a seat.

"I absolutely want the diary," Bellow continued. "The exhibit will be nothing without the supporting elements of various whaling towns involved in these voyages. And reach out to Smith in Hudson for the example of a captain's wife's diary."

Agnes returned to her station, and immediately I noticed her wrinkled brow and pursed lips.

"You're interested in the Cooper Thieves?" she said, placing a piece of paper onto her desk. "Why didn't you tell me?"

Walking back to her desk, I looked at the single page she had produced. I suspected it wasn't Mary Backus's diary, but I was surprised and a little confused, by what I saw. The page contained a list of names, with Agnes's among them. I seemed to be looking at her family tree.

"I can tell you all you want to know," said Agnes. "Patience Cooper was a member of my family."

"Patience?"

My eye fell to the name Patience Hussey Cooper on the paper between us. I let the name settle in. I could almost feel my pupils dilate with interest.

"You know her story?" I said.

"Stella," she said, laying her hand protectively over her family tree, "I'll be honest. Not many of us left are familiar with the story. It's one of those skeletons in the closet we try not to remember. Before I say anything more, why are you asking?"

"I think she might have lived at the Morton house," I said.

"Really?" said Agnes, looking shocked that anything to do with the story was coming up.

Agnes sighed. I knew that she loved a good story. As much as she wanted to let it lie, it would be impossible for her not to tell me more.

"In the 1830s, Patience Hussey Cooper, a motherless only child, worked on Petticoat Row. When she was in her late teens, she fell in love with a sailor, Jedediah Cooper. He was a wash-ashore, arriving on Nantucket from a whaling voyage he'd joined in the South Pacific."

"You know your stuff," I said, genuinely impressed and wondering how Jedediah fit in to Agnes's family story. I still wasn't sure if I'd found the right Coopers, but I was eager to hear more.

"Jedediah wasn't a Quaker, but he was handsome and charming," she said, as if she'd met the man herself. "As you can imagine, Patience wasn't the only girl who had her eye on him. She and her best friend, Nancy Holland, competed for Jedediah's affections. By all accounts, Patience was not the more beautiful of the two, but he chose Patience. Probably because her father had just died, and Jedediah could pick up her family's business and settle down from a life at sea without much difficulty. The Coopers made candles, you know."

"I didn't, but that's a very helpful detail," I said, my confidence rising that I'd found the right Coopers to investigate further. It was a thrilling, yet surreal possibility, since all the characters had been dead and gone for so long.

"Nancy and Patience worked on Petticoat Row together. They were seamstresses. They were also savvy women. Shortly after Patience and Jedediah married, there was a whaling ship about to set sail around the horn of South Africa. The ladies decided to invest in the voyage, in hopes of making a tidy sum if the enterprise went well."

"People could do that?" I said.

"Oh, yes. It was like buying stocks, but you might have to wait years for a return," said Agnes. "Anyhow, Nancy was in charge of taking the women's funds to the vessel's captain on behalf of the investors. Legend has it, she was sick that morning, so Patience offered to conduct their business instead. Nancy gave her the money, and Patience headed off. That night, however, Jedediah told the neighbors that Patience had been beaten and the money stolen as she made her way to the ship. He told everyone he was going to take Patience to the mainland for medical attention on a boat that was about to leave for the Cape. That was the last anyone saw of the Coopers and the Petticoat Row ladies' money."

"The Cooper Thieves," I said, remembering the headlines. "They stole the money and hightailed it. The end?"

"The end. And a terrible end at that," said Agnes, shaking her head in disapproval, even all these years later.

As excited as I had initially been about the candle connection, I now felt I was back to square one. I was looking for a murdered woman, not two con artists who had skipped town. Although both stories in-

cluded candle makers, there didn't seem to be anything in Agnes's tale that ended with a dead body.

"You can see why we like to let this one lie," Agnes
said. "But you think she lived at the Morton house? I
have to admit it's interesting to know that."

"Actually, in spite of the name Cooper and the
candle connection, I don't think it's the same family.
You see, I found a skeleton in their old chandlery
with the sign for Cooper's Candles above it, but I'm
in search of a murderer, not thieves. There must
have been more Coopers on Nantucket than I ever
realized."

"A dead body?" she said. "Oh, lordy. I hope they
didn't kill people while they were at it. I'll keep
searching for you. Maybe I can come up with something that could help."

"Knock, knock," said Bellows.

We turned to find the island's popular historian in
his patched jacket standing at a cautious distance. I
could now see that he was quite tall, which was not
what I had expected, having only seen him hunched
over his books. I wondered when he'd come downstairs, and how long he'd been there.

"I have a list of periodicals and diaries for you to
find for me, Ms. Agnes," he said, and gave us both a
smile. "I don't think we've met," he said to me, handing me his card. "Jameson Bellows."

"Welcome to Nantucket," I said.

"Keep in touch," said Agnes to me.

"I will," I said. "And try the word, layered, for
tiramisu part."

The tightness in her face faded and was replaced
with a smile as she glanced at her crossword puzzle.

"Thanks, Stella," she said.

She filled in the word, then took Bellows's list and disappeared as my phone pinged an update from Peter. His note informed me that I had twenty minutes until maximum low tide, when the "city" of crabs was revealed. It was an invitation I now decided to accept. I nodded politely to Bellows, who seemed to be searching for something else to say to me, and headed out the door.

Chapter 4

The drive to the Nantucket Field Station gave me time to reflect on Agnes's story. Although most of the connections between my skeleton and her family's history were circumstantial, there was something about the similarity between the characters that held my interest. Lost in thought, I pulled into the station's dune road, my Beetle fighting mightily across the sand, and parked when I didn't think the car could make it any farther. I took off my sneakers and threw them in the back seat. I rolled up my jeans for the trek down to the beach, and when I reached the sand beyond the dunes, I took a left, toward an inlet where I would find Crab City and Peter. I was glad the sun was warm; otherwise, my bare toes would have frozen in the autumn sand.

When I rounded the beach to the inlet, I gave out a howl of laughter. At the end of wet, slimy sand, through which small rivulets of water ran, I saw Peter. He was wearing knee-high rubber boots, carrying a net, and scribbling notes with the short stub of his number-two pencil. He appeared, from my angle, as if he were trying to interview the little crustaceans. He looked up and gave me a wave with a huge smile.

"Watch your step," he said.

Indeed, I would have to be careful. Although the sand looked muddy and bleak at first glance, on closer inspection, the ground was in constant motion. This phenomenon was the result of thousands of little crabs, exposed from their snug homes for the period of low tide. They were climbing over each other, ducking in and out of safe spaces, and seemed to exponentially multiply moment by moment. Their activities were warranted too. Above, seagulls flew in droves, looking for a good meal. Fortunately for them, the clams at the shoreline on the other side of the beach were the tastier delicacy.

While the birds made bomb dives into the shallow sea behind me, I skipped from here to there until I reached Peter. By way of greeting, he placed four tiny hermit crabs in my hand.

"They tickle," I said, feeling them crawl over my palm. "I love it. If I didn't know they were crabs, I'd feel really spooked by their claws moving so manically over me. Can we bring a few dozen of them over to Halloween Haunts on Friday and return them before they're in danger? I bet we could use them to make a wonderfully scary spider booth in the Spooks Room. With a blindfold on, they'd feel just like creeping spiders."

"That would be amazing," he said. "Speaking of spooky things, what'd you find out about the skeleton?"

"A lot, or maybe nothing at all," I said.

I told him about my search and Agnes's family story. Peter turned a page in his notebook as I spoke. I wondered how that book would read from page to page. Crabs on one side, skeletons on another.

The tide had already started to return, and the water was cold on my feet, so Peter and I found a patch of sand closer to the ocean where we took a break. He handed me half of a turkey sandwich, which made me realize how hungry I was. We ate as I finished my story.

"I think there are too many parallels between Agnes's family history and the skeleton you found to drop the lead," said Peter when I'd finished. "Agnes was told that the two con artists made up the story of the attack and used it as an excuse to leave town, but maybe Jedediah really left alone."

"I see you're coming around to my murder theory, but I'm not following you. Why would Jedediah kill Patience before leaving the island? They had the money."

"Actually, it's not a murder theory," said Peter. "Patience was probably attacked, somehow held on to the money, but then died from her wounds. Jedediah buried her quickly and hit the road, using the excuse of her needing help to avoid suspicion. People are susceptible to stories."

Peter lay back on the sand, and I joined him, tucking my head into the crook of his arm. For the second time today, I watched the clouds roll by.

"I still think it was murder. Maybe someone else left Nantucket with Jedediah," I said. "What if they killed Patience and hid her in the fireplace?"

Before we could explore the idea, my phone rang.

I looked at the screen to find the words WICK & FLAME.

"It's Cherry," said my assistant's bright voice when I hit ACCEPT. "Everything's going well today. I sold a Tinker Special. A tourist came in and snapped him up. Said she has a black tabby at home."

"That's great," I said.

"Also, I have a phone message," said Cherry. "The ghost tour lady, Brenda, called. She said to tell you that she went by the Morton house, hoping you'd be there, but that the police were there and a few people she'd never seen before, so she left. She'll be back tomorrow morning."

"Thanks," I said.

Cherry went on to tell me a few more details about our days' sales, but I was focused on one thing only.

"Come on," I said to Peter when I ended the call. I stood and pulled Peter up behind me. "The forensics people are there already."

"I can't," said Peter. "I didn't have a chance to tell you, but my contact at U Mass suggested that I stay here tonight. There will be a waxing gibbous moon, and he said lunar phases affect sea life, especially right before a full moon. He says it's not to be missed. I thought it was worth investigating."

I looked at Peter's gear and noticed that he had brought his sleeping bag.

"You're crazy about this story," I said, in the most loving way.

"A little bit. Are you going to be alright in that old house tonight?" he said, pulling me close to him. "We could always have a campout."

"Not on your life," I said. "But text me a picture of

the moon. Also, you have dried seaweed in your hair."

"It's a fashion statement," he said. "Meant to woo you."

I gave him a kiss to let him know it had worked and headed back down the beach. By the time I reached the car, I was wondering if the body would be gone from The Shack by the time I got home. I knew Andy was a professional, and that duty called, but I also couldn't believe he had moved ahead so quickly. I'd hoped to have information for him before he started to take next steps. I really did feel responsible for the mysterious corpse's well-being.

Fortunately, when I parked in front of the house, Andy's car was still out front. I marched to the back of the house and across the yard to The Shack.

"Hello!" I said, entering the room as the lady of the house.

I noticed that my candles had been replaced by a small generator and three spotlights that lit the room much better. The lights were clamped onto standing rods, so that they could be directed in different places if need be. Another big change to the room was the addition of some white sheets hanging from stands, which broke the space into different sections. A folding table had also been brought in. On top of it was scientific-looking stuff, like test tubes and a box of latex gloves and magnifying glasses and bottles of liquids. Someone had moved the Cooper's Candles sign across the room, where it now lay beside the door.

Andy was standing by the hearth with two people, a man and a woman.

Dressed in forgettable attire, the man had a long, skinny neck upon which sat a head marked by thick, dark eyebrows and round spectacles that were too small for his pale face, in my opinion. If the girls had hired him to pose as a vampire for their event, I'd have thought he was the perfect find.

In contrast, the woman was a knockout with straight black hair and perfectly trimmed bangs. Somehow her features were unmistakably of Korean descent, unlike my hodgepodge of features, from my Irish heritage to my dark mane and olive complexion. I don't know anything about my dad, but I bet he had some kind of Mediterranean background.

Andy took a step toward me.

"Remember, Stella," he said. "No one near the body until an anthropologist has looked at it."

"You might as well count me in," I said. "I've been looking into the story at the library all day."

"We don't mind an audience," said the woman.

I immediately liked her.

After a beat, Andy stepped aside so I could greet our newcomers.

"If you two don't mind, I don't mind," Andy said to the couple. "As long as you have something to add, Stella."

"You know I'm good for it," I said, hoping I would be.

"This is Dr. Robert Solder and his assistant, Miss Leigh Paik, from Boston University," Andy said. "They are part of a world-renowned forensic anthropology department. They took the first flight over to help us."

As Andy spoke, Solder gently leaned his forearm against his partner's. Leigh returned his nuanced affection by dipping her head toward his shoulder. They were a funny couple, but I got it. She loved his mind; he loved everything about her.

"So glad you both could make it, Dr. Solder, Ms. Paik." I extended my hand. "I'm Stella Wright. I live in the main house, so you can always reach out to me if you need anything. "

"Don't worry about us. We have a whole lot of bones to play with. And call me Leigh," said the woman, shaking my hand while her partner got back to work. Although she was the assistant on their team, she seemed to be the public front for the two. "We're setting up the lab. Then we'll examine the body. Your timing is perfect."

I was impressed. It had only been a few hours since the ME had suggested a forensic anthropologist take over, and here were two professionals, world-renowned, on the case. I smiled at Andy, who rubbed his hands together in anticipation of what would come next. I wished Peter was with us too.

"Knock, knock," said a new voice, behind us.

It was the second time I'd heard that phrase today. As I expected, I turned to find a corduroy jacket with elbow patches in the doorway.

"Jameson Bellows," said the historian I'd met at the library.

His introduction was aimed at the scientists, but Solder was now busy instructing Leigh to organize some tools to help him measure the bones.

"I'm the resident curator at the Nantucket Historical Association. Consider me at your service," he said, trying again for their attention. When he received little more than an indulgent smile from Leigh, he turned to me. "Is that you, Ms. Wright?" I nodded, cognizant of the fact that Jameson Bellows's sudden arrival was most likely connected to the fact that he'd overheard me talking to Agnes. I surmised that he had learned the Morton's address from Agnes after I'd left and was eager to get in on the action. I had to admit I respected his ambition to make a name for himself on our island. He definitely wanted to be the Historical Association's new superstar.

"Mr. Bellows," said Andy, "although I appreciate that you've made time to visit, I will ask that you respect—"

"It's really OK," said Leigh, "we're happy that the island's community is interested in our work. Please feel free to observe us."

"But perhaps later," said Solder, as much to Leigh as to Bellows. "We'll have to sell tickets at this rate. Right now, the goal is to discover as much as we can, as quickly as we can. Since the bones have been unearthed, it's important to examine them thoroughly lest the exterior environment contaminate them over time."

I was fascinated to see who would win. Solder bit his bottom lip and looked as if he was going to hold his ground, but Leigh gave him an equally stubborn stare. She had transformed from a dreamy groupie to a frustrated colleague in the blink of an eye, and I realized she must wear a couple of hats in their relationship. I found I was rooting for her and was happy when Solder took a step aside. As he did, he lowered a pair of glasses with magnifiers for lenses, and flipped on a flashlight attached to them. With his eyes looking four times their size, I once again found myself trying to figure out how we could use him at Halloween Haunts.

"Please don't assume this is going to be an ongoing partnership, Mr. Bellows," he said. "This is no more than professional courtesy."

Leigh raised her chin but graciously said nothing more.

In the four or five steps it took the historian to head victoriously to the hearth, he pulled out a small case from his breast pocket. He unzipped it and removed a pair of glasses with a magnifying glass and light attached to them, similar to Solder's own glasses, and took a place beside Solder at the hearth.

"I can already see," said Bellows after only a moment's silence, "that the weave of cloth of the woman's dress places her in an early-nineteenth-century time period."

The two men, with their four collective eyes magnified by their glasses, looked up and gave each other a good, long stare.

"Obviously," said Solder, not breaking eye contact.

"Obviously," said Bellows with equal intensity.

The two men turned and faced the hearth again with the precision of synchronized swimmers. Without speaking to each other, Bellows took the bottom of the skeleton, and Solder took the top. I noticed Leigh shaking her head as she opened a cardboard box at the table.

"The teeth are worn at the incisor," said Solder, perhaps to Bellows, perhaps to himself. "I believe she sewed a lot."

I stepped toward the area of the room where the

investigators were examining the skeleton, fascinated by the suggestion that she was a seamstress. I supposed all women sewed back then, but I was reminded that the Cooper Thieves had stolen from Petticoat Row women, many of whom were seamstresses.

After about a minute, the two gentlemen switched places and continued their scan of the body. I felt like we were watching paint dry, but finally there was some action up front. Bellows reached into the woman's dress sleeve. Solder reached out to stop him, but Bellows had already extracted what looked like a small piece of linen.

"What is it?" I said.

Without a word, Bellows walked to the table with Solder right behind him. Andy and I craned our necks to see, but Leigh was there as well and we couldn't make out much over their shoulders.

"I'd say eighteen thirties or forties, from the embroidery," said Leigh.

"The color choice of the thread is in keeping with that time," said Bellows with a condescending air.

Solder nodded, focused on the linen. While Bellows looked pleased with himself for having had the opportunity to display his knowledge, Solder was in his zone, finding clues from an old piece of cloth. I knew how he must feel. There was a puzzle to be solved, and he had found a solid clue. I'm like that when I'm designing new candles.

"It's in good condition. Aside from the blood," said Solder.

"Did you find many wounds on the body? Other

fractures anywhere?" I asked, thinking of Peter's idea
that Patience Cooper had been attacked by thieves
and had died from her wounds, leaving Jedediah
free to leave with the money she'd protected with
her life.

Solder shook his head.

"Only the wound to her rib cage," he said.

The seamstress connection had led me to think
that the body might actually be Agnes's relative, but
the discrepancy in the wounds left me stumped.

Solder took what looked like a pen from his pocket,
clicked it, and then began to speak into it.

"From a cursory observational examination, I believe the body to be female, from the mid-nineteenth
century," said Solder. "Rib number five on the right
side is shattered, indicating death by blunt force.
The size and rotational fracture suggest a rounded
object, inflicted at close range. Handkerchief—contaminated by modern handling—has minute blood
splatter in upper left corner. Initials PC embroidered
into linen. Tooth erosion suggests a trade in sewing."

"Did you say PC?" I said, almost shouting.

Solder clicked off his recording device and raised
the handkerchief gently, holding it by tweezers, for
us to view. Embroidered neatly in the corner of the
simple linen were two initials: PC.

There was now no doubt in my mind. The skeleton I'd found of a young woman who had once been
a candle maker was Agnes's relative, Patience
Cooper. And given the discrepancy between Agnes's
story that Patience had skipped town and the cold
hard truth that she was lying here with a single stab

wound as her cause of death, something very foul indeed had happened to the woman.

"If I may, I believe the body is Patience Cooper," said Bellows with great authority. "Married to Jedediah Cooper in eighteen forty-seven."

Andy, Solder, and even Leigh looked impressed. Me? I held my tongue, knowing that the only way Bellows had this information was because he'd listened in on my conversation with Agnes. He was certainly trying hard to establish his authority. Luckily for him, I was still too stunned to quibble.

"Your theory is an interesting one, but our focus is on scientific facts, Mr. Bellows," said Solder. "The linen is illuminating, but we may only ever be able to theorize, not prove, that this is someone named Patience Cooper. That's an important distinction."

"Excuse me?" said a voice from behind us.

We turned, startled, to find Agnes.

"I'm related to the Coopers. I came to see if you have found Patience."

"Agnes? How'd you know to come here? And what made you think we'd find Patience Cooper?" Andy asked. Then he looked at me. "Never mind."

Agnes stopped and stared at the skeleton like a deer caught in headlights. Before she could faint, Andy walked briskly to the door, grabbing a folding chair while he did. Reaching her, he opened the chair and led her to it.

"What are you doing here, Agnes?" he said.

"I'm fine," she said, taking a deep breath and composing herself. "I've never seen anything like that before. And to think she could be family."

I joined them and rubbed her back.

"You shouldn't have come," I said.

"But I wanted to help," Agnes said, and looked at me.

Agnes absently touched the glasses that were perched on top of her head as she took a breath.

"I remembered something more about the story of Patience Cooper," she said.

Chapter 5

For a few moments, there was some confusion about Agnes's pronouncement and its relative value to the work at hand. Bellows took the liberty of filling in Andy, Solder, and Leigh about Patience and Jedediah Cooper and the robbery of the Petticoat Row ladies' money. I was happy for him to take the lead. I knew the police and anthropologists would be more receptive to the story if it came from a historian rather than from Agnes or me.

I also didn't mind taking a back seat because, while Bellows spoke, no one was paying much attention to me. Capitalizing on their distraction, I crossed the room. My pretense was to lower the sheet hanging over the skeleton, since it continued to spook Agnes, but I also wanted to glance at the grave itself, which I hadn't done earlier.

"What did you remember about Patience's story?" Andy said to Agnes when Bellows had finished.

"It's something about Nancy Holland, Patience's best friend."

My eye had just caught sight of a stone that was at a funny angle, but I paused to listen to Agnes. Having my own very best friend on the island, Emily Gardner, I know that best friends are a vault of secrets and that they can answer a lot of important questions. For example, if Emily's husband came to me before birthdays and holidays, he'd save himself a lot of hassle when buying gifts.

Agnes shifted in her seat, now that so many eyes were on her. She looked in my direction. I nodded toward her to continue.

"The story has always been that Nancy was racked with guilt about the Petticoat Row ladies' lost funds, and she was devastated by the betrayal of her best friend," Agnes said. "Shortly after Patience and Jedediah left, she killed herself by jumping down the well behind her house out in Monomoy."

"Juicy," said Leigh.

I had to agree. I'd always thought of the old-time ladies on the island as straight shooters and hard workers, but there was a lot of drama going on as well.

"The Hollands lived in what is now Old Holly's house," said Agnes. "You know the one. I guess Holly is Nancy's great-great-grand-whatever nephew."

Old Holly is the affectionate name given to Gil Holland, who lives out by a quiet area called Monomoy. He is a short-tempered fellow, now a retired widower, who had made his living as a mechanic. I knew his family had been on the island forever, but I didn't know him well outside of serving him a Thanksgiving dinner at the Rotary Club once. I remembered him because their stuffing is out of this world and he'd complained that it was too dry. It's the opposite of dry.

"I found an article about Nancy's suicide that disturbed me," said Agnes.

She opened her tote bag and retrieved a photocopy of an article she'd likely found at the library. I was proud of Agnes for bringing evidence with her since there was a circle of curious professionals around her. Since I didn't need Agnes to prove anything to me with a piece of paper, however, I shifted my attention back to the hearth.

"See?" said Agnes. "Nancy jumped down the well behind Old Holly's house. She left a note that said she could not live, having lost her friend and the Petticoat Row money. Aside from the letter, however, all that was found was her cloak, hanging from the well."

"Hello," I said to a small object I pried from behind the rock, at a spot that would have been beside Patience's clavicle. "Check it out."

I held up a small metal tool to the group.

"What is it?" said Andy.

"It's a tong," I said, bringing it over to the still small but growing team. "Used to remove pots of melted wax from heat before pouring it into molds."

"It's from the right period," said Bellows, admiring the piece. "Mid-eighteen hundreds."

Solder took the tool from me and walked back to the skeleton. He removed the sheet that covered Patience and then moved aside her blouse. He held the tong over the exposed rib cage.

"One mystery solved," he said. "The injury and the tool match. Combined with the blood spatter on the metal, I believe she died from a wound inflicted by this tong."

"The handkerchief's initials suggest that the body is Patience Cooper, and the hidden blood-spattered tongs suggest someone used them to kill her," I said. "Given that there are no signs of a brutal attack from robbers, I think there's more to the Cooper legend than anyone ever knew."

"It's just as I feared," said Agnes. "You know, I was at Old Holly's house once. Years ago, before his wife died. We were making jams for the cranberry festival. Holly's wife said that when he inherited the house there was a stipulation that the well remain untouched, as it had been for decades, because Nancy was down there. She thought it was creepy that the body of a dead woman was in her backyard, but she said no matter how much she complained, Holly would never go near the well."

"There are many fascinating tales of inheritance restrictions," said Bellows with an air of self-importance that fell flat. He seemed to realize it too and stopped his monologue.

"I can't believe I didn't think of it sooner," Agnes said. "I can't find my glasses, but sometimes I'll remember something out of nowhere."

"They're on your head, dear," said Leigh, bringing Agnes a cup of water.

"Thank you," said Agnes.

"Nancy Holland reportedly went down the well, but her body was never recovered," I said, catching on to Agnes's line of thinking. "Jedediah left the island with a woman, who was clearly not Patience.

Agnes, you told me that Nancy and Jedediah had had a thing before he'd married Patience."

"Do you think that Nancy staged her own death after she and Jedediah killed Patience, and then they left the island together?" said Andy.

"It seems possible," I said. "Nancy Holland and Jedediah could have killed Patience Cooper and made up the story about the attack."

"Meanwhile, my poor family has had a black stain on it for generations, while the Hollands were the real criminals," said Agnes.

"It would explain why people thought they saw Jedediah leave the island with a woman," said Bellows. "And it would explain why the Holland family didn't want to disinter Nancy's body after she allegedly went down the well. Better that the Coopers be the bad guys."

Agnes nodded vehemently. I could see that my morning's discovery and subsequent investigation had had a profound impact on her. What had started for me as an otherworldly connection to Nantucket's candle-making past had led to a much deeper significance for Agnes. I admired her pride in her family, but also feared that without some closure, she might be haunted by the story in a very unhealthy way.

"Why don't we clear this up," I said. "Couldn't we find out if Nancy is down the well?"

"Could we?" said Agnes, a tear springing to her eye. "If she's not, you may find you have a cold case with poor Patience."

"As one of the island's historians, I'd like to second the motion that we explore the well," said Bellows. "I am humbled and thrilled to have arrived on Nantucket at a time when this discovery has been made. I will make it my mission to see it through."

"Mr. Bellows," said Solder. "This is a scientific endeavor, not a storyteller's indulgence."

"I beg your pardon," said Bellows, his eyes practically dropping from their sockets.

"I'm sure this could be a great scientific discovery for us, as well as a wonderful story for Mr. Bellows to add to the history books," said Leigh. "We could get our equipment together by tomorrow and explore the well with no problem if Mr. Holland agrees."

"Old Holly is under no obligation to open up his well," said Andy. "Especially for a rumor we're starting."

"I'll take care of that," said Agnes.

She whipped out her phone. She had dialed before anyone could argue.

"Holly? It's Agnes," she said.

I motioned for her to put the call on speaker.

"What do you want?" said a gruff voice.

"You lying, stinking cheat," she said. "I just found out that Nancy Holland never killed herself. In fact, she had a hand in killing Patience Cooper, and then took off with her husband. I wouldn't put it past you to have known all these years."

"What the hell are you talking about, you old bat?" he said.

"I'm talking about the fact that I'm standing next to Patience Cooper's skeleton."

"I don't believe you," he said. "And I couldn't care less, even if you were standing next to the bones of your family's good-for-nothing thief."

"I'm with a specialist in bones. We're coming over tomorrow morning to open up your well to confirm that it is empty."

"Like hell you are," he said.

"Wait!" I said, before Old Holly could hang up. "Hi! It's Stella Wright. I'm here with Officer Southerland and someone from the Nantucket Historical Association too."

Old Holly cleared his throat.

"Hello," he said, more politely. "I appreciate your interest, but I am not opening my well."

"I can understand," I said. "But you know how stories fly. If it turns out Nancy's body is there, as you believe it is, then we can put Agnes's suspicions to rest. However, if we let the story marinate, you'll have all sorts of people showing up at your house, looking for access to the well, wanting to know about the story. It will never end, and you'll never have a moment of peace."

"Goddamn, Agnes. What have you done?" said Old Holly. "I was planning to watch baseball tomorrow."

"Mr. Holland," I said, thinking of something that might put him over the edge. "I can have my cousins out to your house today to clear the backyard for you, to create easy access to the well."

"I'll ask the Historical Association to consider covering the costs," Bellows said.

"Not necessary," said Solder.

My cousins, Ted and Docker Wright, are the proud owners of Wright Brothers Carting Company. They recently bought an extra truck and had hopes for further expansion, so I knew they'd be happy for the extra income. Clearing yards isn't part of their usual scope of work, but they were used to adding extra tasks to get the job done, especially while they were building their business. Hopefully, it would be a win-win opportunity for everyone.

"Yard work?" said Old Holly.

There was a pause. We all stared at Agnes's phone.

"Fine," he said. "But don't remove the body. I'm not allowed. Family rules."

"We'll be there tomorrow morning for the excavation," said Leigh. She looked at Solder with a pleased expression, but he had begun to measure Patience's bones.

"Wonderful," I said.

Agnes hung up and looked at me. The laugh lines around her eyes had disappeared and a hollow darkness was left behind. I squeezed her hand reassuringly, and hoped tomorrow would give her peace.

"Up you go, Agnes," I said. "Let's leave the experts to their work. I'm going home to pack up a few items for my stay at the Morton house."

"Honestly, I'm nervous about what we might find tomorrow," said Agnes when we reached our cars. "I'm heading back to the library to get you that diary you asked for earlier."

Agnes started her car, and I could see that there was nothing I could do to stop her. I decided that a little routine might steady her nerves, so I made her promise to attend our regularly scheduled candle class tomorrow morning before she drove away.

Andy and Leigh walked up the lawn to me.

"We called your cousin Ted. He said thanks for the job," Andy said. "The chief also assigned me to be at

Old Holly's tomorrow. You should have some official presence around."

"What are you going to do with Patience's body now that we're looking into Nancy too?" I said, impressed by how my town was coming together so quickly to learn more about these women.

Andy pushed his cap up his forehead an inch or two.

"Bellows was on the phone with the Historical Association," he said. "He was angling to move the body over to the museum by the end of tonight, but Solder put his foot down."

"From a scientific perspective, we'd like to keep the body on site, in case we find another tomorrow and there are points of comparison to make," Leigh said in Solder's defense.

I was thinking about my impending slumber party with Patience as I headed home to pack a few clothes for me and provisions for Tinker. I really hoped my stay at the Morton house would inspire the Girl Scouts to turn their fear of the skeleton into fascination. We couldn't let all of the work they'd put into Halloween Haunts go to waste. And I didn't want to let down the towns' neediest.

Chris had put up a garbage bag over my broken kitchen window, but it wasn't as creative a solution as I'd thought it might be. The bag kept the leaves and birds from flying into my apartment, but it was awfully cold inside. I was glad I had the Morton house to call home, especially if Peter was planning to spend the foreseeable future camping out at the beach.

On the way back to my new house, I stopped by

the Wick & Flame. My day so far had had many unexpected twists and turns, so I used the afternoon to
do what I know best. I made candles, and another
Tinker Special, and closed up for Cherry. When I finally shut the door and turned the key for the night,
I marveled over the fact that I'd unlocked a door to
another world this morning.

I also realized that there was nothing in my fridge
at the Morton house, so I had a bite to eat at the Nantucket Pharmacy on Main Street. When I finally arrived at the house, it was well after dark. The Shack's
door was chained and locked. Everything was quiet
but for the wind, which was picking up.

The moment I stepped into the house, I realized it
was almost as cold as the apartment I'd left. I flicked
on the lights, then turned the knob of the radiator
by the front door, hoping for the best. To be on the
safe side, I found the linen closet on the second floor
and pulled out every blanket I could find.

When I entered the bedroom carrying bedcovers
piled up to my chin, Tinker was curled up under a
pillow, with his nose and whiskers sticking out. He
licked his paws and rubbed them over his head as I
changed into my pajamas.

"Since when are you a fraidy cat?" I said, snuggling
up next to him, and hoping the scent of mothballs
from the blankets would dissipate sooner than later.

Tinker gave me a purr filled with indignation at
my accusation.

"Holding down the fort then?" I said.

He whisked his tail and closed his eyes.

"That's a good idea," I said, turning out my light.

As the radiator's first *bang!* echoed throughout the house, I shut my eyes. Under the waxing gibbous moon, the chain across the old chandlery outside banged against the door in the wind. As I turned this way and that throughout the night, I felt that Patience herself was calling to me.

Chapter 6

I woke up the next morning to a soft sensation hovering above me. Slowly, I opened one eye.

"Holy—" I said, falling backward out of bed, throwing pounds of blankets off of me and into the room in the process.

"Whoa—" said Peter, fending off the blankets as they flew toward him. His hair was everywhere, and his face flushed. "It's like a sauna in here."

I looked around the room, lit by the rising sun. Peter was right. It was very hot. The heater had been stronger than I'd expected. I pushed my hair back and noticed I was a little sweaty.

"You startled me," I said.

"I noticed," said Peter.

He put the blankets back on my bed in a way that indicated he thought he had made it.

"Sorry I snuck up on you like that," he said, "but you didn't answer when I knocked. I found the key under the rock out front. It's almost eight thirty."

"Oh, no," I said. "Be right back."

I immediately ran to the bathroom and turned on the shower. The water was ice-cold from the morning's chill, but I held my breath and jumped in. I had my candle class at the Wick & Flame in thirty minutes. It would only take five minutes to walk to town, but I like to arrive early to set up for the day.

Peter was lying on my bed when I jumped out, his arms crooked behind his head, staring at the dust particles that floated in the air. Tinker was beside him, doing the same. What a pair.

"How was the beach?" I said.

"I was hazed by the scientist who lives in the cottage out there," he said with a good-natured laugh. "The crabs slept, safe and sound. The gibbous moon had no effect on them. At about four in the morning, I knocked on his door, feeling hypothermic, and had a strong shot of whiskey. I was so tired I fell right back asleep on his beat-up sofa."

I sat on the bed in my Sunday attire—jeans, sneakers, and a sweatshirt; not my usual work look, but this was a special day.

"You should have stayed with me," I said. "We have quite an exciting morning ahead of us."

"I heard," said Peter. "I bumped into Andy at The Downyflake on the way home. He told me to tell you to let the pros do their thing when we get to the well."

We both laughed at the thought.

"Meet me at Old Holly's in a couple of hours?" I said.

"You mean we aren't heading out there now?" said Peter, looking as if I might actually be following Andy's orders.

"First, I'm teaching a class," I said. "I thought it would be good for Agnes if we kept everything as normal as possible. She's nervous about the family stuff."

"I'll feed Tinker," said Peter.

"Thanks," I said. "You look very cute in a Victorian bed."

"Hold that thought?" he said.

I reluctantly left him and bounced along the rickety cobblestone road to town in the Beetle. When I unlocked the door to my store, I decided the Wick & Flame had the perfect air of both wicked and cheerful. As many days as I've walked into the store, I never take the Wick & Flame for granted. I am filled with appreciation that I have been able to turn my passion into my livelihood. I spend every day surrounded by an array of candles in every size, scent, and color. My simple white walls are filled with shelves that display my wares for my loyal customers and appreciative tourists. And if someone can't find what they want, I'll make a personalized creation for them. If you ever have a chance to stop by, I promise I'll make sure you leave with something you like.

The teapot was starting to sing when I heard a knock on my door. Agnes, Cherry, and their friend Flo, a group we've aptly named the Candleers for all of the classes they've taken with me, peered in through the window with expectant smiles. I returned theirs and opened the door to let them in.

"Here," said Agnes, handing me a yellow envelope. "I found Mary Backus's diary for you. Who says librarians aren't relevant?"

"No one says that," said Flo.

"I couldn't sign it out; it's too old. So I made a copy of it," Agnes said.

I took the envelope, impressed by her legwork. It was about a half inch thick. I'd have a lot to read.

"Agnes told us everything," said Cherry. "Before you say a word, we've called Lucy. She'll cover for me today. We can't let Agnes go to Old Holly's alone."

"I need my girls," said Agnes, nodding.

Lucy is a recent graduate of the high school who is heading to college in a couple of months. She was my helper for two summers, during the busy season. If Cherry was willing to give up her shift to Lucy, I knew she was worried about Agnes. Cherry loves to help at the store and is somewhat possessive of her job. She feels that work is the key for an aging woman to stay healthy and feel in the game.

"How was it to stay in that haunted house last night?" said Flo as we headed to my back workroom. "It sounds so creepy."

"It was old," I said, remembering the creaks and bangs of my night's sleep.

"I love old houses," said Cherry. "They make me feel young."

"True enough," said Flo. "It's not often you find something more wrinkled than you are."

The three of them cackled with laughter at their joke.

"How about we get to work?" I said, starting our day.

For my latest class, on the theme of candle clocks, I had been inspired by an ad I found on eBay for two hundred candle clock holders at an insanely good clearance price from a junk shop in Illinois. The concept of a candle clock was new to me, and the deal was so good that I couldn't resist tinkering around with the idea.

I quickly learned that these clever devices have been around since medieval times, before mechanical clocks had been invented, and were useful for marking time indoors or during cloudy days when following the sun was hard to do. At its simplest form, evenly spaced markings were made on a candle so that as the wax burned past each marking, the owner could follow the passage of time. When a nail was inserted into one of the markings, the candle could also be used as an alarm clock, since the nail would fall and make a clattering sound when the wax around it melted.

The holders I found could turn these candles into timers as well. This invention struck me as more romantic than a smartphone, but just as technologically practical. In this form, the candle is made of long, beeswax coils which wind their way up a base and are threaded through a metal clip at the top. The user decides how long the candle should burn by adjusting the length of wax above the clip. Then, when the wax melts down, the candle self-extinguishes. Brilliant.

We'd spent the first couple of classes doing the hard work of creating what seemed now like miles of wax coil, and then we did the math, testing how long the wax burned at different time intervals and marking the coils accordingly. Now we were getting creative. The fun part about the coils was that we could wind them into fun designs. Cherry, for example, had died her wax orange and was planning to sculpt her coil into a round shape with added decorative pumpkin eyes. She thought it would be a perfect Halloween candle for her windowsill, and one she could time to "die" at midnight.

While the women busied themselves, I opened the envelope Agnes had given me. From inside, I extracted a thick document on letter-sized paper that contained colored copies of Mary's small book, an item of no more than about five by seven inches. From the images, I determined that the diary had been covered in tan leather and was embossed with the initials MB. Overall, the book seemed in good shape, although the edges of the interior pages looked worn from Mary's days recording her thoughts of the world around her. Although the pages were yellowed, they were otherwise legible.

Carefully, I began to turn the pages of Mary's diary. I was keenly aware that I was looking at someone's private papers. Even though the book had been written well over one hundred years ago, I treaded lightly.

At first.

Before I knew it, I was absorbed in the beautiful handwriting and lovely details of a much-forgotten past. I learned that a family named the Piles had purchased a new workhorse and that the rose of Sharon had blossomed early the following year. There was sad news of a ship lost at sea. In honor of the lost men, Mary had written a poem. Many pages were filled with sketches of friends, flowers, and cats. One drawing even looked like Tinker.

Near the end of the book, I found the only mention of the Cooper Thieves. It was a short entry, but I pored over the words.

The Coopers have lost their children to greed. I fear for Patience's soul and that of her offspring and husband. I grieve, mightily, for the women she betrayed as well. Nancy Holland looks like the walking dead. She shivers and passes with the graveyard in her eyes. Her heart is broken.

There were only two more pages after the entry. They mostly included details about a trip Mary Backus planned to take to see a cousin off island, but two items in the mention about the Coopers resonated with me.

First, Mary's version of the events included an interesting detail: Nancy was seen on the island after Patience and Jedediah had left. It didn't support our theory that she'd taken off with Jedediah. Adding to this point was Mary's description of Nancy. She sounded like someone in deep despair, perhaps someone who might kill herself. I was more curious than ever to see what we would find in Old Holly's well. Perhaps we would discover a body after all.

I was also surprised by the suggestion of offspring. Was Mary alluding to an existing child, or was she fearful that the Coopers, having left Nantucket, would be cursed forevermore?

"Did Patience have children?" I said to Agnes as we were cleaning up.

"I've never heard of it," she said. "Why?"

My store was still closed, but I heard a rap at the door. Shelly was peering through the glass.

I opened the door for her.

"Not that it surprises me, but the girls are spreading news all over town about the skeleton in The Shack," she said, entering my store. "I came to see if the horrible thing is still there. If it is, the girls said they might not come today."

She seemed as overwhelmed as she'd been yesterday.

"I will say, they think you're brave for staying there," she said. "My daughter and her friends keep saying to everyone how they've been working in a house with a dead body, and that you now live with it. Drama, drama. Meanwhile, I'm left with these decorative spider webs and no girls to help me hang them."

Shelly's bag was huge and bursting with decorations.

"Let me see those cobwebs," said Cherry, coming up to Shelly with a disapproving stare. She gathered the gauze hanging from Shelly's bag as the other Candleers gathered around with a chorus of *tut*s and *oh no*s.

"Shelly," said Flo, "we can whip up some cobwebs for you that'll have the town quaking in their shoes. You should see what we can do with a little silk thread and a crochet hook."

"And don't worry about Halloween Haunts," said Flo as she walked Shelly to the door. "We're going out to Old Holly's right now. Once we find the other skeleton over there, the discovery of Patience Cooper will look like nothing."

"Who's Patience Cooper?" said Shelly.

"Your dead body," said Flo.

"Patience?" said Shelly. "The skeleton has a name?"

Flo nodded cheerfully and closed the door on Shelly. She waved at the woman, who was now lost in thought about having a skeleton with a name on her hands. Flo hadn't finished waving when Shelly paused mid-step on her way back to the sidewalk and turned around abruptly.

"There's another skeleton?" Shelly said through the glass.

Flo held her hand up to her ear as if she couldn't hear. Then she rejoined us with a giggle.

"Shelly should follow the troop's Instagram posts," said Cherry. "The girls already know all about Old Holly's well. The brave ones have probably already been down the old thing this morning to check it out."

"From what Shelley said about the girls, I doubt they'll ever go near any of these houses again," I said, putting the diary back into the envelope.

"I can't wait to get to the bottom of this," said Agnes.

It felt like it took an eternity for Lucy to arrive, but I think it was only about ten more minutes before we all jumped into our cars and hit the road to Old Holly's. The morning sun had been swallowed up, and the day had turned foggy, which somehow suited the vibe for the impending excavation.

When I pulled up, I saw Andy's patrol car, along with four others, parked in the driveway. I supposed one was Bellows's car. It was a safe bet that the second one, a well-worn pickup truck, was Old Holly's. The other two were rentals. I assumed Solders and Leigh had picked up one of them. I wondered who had rented the other.

The answer came quickly. I stepped out of the Beetle as the screen door of Old Holly's front porch slammed open and shut. I turned, expecting to see the master of the house, but instead I was met by a dark-haired fellow, about ten years older than I, with slicked-back hair and a moustache. He was wearing a blue, pinstriped suit that looked really out of place on our quiet island.

"Hugh Fontbutter," he said, walking toward me with outstretched hand. "I hear you're the one who found the body. It's a pleasure to meet you. Your discovery is huge. Huge."

I extended my hand and shook, feeling I had no choice but regretting that I was now trapped in the strong grip of this stranger. As we shook, Old Holly himself stepped onto the porch above us. He smiled at me and wiggled his eyebrows up and down, like he'd won the lottery.

"You'll be perfect," Fontbutter said to me. He raised his hands into a triangle shape and looked at me through them.

"Excuse me?" I said, my confusion increasing by the moment.

"Mr. Fontbutter is a producer. He makes adventure stories about the supernatural for Netflix," Old Holly said. He leaned against the railing on his porch and kicked the ground with a puffy slipper. I could see he wasn't planning to join us down at the well. Nor had he made much effort to greet his company for the day. His face was unshaven, and he was still in pajamas under his warm jacket. The two men were a picture in contrast. I wondered what they were up to. Mostly, I just wanted my hand back.

Just then, Bellows joined us from around the side of the house. Today he was wearing what I assumed was his outdoor gear. It consisted of a pair of faded khakis and a gray fleece hoodie that looked as old as the patched tweed jacket he'd worn yesterday.

Before he could say a word, Fontbutter released my hand and headed right for him with a pitch about his show.

"I'd be happy to add some historical flourishes," said Bellows with some authority. "I don't have much experience on camera, but I can tell you a lot about history. For example, I am working for the Whaling Museum right now, putting together an exhibit about whaling captains' logs and the ships' voyages. Did you know—?"

"Very kind of you, but that's usually my part of the show," said Fontbutter. "I will want to interview you for information about the bodies and the island. And I'll be happy to give you a credit at the end."

"A credit?" said Bellows. "But I am sure you'll want to include an authentic historian."

"People like a bit more flash these days," said Fontbutter, twirling his moustache. "It's a downright shame, of course. The real heroes never get the credit."

Bellows looked aghast. I could see he was about to

protest when Leigh rounded the house as well. She ignored both men and headed straight to her car with a spring to her step.

"Good morning, Leigh," I said. "How's it going?"

"Great," said Leigh as she opened the back of her car and began to extract some ropes and harnesses, all of which I assumed were for the excavation down the well.

Fontbutter did not attempt to shake Leigh's hand, so I assumed they had already met before I arrived.

"Will your descent be so deep that you'll need all of that equipment?" I said. "That looks like a lot of gear."

"It's to lower ourselves down the wall of the well. Belaying is a way to safely descend a deep drop using ropes. I don't have many opportunities to belay down to sites, and it's my favorite kind of work. Haven't done anything like it since my trek to Egypt. I studied in Cairo under a wonderful Egyptologist in college."

"I've tried it. It's fun," said Fontbutter. "Perhaps we can do a segment on my show about scaling sites."

"We should," said Leigh, brightly.

Bellows paled.

"I have lots of tips of the trade I'd be happy to share," she said, "along with some great stories about Solder's work and some digs we've done together."

"I can't wait to meet this Solder of yours in person," said Fontbutter. "I heard him speak once. Not the most commanding of speakers, but I could tell he's a brilliant guy. I'd love to share some ideas with him on how to promote his work."

"He won't be interested," said Leigh, in a tone that suggested we should all know this fact by now. "He hates publicity. He does it all for the love of the work, not headlines."

Having gathered yesterday that Leigh felt she and Solder should make more of an effort at promoting their work, I suspected she'd try her best to include Solder in Fontbutter's production. I wondered, in fact, if the spring in her step had a bit to do with Fontbutter's arrival.

Perhaps reading my mind, or feeling she had betrayed her man by sharing her disappointment that he did not do more to put himself in the spotlight, Leigh shut the car trunk and scurried back around the house. Fontbutter's eyes followed her. It was obvious to me that he found her attractive.

I quickly averted my stare when he turned back to me.

"Leigh will be a great addition to the production," he said to me. "She has the right vibe. And you! You are small-screen eye candy."

Fontbutter was lucky that my cousins appeared from the backyard at that moment. Had I had another second with the man, I'd have given him an earful of my thoughts on being eye candy for his show. Eye candy? Really? As it was, I gave him my best stare-down. Old Holly and Leigh might welcome his arrival, but not me.

I'd been excited to pursue the mystery of Patience Cooper and Nancy Holland. I'd thought we could save Agnes from living with doubts about her legacy, and that we might even help Halloween Haunts get back on track. I confess, I was also excited myself to learn more about these women with whom I felt so many connections. Now, however, I could see that many others stood to benefit from our discovery of her skeleton.

Patience Cooper had died a violent death. Rather than letting her rest in peace, I hoped I hadn't resurrected her to new troubles.

Chapter 7

"Hiya, Stell," said my cousin Docker.

Strong and stout, Docker dragged behind him something that looked like a small tree, but that I knew was actually a gargantuan weed. I'd had no idea that so much work would be needed in order to clear Old Holly's property. Ted, longer and leaner but equally strong, followed behind with another weed. Both were wearing blue fleeces with the name WRIGHT BROTHERS CARTING on them.

"Everything good?" I said to my cousins.

"Well, you have a path to the well," said Ted. "It took us a while to get to it, but we teamed up with Kyle Nolan from Kyle's Gardening to clear off about two feet of vines around the well, and we added a pathway leading up to it from the lawn."

Ted looked at Old Holly and leaned into me.

"And before you start complaining that we should have done more," he said in a low tone, "this job was really something for a bigger team with more time. The thicket around the well is actually quite deep.

Kyle finished the pruning, though. We had to borrow an axe from Old Holly to get some of it done. It was that thick."

"You guys are the best," I said to both Ted and Docker. I didn't know Kyle Nolan, but I knew his wife, Clemmie, since she was a barista at The Bean.

"Anything for you," said Docker as Agnes and the other ladies pulled up and parked their trio of Toyotas. "And anything for Agnes."

"Hello, boys," said Agnes from her open car window. She jumped out of her car with a box tied with twine.

"You didn't," said Docker, putting his hand to his heart.

"I did," she said. "Lemon bars. Your favorite. I remembered from when you came to clear away my old wood fence last fall."

She looked over at Old Holly. They didn't exactly greet each other as much as acknowledge each other's presence.

"I figured Mr. Holland wouldn't have anything for you to eat, in spite of your labors," she said, turning back to my cousins, "so I wanted to make sure someone was keeping an eye out for you."

"You're the best," said Docker.

My cousins took the box and headed to their truck, which was overflowing with shrubbery. As they pulled away with the last of their load, I watched Ted pop one of Agnes's treats into his mouth with a smile.

"Ready?" I said to Agnes.

"Ready," she said, her friends coming up beside her.

"Ready," said Bellows. He might not have convinced Fontbutter to put him in his production of this
Nantucket mystery, but I could see Bellows wasn't
going to relinquish the opportunity to be part of our
discovery without a fight.

For different reasons, we all took a deep breath.

"Are you coming?" I said to Old Holly over my
shoulder.

"Nah," he said. "I've got baseball to watch. I told
Andy, when you find Nancy you can take your snap-
shots or whatever you want to do. I guess you can
take a couple of artifacts for Fontbutter, too. But at
the end of the day, I want you all to leave her be."

"Will do, Mr. Holland," said Fontbutter, raising a
handheld camera. "I'll keep an eye on everything for
you."

"As will I," said Bellows.

"Who is he?" said Agnes, as we all headed to the
back of Old Holly's property.

"He's a filmmaker," I said. "Old Holly called him,
and he was apparently on the first flight here to
make a movie about the excavation."

When we rounded the house, we found ourselves
in a clearing of about three or four acres. Old Holly's
land included at least a dozen acres more, but unfortunately for him it was mostly wetlands. As a result,
he was stuck with undevelopable land on an island
where acreage was more valuable than gold.

"Leave it to that man to try to make some money
off of this," she said. "Who cares about family pride?
Or facts? To him, this is a chance to have his yard
cleared for free and make some money in the
process."

Cherry put her arm around Agnes, and we all continued toward the well. As Ted and Docker had forewarned, the lawn, if that's what you could call it, given that the grass was half-dead, ended with a wild, dense thicket and stalky pine trees. In the midst of this Northeastern jungle, the team had made their path to the well.

I noticed that a long folding table had been erected on the lawn. It was covered in some of the climbing equipment Leigh had removed from her car, along with a few other odds and ends for the excavation. I wondered why they had chosen a place so set back from the well to set up a command center.

Andy stood beside the table, on the phone, and I could hear him giving his chief a collegial update about the work that had been done. He gave a nod of recognition to all of us as we passed him.

When we reached the old structure, I understood why the table was so far back. My cousins and Kyle Nolan had only been able to clear a limited space around the well, which remained surrounded by thick, high brush. There was not room for all of us and a table. Solder and Leigh were huddled to one side, reviewing a checklist. They looked up at us, and I could tell we had little time to see the site before they'd want us out of their space.

The well itself was a humble, round structure. About six or seven feet wide and made of the same stones as Cooper's chandlery, it came up to my waist. If Nancy was below, I could see how her cloak could have been caught against the stones as she lifted her leg over the cumbersome edge.

Several boards that had covered the old structure

for many generations had also been removed. They
were shoved into the thicket behind the well. As I'd
done with the Cooper's Candles sign, I walked over
to the old slats to examine them. I noticed a few of
the old nails on the ground beside them. They were
rusty from the elements. Some were machine-made,
others were as old as the ones I'd found back at the
Morton house. The Hollands had taken care to keep
the well sealed over the years.

Agnes leaned over the thick, rough edge of the
well and looked down.

"Can you see her?" she said. "Oh, you can't see
anything. My word."

I joined her in staring into pitch-blackness below us.

"Hello," said Cherry into the well. "Anybody
there?"

She looked at our confused faces.

"I was checking for an echo," she said. She picked
up a pebble and dropped it down the well.

We didn't even hear it drop.

"No tampering with the equipment along the side,
please," said Solder, politely but firmly. He put on a
bright yellow windbreaker with many pockets and
checked to make sure he had his gloves with him. His
expression was both serious and excited. I had a feeling that, except for his concern about us tampering
with his site, he was not quite aware of any of us.

"Good luck," Fontbutter said to Leigh.

"You're not really dressed for our outing," said
Bellows to Fontbutter, perhaps noticing his attempt
to flirt with the scientist.

"I'm right off of an event in Virginia and not

dressed appropriately," Fontbutter agreed, "but my enthusiasm runs wild when I find a good story. This one has the potential to be the biggest hit I've ever had."

"How's it going?" said Andy, joining us.

"Considering my connection to the island, and my expertise in history," Bellows said to him, "I would like to propose that I accompany Mr. Solder."

"That will not be necessary, but thank you, Mr. Bellows," said Solder.

"With all due respect, I insist, Mr. Solder. This is as much a historical matter as a forensic one. I am sure I will have information to help you. Any scientist should welcome the offer of help from someone who knows the context of the geography and the culture."

Andy took a step between the men.

"Mr. Bellows, if there is a reason for you to go down the well after Solder's initial investigation, we can discuss it at that time. Although your expertise in archaeology, especially with regard to New England in the nineteenth century, is especially appreciated, given the situation with the body, I only have permission from Old Holly and the chief of police for Robert Solder and Leigh Paik to descend."

I thought Andy did a bang-up job at being diplomatic.

Solder took off his spectacles. Bellows straightened his fleece.

"Of course, I have permission to descend the well for filming," Fontbutter said to him. "I'll take all the photos you'll need."

Solder raised his eyebrows. Bellows clenched his jaw.

"Mr. Fontbutter," said Solder, "I'll be sure to be down the well each time you descend to film. I'm concerned that someone like you might contaminate the body."

Bellows smirked at Fontbutter. Then he bowed to the group and retreated down the path. Leigh handed Andy a walkie-talkie.

"Alright, everyone," Andy said. "Let's clear out. Leigh has given me your walkie-talkie, Solder, so we can stay in touch while you are down the well. She has me on channel two."

"Roger that," said Solder, clicking a rope attached to a belt around his waist to a rope he had secured to the ground.

Leigh began to do the same. The anthropologists adjusted their helmets, checked their headlamps, and did one last check of their ropes. The rest of us all turned and headed back, single file, to the camp table in Old Holly's yard.

"How did Mr. Holland find you?" I asked Fontbutter as we walked up the field.

Fontbutter gave me a mischievous look.

"He didn't find me," he said. "I found him."

"So quickly?" said Agnes.

I thought her question was a good one. It had been less than twenty-four hours since we'd decided to unearth Nancy Holland, and here was Hugh Fontbutter, making himself right at home.

"I'm connected to a lot of social media," he said.

"You should follow me," said Cherry. "I have over

three thousand followers. I'm aiming to be an influencer."

"I'm sure you are," said Fontbutter, with an amused glance at her wardrobe, much of which was hand-crafted and quite colorful compared to his urban style. "But it was your Girl Scouts who tipped me off. They had several hashtags about a dead body, and one was about the well at Mr. Holland's house. Anyone who follows stories on ghosts will have heard about this one by the end of the week."

"Oh, no," said Agnes. "Think of all the crazies about to visit the island. Clairvoyants and ghost whisperers."

"I know," said Fontbutter, looking very excited. "The royalties should be very tidy on this one."

Bellows was pacing in front of the command center. Flo set up three folding stadium chairs. The Candleers took their seats and stared at the brush, as if they were at a sports event that was more exciting than Old Holly's Red Sox game.

The walkie-talkie that Andy was holding blasted white noise as he turned up the volume.

"Testing," said Andy.

We heard a whirring noise, and then a voice broke through.

"Over," said Leigh. "We're heading down. We'll be in touch when we reach the bottom of the well."

"Over," said Andy.

Flo took out a can of nuts and opened them.

"Have something, Agnes," she said.

The sound from the walkie-talkie whirred again, this time more loudly.

"—I think a flashy show is a complete betrayal of our work," we heard Solder say. "It's a good thing the skeleton is under our jurisdiction. Another forensic anthropologist might not be so diligent, but I won't allow Fontbutter access to the Cooper specimen. And if he does manage to find a way in, I'll make sure it will come with a large donation to the university. And neither of us will be doing interviews, that's for sure. At least I know you'll agree."

From the way the two scientists were speaking, we all realized we were listening to a private conversation.

"I don't agree," said Leigh. "But it doesn't surprise me. You don't think even the curator from the Historical Association has the right skills."

Everyone looked at Bellows, who quickly looked at his phone, as if he hadn't heard a thing.

"Leigh, this is Officer Southerland. Do you read me?" said Andy.

There was no response. I gathered that something was pressing against Leigh's walkie-talkie, so that it was only able to transmit to us.

"Bellows," Solder said, "plucked the linen from the body yesterday with his bare hands. Historians should leave the field work to experts. I held my tongue only because I knew you were trying to be nice to the locals."

"I only want to be out in the world, my love," she said.

The conversation stopped for a few minutes. We could hear heavy breathing of the two partners as they shimmied down the well.

"Anyone can go down that well," said Fontbutter,

somewhat to himself, as he rubbed his finger around the collar of his button-down shirt. "I don't need to make donations."

No one answered him. By now, we were all pretending to be busy. The conversations both below-ground and above were not what anyone had anticipated.

"All I'm saying is you can't live in a bubble forever," Leigh said. "The real world is passing you by, Robbie. And now you won't even tell me what you're working on. Why not? What could you possibly be working on that you can't tell me about? I thought if we came here you might tell me."

There was the sound of equipment being unharnessed, and then the line went dead.

"This is Officer Southerland," Andy said again. "Can you read me?"

"Loud and clear," said Leigh in a chipper voice that contrasted noticeably with the tone she had taken with Solder.

"We have quite a discovery down here," said Solder.

Any interest we'd had in the pair's private conversation dissolved. We were on pins and needles.

"There is a skeleton dressed in female attire," said Leigh.

"Nancy," said Agnes, covering her mouth. "She was down there. She really killed herself."

We all looked at Agnes, not sure whether to celebrate the discovery of another historical find on Nantucket or to acknowledge the reality that, one way or another, Patience Cooper was back on the hook for the loss of the Petticoat Row funds.

Cherry was the one who broke the awkward silence.

"That's good news," she said to Agnes. "Now you can focus on Patience and figure out what happened to her. Someone killed her."

"That's right," I said. "It's like crossing off a suspect. This is an old case; it had unanswered questions, and now we know more."

"Plus we've opened a discussion about Nantucket's hidden history," said Bellows. I was impressed that Bellows hadn't let Solder's criticisms knock him off balance. Once again, I could see that the man wasn't going to go down easily.

"Nantucket's hidden history," said Fontbutter. "I like that as a tagline."

Agnes and Bellows visibly cringed.

"I'm setting up the lighting right now," said Leigh over the walkie-talkie. "The conditions here are favorable. The well was sealed tightly. We'll have a look and see what we can determine. Over."

From across the field, we heard Gil Holland yell at his TV, "Run! Run! Yes!"

The Sox were having a good day.

"We've set up the lights," Solder's voice broke through a few minutes later. "I'm examining the body. This is an amazing find. Over."

"Can you tell us what you see?" said Andy. "Over."

"It—a—similar to—"

"We're having a hard time hearing you. Over," said Andy.

"Can you hear m—?"

"A little better," said Andy.

"Confirming from preliminary observation that the body is a woman's," he said.

We all looked at Agnes. Flo and Cherry put their arms around her.

"What happened to Patience Cooper?" she said, her shoulders sinking.

I was thinking the same thing. If Nancy was down the well, and Patience was in her makeshift grave, I wondered if Jedediah had taken the money and left town with some other woman he'd wooed. What a cad.

"There are intact remnants of clothing," said Solder. "She seems to have been carrying a canvas pouch that, because of the strong material, is almost entirely undamaged. That is very rare."

"What's this?" said Leigh from what sounded like a few feet away from Solder.

There was silence for a moment.

"Remind—had—house," said a voice. At this point, we could not even tell who was speaking.

"Hello?" said Andy.

"Can you hear—?" said Solder.

"We keep losing you," he said.

"There—and—a piece of embroidery in the sack. It's similar in style to the linen and needlework we found at the Morton house. I believe it's safe to say the two artifacts are from the same period. It seems to be a map."

"That's not an unusual choice of subject for that type of needlework," said Bellows. He leaned toward the walkie-talkie. "I'll need to see that."

"Mr. Bellows would like a look at the embroidery.

Can you bring it up? Over," said Andy. I could see Andy was enjoying the excavation.

I was surprised Old Holly hadn't stuck his head out at this point, to gloat about Agnes's silly ideas. As far as he'd been concerned, he'd received free lawn work and booked a Netflix special without having to get out of his pajamas or leave his chair.

"It looks like a map—Nantucket," said Solder. His voice was fading. Andy turned up the volume. "There's an X at one point of the island. I am not familiar with the geography, so I don't know where it is. We're packing it to bring up, along with Nancy's bonnet."

"It's a treasure map," said Cherry, her eyes bright with interest.

"There's a saying across the top: My Love, My Treasure," Solder said. We strained to hear the words. "Battery is—Leigh will—pack up what we can take with replacement—."

The line went dead. Andy put down his walkie-talkie.

"Stay here," he said to all of us as he walked down the path to the well.

We watched him leave.

"Maybe Nancy was guilty after all," said Agnes, hopefully. "If she felt remorse after doing the dirty deed, she might have hidden the money from Jedediah and jumped down the well with a map that marked the spot."

"That trove would be worth a fortune today," said Bellows.

"Who gets the treasure if someone finds it?" said Flo.

"It would be up for grabs," said Fontbutter.

"It would be a historical find for the island," said Bellows with a sharp look at Fontbutter.

Andy walked out of the clearing to the table.

"Leigh's coming," he said, looking through one of her bags. "We were able to call out to each other as she was climbing up. They tried to change batteries, but something isn't working with the walkie-talkie. She's going to swap it out, go back down to help Solder package up what they found on the body, and we'll call it a day."

"Should we get some lunch somewhere?" said Flo to her girls.

At that moment, a groaning noise wafted across the field. We looked over to the path by the well's entrance. In stunned silence, we watched as a tree on the right side of the pathway began to sway and then fall with tremendous force across the entrance to the well that my cousins had cleared. When it landed, birds flew to the sky, calling out danger. A rabbit scurried furiously out of the brush. Leaves flew up and across the field in every direction.

Then, Leigh Paik let out an earth-shattering scream from behind the blockade.

Chapter 8

"Leigh!" I cried.

"Can you hear us?" said Andy.

When she did not respond, I knew we were all thinking the worst. The tree's trunk was not particularly thick, but it had many branches, all of them long and filled with sharp limbs. If any of them had hit her, Leigh Paik could be in serious trouble.

Andy, Bellows, Fontbutter, and I ran to the tree, which now barricaded the path. Collectively, we tried to move the timber. The branches, however, had tangled themselves into the extending brush and nothing was moving. We called out to Leigh as we worked, but she still did not answer. Cherry joined us with a small first-aid box she'd found at the table, but I suspected we might need more than Band-Aids.

"Miss Paik," cried Bellows.

"Hello?" said a woman's voice, finally, from the other side of the brush.

A flood of relief washed over all of us.

"Leigh?" said Andy.

"Yes," she said. "I think a tree fell on me."

"It did," said Cherry. "You're lucky to be alive."

"The fire department will be here shortly to help clear away the tree," said Andy. "Are you hurt?"

"I don't think so," she said.

"Can you get to us from your end?" said Andy.

We heard some rustling. Things went quiet for a while. Then we heard some more rustling.

"No," she said. "I'm stuck in some brambles. I think you're going to have to cut me out of here."

"OK," said Andy. "Sit tight."

"I want to make my way around the brush, to see if I can get to her," I said. "There might be an opening on the other side of the well from which it would be easier to reach her. No reason she has to be stuck in there."

"I'll help too," said Fontbutter. He tossed off his suit jacket.

Andy was already kicking around the brush's perimeter, in search of any entry.

"You ladies stay here and wait for the firemen," he said to Cherry, Flo, and Agnes before they offered their services too. I was glad he didn't give me the same instructions. There was no way I was going to sit around while poor Leigh Paik was trapped.

"Wait a minute. Solder must be worried, too," said Bellows, with less enthusiasm about our plan. "I'm sure he'll climb up and get to her first."

If Bellows was trying to dissuade us from the search, he changed his tune when he saw Fontbutter roll up his sleeves. Not to be beat, Bellows found a stick, long and sturdy, left behind by my cousins. He shoved into the brush beside the former path. Fontbutter followed but took a wider path, which started in what was high weeds rather than the bramble Bellows had chosen.

Andy followed Fontbutter's strategy of taking a wider loop in hopes of spotting an opening from the less-dense foliage. Whereas Fontbutter had gone right, Andy went left. Hidden by the brambles, we could already hear Bellows whacking away and grunting with his stick to try to clear a path.

I took one more look at the landscape and then decided to enter through a small opening, of where my cousins' path had been. Before diving in, however, I remembered an extra helmet with a lamp on top that was on the equipment table. I doubted I'd need the light, but I decided head protection couldn't hurt. I put it on.

"We're coming," I called out to Leigh.

There was no answer this time. I hoped she hadn't fainted.

As I stepped into my chosen path, the ground was thick with twigs, leaves, and vines that were tricky to traverse. The vines looked easy enough to cross, but at each step they somehow seemed to grow around my feet and keep me from moving forward. I was immediately glad I'd taken the helmet. With it, I was able to hunch down, below some branches, and plow through the lower brush. I couldn't see anyone, but from the grunts and curses echoing around me, I could tell we were all having a tough time.

My efforts to take each step became a methodical task. One hand would reach forward, pushing aside the brush ahead, then, head down, I'd find a spot for my foot. Once I succeeded on one side, the other hand and foot would echo the routine. Left. Right. Left. Right. Branch in the face. Foot in a puddle. Left. Right. Soon my pattern became automatic to the point that I had time to think about Solder's find. We had all been so excited yesterday by the idea that Nancy Holland might have duped Patience. We were so caught up in history. Now I feared we had done nothing more than invite a Netflix producer to the island to exploit the story of two women who'd had a bad ending. I felt badly for Agnes too.

My thoughts had returned to Solder's interesting discovery of a map when my path became less dense. I thought I'd somehow reached the back of the well and the brush that my cousins had tried to remove. When I began to notice the growing scent of the harbor's waters, however, I realized I had somehow veered off my path and had headed farther away from the well and to the outskirts of Old Holly's property.

Turning around, I retraced my steps until I reached the point that had led me astray. Then, I crouched down and continued. Beyond the miniature forest in which I'd found myself, I heard the fire trucks arriving. I wondered if they'd have to rescue our crew as well as Leigh at this point. Our united grunts and groans were increasing as the search continued. I tried to see someone through the brush, but between the thick foliage and the gray day it was impossible to see far ahead.

I could hear Cherry giving the firemen details on how the tree had fallen and who was underneath. The men called out to Leigh, but again she said nothing.

"She's right through there," I heard Cherry say from my left. Or was it my right? I couldn't tell.

"Under the tree," said Agnes.

Suddenly, the whole of my journey eased up. The ground was not as rough. The brush was not as foreboding. I saw light ahead where the foliage was clearer. In my excitement, I took a couple of steps forward, more quickly than I should have. The first step or two was fine, but on the third, I felt my foot get tangled in a vine I had not noticed until my opposing leg was already in midair. I flew ahead, my sneaker falling off behind me, and landed face down in front of the well.

"I made it," I called out. My cheek was pressed against dead leaves and twigs, and my helmet had fallen off, but I was in one piece. "Leigh? Can you hear me?"

There was no response.

I turned my head as I slowly began to sit up. I expected to see the wall of the well. Instead, I saw a bright yellow wind breaker and realized I was looking at Robert Solder.

He lay next to me, his eyes closed.

"Robert?" I said, sitting up quickly. "Hey, buddy."

I shook the man's shoulders, but I got nothing. He was out cold.

"Andy?" I called out, remembering the CPR I'd learned in high school. All those years of lifeguard training were about to pay off.

"Stella? Sit tight" I heard Andy call, his voice becoming louder with each word.

I pinched Solder's nose and leaned over to begin mouth-to-mouth, wondering what had happened to him. Perhaps he had been hit by some branches as well. I hoped I hadn't knocked him out in my fall.

I was about two inches away from the man when I noticed something was very, very wrong. I unceremoniously dropped Solder's head back down to the ground. When his head hit the dirt, his eyes opened and looked straight into mine. I pulled my hands to the sky as if I had been caught red-handed.

The movements were purely instinct, but they weren't unfounded.

Around Robert Solder's neck was the rope he had used to climb the well. It was pulled tightly against his skin, and his skinny neck bulged over the fibers of his noose.

"What happened?" I said, not so much to him as an expression of pure shock.

I reached my finger out to Solder's neck, to check his pulse, but I couldn't bear to touch him there. Instead, I moved my fingers on his wrist.

"Hurry," I said to Andy, but then realized there was no rush.

Robert Solder had no pulse.

From behind me, Andy emerged from the trees. Ahead of me, Bellows fell forward, in similar fashion to my arrival, and landed right in front of the body with a scream.

"Where are you?" I heard Fontbutter cry out from the dense forest.

"Is he—?" said Bellows, stopping himself.

"Yes," I said.

Bellows stood up and took several steps away from Solder. From across the harbor, the sound of the Sunday church bells chimed twelve noon. Fontbutter suddenly dashed into the open area. I was not surprised to see that he had snuck his camera into the brush. He dropped it, however, when he saw the dead body. He then began to shiver, quite uncontrollably.

I looked at Robert Solder's dead body. I did not see any signs of struggle. He still wore his glasses. Whoever had killed Solder had come upon him in surprise.

A couple of feet next to the dead man, I saw a small satchel that had fallen open. I remembered Leigh carrying the empty bag when the two had descended the well. Now it looked full. I went over to take a look. Inside, there was a filthy canvas bag that appeared to be the one Solder had described as being next to Nancy. There was also a bonnet, similar to Patience Cooper's. Each was in a container, and marked. Interestingly, there was no map.

"Everyone put your hands in the air," said Andy.

Chapter 9

I let go of the bag and raised my hands, along with Bellows and Fontbutter.

"What's going on?" said Leigh, behind us.

I was relieved she was unable to see us from her confinement, but I noticed that there were enough loose branches on our side that we might get her out. I motioned to Andy to indicate the fact, but he shook his head.

"Stay put, Leigh," said Andy.

His gun was still raised.

"I want you all to turn around and face away from each other," Andy said to us.

Once we did, I heard Andy discreetly call in to headquarters from the other side of the well with details of the situation. Following his call, I pieced together noises that sounded like Andy was patting down Bellows and Fontbutter. It took all of my respect for Nantucket's finest to stay turned away.

"What's this?" said Andy, at one point.

"My inhaler," said Bellows. "I think I need it."

A few moments later, I felt Andy behind me. It was his official duty to treat all of us as suspects in the murder of Robert Solder. Technically, I had had the opportunity to kill him.

"I'm going to pat you down your sides," he said. "If you would like to wait for a female officer, we can."

"I think I can handle your hands on me," I said.

Next thing I knew, Andy's hands were making their way down my sides. He took my phone, which did not please me, but his hands were warm and strong, and his measured breath made me realize that I was a bit more frazzled than I had realized. I felt that he sensed this in me too, because he put his hands on my shoulders when he finished. The gesture lasted for only a second, but it helped me steady myself. Once I did, I wanted a look around, so that I could figure out how someone had killed Robert Solder almost in front of us, but without anyone seeing the violent act.

"May I get my shoe?" I said, offering my unshod foot as proof that I needed to move.

"You may sit down. All of you need to sit down," Andy said. "I'll get your shoe."

He walked to the edge of the brush and picked up my sneaker. When he handed it to me, he barely made eye contact. I knew Andy had the task of rescuing a wounded woman, protecting a crime scene, and keeping all of us calm—in the presence of someone who had likely just committed murder.

We both knew, however, that I had none of these official concerns. The one and only thing I cared about was justice for the man beside me who had climbed down a well this morning, with a promise to solve the mystery of Nancy Holland, and had never made it back alive.

"Nobody speak," Andy commanded us. "Even you, Stella."

Sitting in silence, I tried to remember who had suggested we head into the brush to find Leigh. I put my head into my hands when I realized it had been me. I had handed a murderer the opportunity to kill.

"Hello?" Leigh said again, now with a whimper.

"Are you OK?" I said before I remembered I wasn't allowed to speak.

"I heard yelling and a fall," she said. "Is everyone OK?"

"We won't be able to get you out from this direction," said Andy, ignoring her question, "but the firemen are making headway to you."

"OK," she said.

We listened as the firemen slowly reopened the path my cousins had made. I hoped they would reach Leigh quickly. It was only a matter of time until she asked for Solder. If he were alive and healthy at the bottom of the well, he'd have surely climbed up by now.

While we waited, I decided to disobey Andy's orders the tiniest bit. I gathered my courage to look at the body. Not easy. I hate looking at dead bodies.

Robert Solder was lying on his back, as straight as a log. His left arm was outstretched above his head, and the fingers on that hand were open. His right arm, in contrast, was over his chest, and his hand was clenched in a fist. It was a funny combination, both defensive and submissive.

My eyes were drawn to Solder's skinny neck and

the rope around it. I thought that it wouldn't have been hard to squeeze the life from him, especially if he were attacked from behind. A bruise was beginning to form in a ring around his neck, which made me feel a little sick, so I looked at his clothes. They were somewhat dirtier than when he had dropped down into the well, but the damage could have been from his climb as much as from a struggle with his killer.

I could hear Andy taking photos of the crime scene, in anticipation of the firemen arriving and the activity that would ensue. Unfortunately, I didn't think his photos would reveal much. The ground was already covered in footprints from all of us. Both Bellows and I had fallen, so the area beside the body had been contaminated as well.

It wasn't until the firemen had extracted Leigh that they made the final cut through the foliage to the well. At that point, Andy made each of us exit, single file. We were marched straight up to Old Holly's house as the medical examiner passed us and headed toward the well.

Ahead, I saw Leigh, who was sitting on the edge of an open ambulance in Old Holly's driveway. She had a silver Mylar blanket around her, and she was crying hysterically. An EMT was standing beside her with a vial and needle, but she pushed him away.

"The chief tried to talk to Leigh," Andy said, coming up next to me, "but she can't put two words together. I think they're going to give her a tranquilizer and try again later."

"Don't," I said to Andy, my hand instinctively finding his arm. "Let me try to talk to her. Right now, I feel certain she'd rather talk woman-to-woman than to a man in blue."

Andy looked across the field at Leigh's sobbing figure.

"Alright," he said. "But go strictly for comfort."

"You got it," I said.

Andy rubbed his hand over his short hair. He looked at the chief, who was now headed to the well.

"And don't get me in trouble," he said. "If you can, see if she heard Solder climb up the well. Or if she spoke to him."

"Or if she pushed over the tree so she could kill Solder without us seeing?" I said.

He nodded in agreement.

"That too," he said. "Anything you can get on a possible motive, but tread lightly."

"I'll need my phone back."

"Why?" said Andy.

"Girl things?" I said.

"You'll have to do better than that, Wright," he said.

"Maybe I'll have to google something with her," I said. "Like Solder's family or something."

"Not your best," he said, "but here."

I took my phone and headed toward Leigh. As I walked to the ambulance, I made one quick call to my cousin, Kate, who works at the Nantucket Cottage Hospital.

"Hi," said Kate when she picked up. "I'm starting such a long shift, and I'm trying to cut down on coffee. Can you hold some of those pumpkin-spiced latte candles for me? I'm thinking the aroma might trick me into thinking I've had some coffee."

"I don't think it will work, but it's worth a try," I said. "Meanwhile, I need your help. I found a dead body."

Kate is a woman with a serious demeanor. Her greeting about the coffee was as close to stand-up comedy as she got. I could imagine her pushing her glasses up her nose.

"What happened this time?" she said.

"I don't know yet," I said. "His name is Robert Solder. The body is still here, but when it gets to you guys, let me know if there's something interesting I should know. There's free pumpkin-spiced latte candles with a custom espresso shot aroma in it for you."

"I'll hold you to it," she said.

I hung up as I reached the driveway. Ted and Docker's truck was parked there too. Once again, I considered how my proposal to excavate the well had gone so wrong.

Ted lowered his window.

"We heard the news. The police called us back to check out the work we did," Ted said. "They seem very distracted by how the tree fell."

"Why?" I said, confused.

"You got me," said Ted. "I swear none of the trees was in any sort of precarious state when we left. And there's no way anyone could time the falling of a tree to hit the lady."

"All that means is that no one was trying to kill Leigh," I said.

"Still don't know what that has to do with us," said Ted.

"Because if someone planned to fell the tree to

block our access to the well in order to kill Solder, it would suggest premeditated murder."

I left my cousins and walked over to the ambulance, wondering who would have planned to kill Solder.

Leigh was seated at the edge of the truck with a box of tissues, which was doing little to mop up the flood of her tears. When she saw me, she looked as if she wanted to say something, but the words could not come out. Instead, she lifted a shaky hand and crumpled tissue to her nose.

"I'm so sorry," I said.

"Thanks."

Leigh pulled her blanket around her.

After a moment of silence, I ventured a question.

"How did you meet Solder?" I said.

She smiled, and I felt I had started in the right place.

"I was his teaching assistant," she said. "It wasn't a creepy power-play thing on his end. We were not that far apart in age. Compared to the men who were knocking on my door, he was a solid guy. He took his work seriously, and the passion he had for his craft took my breath away. And it spilled over. I mean, he was not your usual let's have a glass of wine and get to know each other kind of first date. We went to a restaurant in Boston where we were like the youngest people by decades. I think he must have looked up how to impress a lady. He barely spoke the whole evening, but then when he dropped me home, he gave me the most passionate kiss. And the next day, a dozen roses without a note arrived at my door."

She wiped her eyes, but she was calmer now.

"We'll have to contact his family," I said. "Are you close to them?"

She shook her head.

"His father passed away. They were close. His mother has dementia. She's in a nursing home. It'll be a strange blessing that she won't be able to connect the dots. He has one older sister, but she's married and lives in Australia. It was mostly just the two of us."

"What about work people?" I said.

"Of course," she said. "But I wouldn't call them friends so much as colleagues. I dealt with our social lives. Solder didn't care much about people. He didn't care much about fame or fortune. Just the work. The mystery. The puzzle."

I nodded. We sat for a few moments, once again in silence, before I continued with my questions.

"I know this is hard," I said. "But can you tell me what happened down in the well?"

I wasn't sure if Leigh would answer, but after struggling with her emotions for a bit, she looked at me.

"When the walkie-talkie died," she said, her voice catching on the last word, "Robbie was much more interested in the body than in talking to you guys. He got on his knees and started examining the girl, so I decided to switch out the walkie-talkie. I just can't remember what happened after I got out of the well."

"If you close your eyes," I said, "maybe you could remember."

Her chin quivered.

"I can try," she said.

She wiped her eyes once more and then closed them. She looked scared, but brave.

"When you climbed out of the well, did you see anyone?" I said. "Maybe by the tree that fell?"

"I thought I might have seen a deer run away," she said.

"Before the tree fell, did everything look like it did when you'd descended?"

Leigh shrugged.

"I guess," she said. "But then the tree fell over, and I was trapped."

"What happened after that?" I said.

"I don't know," she said.

I wondered if she was blocking out the events, since they were so painful to recall. If she was telling the truth and had nothing to do with the crime, I realized that the more time that passed, the easier it would be for her to bury the memory.

"Can you describe what you saw after you were trapped?" I said.

"There were leaves and branches all around me," she said. "One big one pressed against my arm. I wasn't sure what happened, then I heard you calling my name."

I was still interested in why she'd stayed put.

"Did you try to break free?" I said.

"I was afraid to move at all," she said. "I tried to stand up, but immediately I knew I couldn't, so I just sat there. You all told me that you'd come to get me, so I tried to stay very still. My knees began to ache a little from the position I was in. And I felt sleepy."

"Did you hear anything?" I said, accepting her explanation for now. "Any signs of struggle?"

She opened her eyes, her breathing becoming sharp and labored.

"No," she said. "Did I pass out when Robbie was murdered?"

The EMT looked around the truck, and I saw he still had the vial in his hand. I waved him away. The last thing we needed right now was for Leigh to take a tranquilizer. She was upset, to be sure, but she seemed to remember the events better than she thought she did.

"I think you might have fainted," I said, rubbing her arm until she composed herself again. "Solder probably climbed up the well when he heard us calling for you. We were making a lot of noise."

Leigh closed her eyes again. I could see that anger now replaced her fear.

"I heard you all walking through the forest," she said. "Everyone was shouting. At one point, I heard the museum guy, Bellows, call my name. He asked if I could see anything from where I was sitting."

I did not remember hearing Bellows say this to Leigh, but his question might have come when I'd left the path and headed in the wrong direction. I wondered if Bellows, in asking the question, had been trying to make sure no one could see him attack Solder. Of course, Fontbutter might have heard her answer too.

"I did hear a lot of noise," she said. "A lot of rustling about. A lot of noises as you all tried to find me. Then I heard a few heavy falls."

She opened her eyes and looked at me.

"The chief told me you fell beside Robbie," she said. "It must have been horrible."

"Don't you worry about that," I said. "You said you heard a few falls. Can you think how many?"

Leigh shook her head.

"The sounds were confusing," she said. "Sometimes I couldn't tell where they were coming from. I felt trapped. As if I were in a box."

I remembered my own confusion over the direction of sounds and nodded to her, reassuringly.

"I know the police will ask you this," I said, "but it might be easier to tell me. Do you know if Solder was involved in any criminal activities? Or if he had any enemies?"

Unexpectedly, Leigh laughed.

"Solder was a genius," she said, "and he was quickly able to solve the riddles that stumped many of our colleagues. Our peers might have begrudged his talents, but often they benefited from them. And the last time we spoke, we were quibbling over batteries."

They had been quibbling over more than batteries, but I did not let on that I knew that.

"Who would want to kill him?" she said.

I was wondering the same thing.

"This might sound strange," she said, "but I want to finish the job here. I want to go back down the well, to where Solder and I were last together. There's still work to be done. I'd like this excavation, and Fontbutter's film, to be in his honor."

"Stella?" said Andy.

He was standing at the doorway to Old Holly's house, but he motioned slightly toward the well, where I saw both the chief and the ME heading up the field. My time was up.

"One more question," I said, slipping off the edge of the ambulance. "Do you have photos of Nancy Holland's body or any of the items you found?"

Specifically, I was thinking about the map.

"No. Normally that would have been my job," she said, "but after I set up the lights, I headed up the well. I assumed I'd have time for photos when I returned. As for Robbie, he didn't stop to document anything when he was working. He thought it broke his flow. Should I have taken photos? Would it have helped find his murderer?"

Leigh began to cry again, and this time her emotions got the best of her. The EMT came around the truck again with his syringe, and Leigh stuck out her arm without having to be asked.

I headed to the house.

Everything Leigh had said seemed honest and logical enough, except for one thing. I thought about her interest in getting back to work so quickly in light of the argument I'd heard between her and Solder on the way down the well. From what I'd learned, he certainly did not appreciate Fontbutter's arrival. I doubted he'd have considered a posthumous connection to the producer as an honor. I also realized that with Solder gone, Leigh might now have her opportunity to move into the limelight. Especially if she could star in a Netflix special.

Chapter 10

"I told you to leave well enough alone," Old Holly was saying to Agnes when I entered the living room of his house a few minutes later. Before I could say hello to him, he stormed out of the room and into his kitchen, slamming the door shut behind him.

The Candleers were seated on Old Holly's sagging sofa, under a bay window at the far side of the room. They clucked among themselves over Old Holly's rude behavior. Fontbutter was staring out of the window at the other end of the living room, looking at the police and firemen scouring the area for clues. Bellows was pacing in the dining room, looking nervous. Very nervous.

I stepped forward into the living room, but Andy interceded, cramping my style.

"How's Leigh?" he said.

"I don't know how much help she'll be to you," I said to him. Nobody was looking at us, but I spoke quietly. "If she's telling the truth, she says she heard noises, but could not tell who made them or what they represented. Could have been any one of us, or the killer. You'll need to contact his sister in Australia about the death, but otherwise Robert Solder kept to himself. His world was Leigh and forensic anthropology. No enemies she could think of. In fact, I have a feeling that a few of the trickier cases in the forensics anthropology world might not get solved now that he's gone. From Leigh's perspective, his colleagues considered him a genius. The only thing I don't like is her eagerness to get back to work."

"People have a lot of different ways to deal with grief," said Andy as he pulled his ringing phone from his pocket.

"Hi, sweetie," he said into the phone. "Hold on a sec?"

I assumed he was speaking to his girlfriend, Georgianna. He put his phone on his shoulder to muffle the sound and looked back at me.

"I've got to take this," he said. "Can I trust you to lay low? The chief has a lot of questions for everyone."

"I was going to chat with Fontbutter and Bellows," I said.

There had been no arrests, but at this moment Old Holly's house was as good as a detention cell for all of us. As a fellow suspect in what was now the Old Holly jailhouse, I hoped a sense of camaraderie would enable me to learn something from my fellow inmates.

"I don't like the idea of you talking to them before the chief joins us from the murder scene," he said.

"Promise me you'll stay out of trouble. I've got my own problems to deal with."

I knew we had different ideas about what my getting into trouble might look like, so I wasn't going to pick a fight. Instead, I gave him a wink and then crossed my arms. He looked confused by my two opposing actions.

"I'm not talking to you about anything without my lawyer," I said, a decibel higher than necessary. My goal was to give the impression to the others assembled that Andy had been hassling me about the case, especially since I had been seen speaking to Leigh. There was no need for anyone to know that Andy and I were trading information. I didn't want to risk losing anyone's confidence.

He matched my glare with a respectable one of his own and then stepped away.

"I told you I'd call you back." I heard him say to Georgianna. For the second time that day, I realized I was in the uncomfortable position of overhearing strained words between lovers. Listening to Solder and Leigh quarrel had been awkward, but also, frankly, interesting. Especially given how events unfolded. I did not, however, want to hear any details between Andy and Georgianna. We live in a small town, and sometimes you need to maintain boundaries in order to keep the balance between everyone. Like a good family might. Fortunately, I saw Cherry looking at me.

"Stella," she said motioning to me.

Agnes, Cherry, and Flo sat shoulder to shoulder, not far from Old Holly's empty recliner. Agnes was in the middle, and her friends' hands were reassuringly pressed against hers. Escaping the proximity of Andy, I entered the living room and sat on the arm of the recliner next to them.

"We saw you talking to Leigh," said Cherry.

Agnes adjusted her pearls.

"Poor girl," Agnes said. "Oh, what have I done? I was so darn sure I was going to protect Patience and the Coopers' legacy. Instead, a man is dead."

"There, there. It was Stella's idea, not yours," said Cherry, summing up my fears nicely.

"What happened on your side of the yard after we all left you and went to look for Leigh?" I said.

The ladies shook their heads.

"We sat there, feeling helpless, until the firemen arrived," said Flo.

"It was terrible," said Cherry. "We could hear you all banging away in the brush, trying to get to her. Then we heard falling and yelling. We thought you'd gotten to Leigh, but then that man Bellows gave such a shriek."

"We knew something was wrong," said Agnes. "But all the action was on the other side of the fallen tree and brush. We had no idea what was going on."

"So no one saw anyone else join us in search of Leigh?"

The ladies shook their heads. I knew they didn't have the best eyesight. Someone who was moving stealthily might have been able to join us in the brush without their noticing. I hoped that wasn't the case. The fewer the suspects, the better.

At that moment, my cousin Docker stuck his head inside the house.

"Andy," he said, "can we speak with you outside?"

Another officer, who looked younger and slightly overwhelmed, took Andy's place in the house. I knew his job was to make sure none of us left.

"Who do you think did it?" said Cherry, eyeing Fontbutter and Bellows.

I joined them in looking at the two men.

"My money is on Fontbutter," said Flo. "No one can really shriek like Bellows did and be guilty of committing a murder."

"I think it was Bellows," said Cherry. "I could see it in his eyes the moment I saw him. I'm good at reading eyes. Plus he has a motive. Solder was going to rat on him to the Historical Association about his unprofessional behavior at the Morton house. And he wanted to keep him from participating in any of the excavations. We all heard it."

"His reputation is all he has," I said, agreeing with the ladies. "Plus, with Solder now out of the way, he'll probably be able to take over the case of Nancy Holland and Patience Cooper."

"I'd be willing to wager my new, hand-quilted jacket that Fontbutter did it," said Flo.

"I love that jacket," said Cherry.

"Ladies!" I said. "Betting on murder? What's become of you?"

"I'm sorry," said Cherry. "But I do love that jacket."

"I agree with Stella," said Agnes, looking very agitated. "A man is dead."

"There, there," said Flo. "Too soon. I see. I was just trying to lighten the mood. I'd never part with my jacket."

I was tempted to share a giggle with the ladies, but I noticed that Agnes flinched when Flo touched her.

"What's wrong with your arm?" I said to her.

"I must have hurt it moving some firewood yesterday," she said.

Cherry suddenly became very interested in straightening some fringe on the throw pillow that was shoved between her and Agnes.

"You know Agnes," said Cherry.

"Such a flibbertigibbet," said Flo.

"That's exactly what I am," said Agnes, touching her pearls again.

"Flibbertigibbety?" I said. "You gals might trick everyone with your old-lady bit, but I know you better. What are you hiding from me?"

"Would you like an Altoid?" said Agnes. "I have spearmint."

"This must be bad," I said.

"Oh, just tell her," said Cherry. "It's Stella. You can trust her."

Agnes clasped her hands on her lap and looked at them.

"I went into the woods," she said.

"Not long after you all went in," said Flo.

"Tell her what happened," said Cherry.

"I wanted to try to help, so I went into the woods," said Agnes, lifting her eyes to meet mine. "I took the direction of Fontbutter's path, because there was more room to walk there."

"And because we thought he'd just film the search but not really look for her," said Cherry. "They call it B-roll."

"Fontbutter was faster than I was, and I couldn't keep up," said Agnes, "so I decided to try to make my way to Leigh on my own. Then I tripped and fell and hurt my arm. I didn't want to return to the girls empty-handed, I guess. I sat there for a long while, so they thought I was on the track to finding her. When I heard the firemen come, I stepped back out to the yard."

"Why didn't you tell Andy?" I said.

"Because I don't have anything to add, and I don't want to be a suspect in a crime that I know I didn't commit," said Agnes.

"OK," I said, ignoring, for the time, the fact that she was withholding information from the police. "Then tell me. Are you sure you didn't see anything while you were in the woods?"

"Not a thing. I mean, I might have," she said, "but it was hard to tell anything. It could have been one of us searching for Leigh, or even a deer."

"Don't be embarrassed. Tell her what you saw," said Flo.

"Oh, fine. I saw something that looked like a ghost. Are you happy?" she said. "But it's very gray outside, and it was a little foggy out there. I'm sure it was something real and not a ghost."

"But it looked like a ghost," said Cherry.

The kitchen door opened, and Old Holly stepped into the living room.

"The next game is on," he said. He shoved me off of the arm of his seat and settled into his La-Z-Boy chair, pulling a lever that raised his feet. Then he popped open a beer.

"I wouldn't be surprised if Gil Holland did it," whispered Flo, looking at our host with some suspicion.

"It would take too much effort for him to get down the hill," said Cherry.

Flo had a point. Old Holly had been MIA during the entire excavation—from the moment we headed to the well until the moment people were ushered into his house after Solder's body was found.

Motive, however, was the question. I tried to think of any reason why Old Holly would want Solder dead. I considered that with a murder on his property, Fontbutter's movie had more value, which would translate to more money for him. The idea seemed extreme, but my list of suspects was growing. I added Old Holly to the lineup.

Reluctantly, I also added Agnes to the list now that I knew she had been in the vicinity of Solder as well. I found it hard to believe she could be a suspect, but she had been in the right place at the right time, and she'd chosen not to tell the police.

"Oh, look," said Flo. Her gaze was through the window. "They're taking Leigh's fingerprints."

"They'll probably take all of ours," said Cherry. "And I just had my nails done."

I looked at the officer who had taken Andy's place in Old Holly's house. He was distracted with the activity outside the window too.

"Excuse me," I said to the ladies, and headed to the dining room while everyone was looking out the window.

I found Bellows picking at a thread on the hem of his tattered fleece.

"How is the Paik lady?" he asked, straightaway.

"Fine. You know, I heard Fontbutter saw Solder speak once. That'll probably put him at the top of the suspect list."

"You think if he met Solder before today he'll be on the top of the list?" said Bellows, turning paler.

My comment was meant to put him at ease and to make him think I was suspicious of Fontbutter. Instead, he seemed even more alarmed.

"Have you ever met Solder before today?" I said.

"As a matter of fact, I have. Last year," he said. "Solder was among a panel of experts at U Mass, and I was interested in learning more about new discoveries. Actually, I'll admit it. I was out of work and had time. It was a rare appearance, I hear. Arrogant fellow. I shook his hand afterward, but obviously he didn't remember when he met me again yesterday."

I was fascinated. Both men had a previous history with Solder. I wondered if there was a connection to one of their past meetings and the murder.

"What was Solder talking about at the conference you attended?" I said.

"The risk of overlaying historical legend with scientific fact," he said. "Didn't surprise me when Solder was skeptical about the PC embroidery on the Morton house skeleton yesterday. He would have probably had issues with today's find too. That's why I wanted to go down the well. I see things differently, but my perspective is equally valid."

His last few words sounded defensive to me, but I supposed I understood where he was coming from.

"What do you think about the map?" I said.

"Good question. Needlework was a popular pastime, although I feel like the map, given the context of the body and whatnot, is odd. Finding anomalies is the most exciting part of a historian's life. I'd like to see it as soon as possible."

"Me too," I said.

"No offense, but I'm having a hard time with small talk, knowing we're with a murderer," said Bellows. "It doesn't surprise me that a man like Fontbutter would be reduced to a murderer. His last production was *Ghostly Ghouls of Georgia*. Let's say he needed a hit, at any cost."

"Do you think you'll be in Fontbutter's film now that Solder is gone?"

Bellows turned red, and did not answer.

Seeing I'd overstayed my welcome, I left Bellows to stew and walked over to Fontbutter, who had taken a seat in an old armchair and was studying Old Holly's bookshelf.

"How are you doing?" I said, quietly.

"I'd like to return to the scene of the crime," he said. "The sun is shifting, and soon the light won't be very good. I want to get shots of the well, and ideally the body too, before they take it away. This is going to be my best show ever."

"You'll have a lot of good interview opportunities," I said, secretly horrified by his cavalier attitude toward filming the murdered body for his show.

"That's for sure," said Fontbutter, quite calmly. "I heard you talking to the Cooper relative, Agnes. She thinks she saw a ghost? That's pure gold for a show like mine. She'll be at the top of my list of interviews."

"Did *you* see anything in the brush?" I said.

Fontbutter tossed off a laugh and shook his head, then crossed his legs and put his index fingers to his chin. His leather-soled shoes were shot. They were both covered in mud and scuffed beyond repair. I had to give the man credit. He was willing to do anything to get a good story. Did that include murder?

"I think the discovery of the map is very interesting," I said.

Fontbutter leaned back in his chair and gave me a cool stare, which I returned.

"'My Treasure, My Love'—with an X for extra drama," he said. "That's an odd line to stitch across a map. What do you think it means?"

"What do you think it means?" I said.

He smiled coyly and shrugged.

"You mentioned that you saw Solder speak once in Boston," I said. "Have you ever wanted to use Solder in any of your shows?"

"No," said Fontbutter. "Solder's not what we call a camera-friendly type."

"Leigh is," I said.

"That she is," he said.

"I'm not the silver-screen-type," I said, "but if you need extra help, I'd love to assist you in production."

"Not a bad idea," Fontbutter said with genuine enthusiasm. "I don't have an assistant on the island with me. This opportunity to work on the show came about quickly. I saw a chance and took it before anyone else could."

"It's a deal," I said to Fontbutter as I stood to leave, pleased with my success at having secured future interaction with the man. I'd know where to find Bellows, but Fontbutter might have been harder to keep track of.

"Speaking as your assistant, I'd talk to the officer over there about what he knows and how much longer we'll be here today. I know those guys. He's more likely to talk than anyone else."

Fontbutter smiled.

"Good idea," he said, and headed across the room.

The moment Fontbutter engaged the officer in conversation, I slipped out of the house.

Chapter 11

I stepped out of Old Holly's house as the ambulance pulled away with Leigh in it. Before the officer inside noticed my absence, I walked quickly down the field. My gait was fast enough to make headway, but hopefully casual enough that I didn't attract attention. As I made my way, I considered the suspects. I knew that people killed for lust, greed, power, and revenge.

Leigh was experiencing problems in her relationship with Solder. Perhaps she had found a way to slip out of the brush and kill her lover. With him gone, she would inherit his reputation and work.

Bellows had felt threatened by science's upper hand in the focus on forensics. He was angry that Solder had not appreciated his ability to piece together the story of Nancy and Patience using historical fact. And had Solder succeeded in taking possession of Patience, and even Nancy, he might also have felt undermined in his efforts to join the Nantucket Historical Association full-time. If so, he might have snapped.

Whereas Bellow feared he was losing power through Solder's work, Fontbutter might have feared Solder would compromise his opportunity for fame. Fontbutter had the best story of his life, but we'd all heard Solder vow to intercept him at every step. We'd also heard him state his ambition to make Fontbutter pay for access to the their work since Nancy's remains would be his property, not Old Holly's. Could that be motive enough for a man like Fontbutter?

Old Holly, the source of Fontbutter's opportunity, might have also come to the same conclusion. After years of being land rich but cash poor, he might have feared his financial opportunity would diminish were Solder to be in charge. Again, motive enough for murder.

I hated to keep Agnes on the list, but experience had taught me that I needed to see every angle through to the end before crossing someone off. I couldn't imagine what her motive might be, but I knew that she was very emotional about the story of Nancy and Patience. I thought for a moment about her observation that a ghost was lurking. Perhaps she had been frightened. If she were the killer, the crime might have been a reaction to her fears, not an act of cruelty.

The most important question to answer first, I decided, was whether the murder was premeditated or spontaneous. Remembering the path that had led me away from the well when I'd searched for Leigh, I decided I needed to make sure there were no other potential suspects who had had access to the well from that direction. The thought made me a bit nervous. If the murderer and I had used the same path, I might have been close to him all along.

When I stepped into the clearing around the well, I saw the medical examiner, his assistant, Andy, and the chief. The group stopped speaking when they saw me. The chief's lips were a straight, grim line. Andy raised a hand to stop the lecture that might be forthcoming and walked over to me.

"I thought you'd like to know," I said, "that I remembered something about the area. When I was searching through the brush to make my way to Leigh, I lost my way. Before I knew it, I was in a more open space that felt like a path but wasn't. With all of the excitement, I didn't think of it until now . . . but if there was a path, why didn't Old Holly tell us? He'd said the area was overgrown and forgotten. Obviously, it was not."

Andy looked over my shoulder to the area where I had been searching. His eyes seemed to see through the trees.

"And your path was on the side of the well where the tree fell," he said. "Interesting."

I could see he was trying to make sense of this new detail, but I still wasn't entirely sure about the police team's interest in the tree.

"Stay here," he said.

Andy walked back to the chief. The two men spoke quietly for a moment or two. The chief looked my way once, but no more than that. I knew they were trying to decide if they needed me or not.

Finally, Andy walked over to one of the firemen

and said something. In return, the man took off his hat and handed it to Andy.

"It's a little big," Andy said when he returned. "But I know you and your hair."

"Thank you," I said, taking the bright yellow hat from his hands and buckling it onto my head. "For the hat, and for trusting me. Shall we?"

"Lead the way," he said.

If anyone had told me when I'd stepped out of the brush earlier that I'd voluntarily return, I'd have questioned their sanity. Here I was, however, angling one foot in front of the other, maneuvering over twigs and vines and brush that made my ankles itch. The first few steps were easy to trace. I'd flattened some of the bushes on one side, so I knew I was heading in the right direction. After a minute or so, however, I stopped and looked around me.

"Does anything look familiar?" said Andy. He was holding back the branches of two trees that were growing so close together he could barely fit through.

As Fontbutter had said, the sun was shifting, so not everything looked the same. I closed my eyes and tried to find the hint of the sea that had made me stop. I inhaled deeply, seeking the scent of salt and fish and shells over the autumn leaves around me.

"This way," I said, opening my eyes.

"That's my girl," he said with a chuckle.

Andy always got a laugh out of my keen sense of smell. It was exasperating. Like him, I was holding a branch that reached across my path. As I took a step forward, I let it go, and allowed the branch snap up. I heard Andy utter an *oomph* behind me as I continued. I knew I should've kept my cool, but it was satisfying.

After taking a few more turns, we found ourselves in the space I remembered. I now walked carefully, searching with each step for a clue left behind by someone else who had used the path. I was looking behind a bush I thought looked unnaturally crushed when Andy made a discovery.

"Look at this," he said.

I was surprised to notice various piles of Marlboro cigarette butts. Andy pulled out evidence bags and collected a few.

"This should get us started," he said.

"Strange, right?" I said. "Do any of our suspects smoke?"

"Not that I know of," he said, "but I'll find out."

Andy continued on down the path, beyond where I had stopped. This time, it was I who followed him. We walked about another twenty yards, through a footpath that was not expertly cleared but definitely had been made into enough of a pathway that our steps were easy. Behind us, we could not see the well. I knew no one could see us either.

Finally, the path opened to a marshy field. It ended at the harbor.

"Did you see any boats when you were here?" said Andy, looking across the water.

"I wasn't here," I said, wishing I could be of more assistance. "Do you think someone could have taken a boat here, knocked the tree over, killed Solder, and retreated?"

Andy tilted his head. His eyes were still on the horizon.

"But who?" he said. "And wouldn't that person have been afraid that Leigh would see the whole thing?"

"That broken walkie-talkie might have saved her life."

"Weird about the cigarette butts," he said, and headed back down the path.

Our return to camp was faster. At this point, we'd made enough of a dent in the trees that we didn't get lost. When we reentered the area around the well, Andy walked directly to the chief. I could see my cousins Ted and Docker had rejoined them. I was curious to know what they had to say about the fallen tree, but I was even more focused on taking advantage of the opportunity to check out Robert Solder, whose body was still in the area. The medical examiner had rolled the body over, onto a cloth sheet, and had moved it a short distance. An officer was taking photos of the ground under the body, while the ME was examining the back of the corpse.

"Start a search for a blunt object," the examiner said to his assistant.

I could see why he'd issued the order. On the side of Solder's head was a gash I hadn't noticed before. I looked at the stone well. I could imagine that if I hit my head against it, I'd get a noticeable wound too. The ME, however, seemed to think he might have been hit by an object.

"What are you saying, dude?" I heard my cousin Ted say.

"Kyle Nolan might be a lot of things, but I don't like where you're going with this," said Docker with an equally animated outburst to the otherwise business-as-usual vibe that had taken over the crime scene as the professionals went to work. Kyle Nolan, I remembered, was the gardener who had helped my cousins clear the well.

The men were standing beside the tree that had fallen so suddenly across Leigh's path. I sidled up next to the meeting, before anyone remembered to send me back to the house. Immediately, I saw that neither a deer nor any other animal had had a part in the tree's collapse. The fall was no random accident. The trunk was cleanly cut about three-quarters of the way through. The rest of the trunk was torn, as if someone had pushed it over. It would have taken strength to do the last bit by hand, but these trees were about as thick as Robert Solder's neck. It wasn't impossible.

"They think one of us sabotaged the tree so that it would fall over," Docker said to me.

"No, they don't," I said. "They just have to follow all leads. Right, Andy?"

But Andy was on his walkie-talkie, sending a message up to the house to find the axe that Kyle Nolan had borrowed yesterday.

As I had instructed Leigh to do not long ago, I closed my eyes and tried to remember watching the tree fall. Our attention had been on Flo who had suggested lunch, so we had not seen the tree moving at first. When we had heard the noise, however, we had all turned. I remembered seeing the tree swaying and groaning.

I had assumed that the tree had fallen by itself and that one of our group had taken advantage of that opportunity to murder Solder. With the discovery of my pathway and the suspiciously cut tree, however, it now seemed possible that the swaying might have been the result of someone pushing the tree over for its final fall, one timed to coincide with the ascent of the forensics team.

I opened my eyes.

"The batteries," I said to Andy.

"What about them?" he said.

"The killer might have tried to get Leigh out of the way by swapping in bad batteries."

"I'll get fingerprints on the batteries," he said. "Good work. Let's head back to the house."

He took a step, but I remained still. There was a neat row of evidence bags on a tarp beside the well. I noticed that the bags included Nancy's bonnet and her canvas bag, but no map.

"Still looking for the map?" said Andy. "Solder said he'd bring it up, but he didn't have it on him."

"That seems important to me," I said. "Bellows said it would be worth a lot in today's market. Perhaps someone was willing to kill him for the map."

"No one had a map when I searched them," said Andy. "And no one has found it in the area."

"But it doesn't make sense for him to have left it down in the well," I said.

"Solder only discovered that map today," said Andy. "Given the clues that this murder was premeditated, I doubt the map has anything to do with motive."

"But if the map is missing, I don't think this murder was planned," I said. "I can't explain the tree, but I think this murder might have to do with Nancy Holland and Patience Cooper's story, and the map Nancy left behind."

"Thank you for your suggestion," said Andy, walking me toward the path back to Old Holly's house before the chief complained about the fact that I was still there. "And I'm sure I don't have to tell you, but you are not to spread rumors about where the map is or isn't."

"I'm just happy I don't have to remind you of that fact," I said. "It's in our best interest to keep quiet about its disappearance."

"I'm sure it didn't disappear," said Andy.

We stopped at the table where I saw the walkie-talkies. I knew Andy had work to do.

"What are you going to do with Fontbutter and Bellows?" I said.

"We don't have enough evidence to arrest anyone at this point," said Andy. "Of course, no one is to leave the island. Including you."

I looked at him, about to share a good laugh, but he wasn't laughing.

"OK," I said, and headed back up to the house.

"Bye, Stell," Docker called out as I left.

"Keep an eye on the police," I called out to him over my shoulder.

"Will do!"

I entered Old Holly's house, this time through the kitchen door instead of the main one. I wasn't sure what to say or do with my suspects right now. I knew none of them would hand me the map if they had it, but I wanted to think about its disappearance a bit more.

"What're you doing, snooping around my stuff?" I heard Old Holly say to an officer inside the living room.

I peeked through the kitchen door, knowing that the search for an axe was now underway.

Old Holly was standing by his television, grabbing for his clicker, which the officer was using to lower the volume.

"I'll have to ask you to step away, sir," said the officer.

I closed the door and headed up the back stairs to find someplace to think.

Reaching the second-floor landing, I looked through a couple of doors that led to musty old rooms. Unlike the Morton house, which had some charm in spite of its neglect over time, Old Holly's house had a sadness to it I couldn't shake. It looked to me like Old Holly had left a wet towel one place, a plate of spaghetti in another spot, and then forgotten about them. I wondered if Fontbutter's call last night, suggesting a show featuring his family's story, had been an opportunity for escape for Old Holly. I could see why he might not be able to handle anything standing in its way, including Solder's lack of charisma, which might have jeopardized the show's success.

When I saw a latch in the ceiling that connected to the house's widow's walk, I took advantage of the opportunity to slip away from the second-floor rooms. It was easy to pull down and open the ladder. In a moment, I was up the stairs and on the roof porch that overlooked Old Holly's land.

I sat comfortably in the center of the small deck, away from the commotion below. From here, I had a solid view of the property and the harbor leading to town. I could see more than ever how buried the well had been before my cousins and Kyle had cleared a path. It was interesting to me that Old Holly had been so clear about where the guys would find it. Although the well had been almost buried by nature, he had certainly known exactly where it was. My cousins and Kyle Nolan had done a great job of clearing what they could in the time that they had had.

Below, I saw my cousins steaming with anger about the discovery that the tree had been tampered with ahead of the excavation today. The search continued for the axe, but no one seemed able to find it.

Was the break in the tree a strange coincidence or part of a plan to kill Robert Solder? This point seemed to be the difference between a premeditated murder and one of impulse. The police were sure the crime had been premeditated, but I decided to keep an open mind. I knew, however, that this piece of the puzzle needed to be solved sooner than later. It was the key to understanding motive and means.

I decided to visit Kyle Nolan, the gardener, to learn more.

Chapter 12

Kyle and Clemmie Nolan live out by the airport. I didn't know Kyle, but I was friendly with Clemmie, who works at The Bean. Our acquaintance began one day when my best friend, Emily Gardner, and I were paying for our coffees. Somehow, Em and I had gotten into a conversation about a bench on Main Street that has the names of beloved Nantucketers inscribed on it. We promised each other that whoever kicked the bucket first, we'd find a way to dedicate a bench to the other. Unbeknown to us, Clemmie was working her first day there, and she was listening.

"You silly girls," she had said with warm exasperation.

Clemmie is about our age, but she looks even younger. Even though her hair was covered in a net while at work, I remembered admiring its pale blue color, which popped against her dark skin and high cheekbones.

"What are you waiting for?" she had said when we

looked at her questioningly. "If you drag your heels like that, the old folks will have snatched up your bench by the time you need it. Mark your territory, women."

You can see why I liked her. After we left, I think I had promised Emily that I'd do the research on how to put a plaque on a bench, but we hadn't gotten around to doing anything about it yet, aside from debating what the plaque should say.

Of course, I never imagined that I'd ever be curious about whether Clemmie's husband had somehow had a hand in killing a man, but Kyle didn't have the same warm reputation as his wife. Kyle Nolan had grown up on Nantucket, his parents having arrived from the Caribbean before he was born, whereas Clemmie arrived here from Florida after high school to live with her aunt. While Clemmie took to Nantucket's life immediately, Kyle always seemed to be a fish out of water, so to speak. Even as an adult with a successful gardening company, the man was known to have a temper, although I'd never seen it myself.

When I pulled up to the house, I realized immediately that the police had already reached the Nolans before me. Kyle was out front. My window was up, but I didn't need to hear Kyle's words to get the gist. A vein on his neck had become so large with anger I could see it from across the street.

I was about to leave—I mean, timing is everything—but then the screen door of the Nolans' house opened, and Clemmie came running out. She headed right to my car.

I opened my window. Clemmie is of average

height; her figure is a healthy plus size, and she rocks it. Right now, she was wearing a form-fitting T-shirt and curvy jeans. She wore no makeup, opting instead for five sparkling studs up each ear, framed by pale blue tresses.

"Hi, Clemmie," I said. "You OK?"

"Hell, no, I'm not OK," she said.

The sunshine I always associated with her had been replaced with a cloud that rivaled the day's fog.

"Do you know anything about why the police are hassling Kyle?"

I turned off the car and got out. Behind Clemmie, their dog barked.

"Quiet, Buster," said Clemmie.

I was impressed. Buster not only stopped barking, but he settled by Kyle's feet.

"Ma'am," said the officer, a man I knew by sight but not by name. "Please get back into your car. You are intruding on a police matter."

"She's intruding on nothing," said Clemmie with a ferocity that could equal Kyle's.

"My wife has a social engagement," said Kyle, backing up his wife. "You have a problem with that? If so, I'll have Clemmie come right here to stand by my side. If you think I'm mad, get ready for my lady."

"Come on," said Clemmie, heading down the road, away from the men. "Kyle thinks the cop is here because he's been double-parking in town all month. He saw on TV that if you don't give the policeman a chance to tell you your offense, then they can't press charges. I think he's confusing that with getting a subpoena. Me? I don't think they send an officer over for things like parking spaces. And it seems an odd coincidence that you chose right now for our first social engagement outside of The Bean. Do you know what's up?"

"Kyle did a job for my cousins, Ted and Docker," I said. "A man was murdered this morning on the site where they worked. Before he was killed, a tree fell in front of him. When the police checked the tree, they found that it had been axed just enough in advance that someone could have pushed it over while we were there."

Clemmie stopped in her tracks.

"Kyle wasn't killing anyone this morning by pushing a tree on them. I've been with him all day."

I looked back at Kyle, who still hadn't let the policeman get a word in.

"Kyle likes a good fight," said Clemmie, as if reading my mind. "This is like a day at the beach for him. He's gentle as a lamb with me, though. As good a husband as there is."

Kyle began to pace around his porch, lecturing the policeman about the problems with piping plovers, a bird that has had protection issues on the island. The policeman crossed his arms but nodded in agreement.

"He would have been a good lawyer," said Clemmie. "Or politician. Instead, he's my crazy husband, who picked a few fights in his younger days and decided to embrace the role. He says it has its perks. He gets to cut in line at the movies, people let him have a parking space. You should see how good our service is when we dine out."

"But does he know that the police are here about murder?" I said. "This isn't a misdemeanor they're checking up on."

"He hasn't stopped talking since that officer arrived, so no. But I'm not worried. And nor should he be. He has an alibi. He was here, and I was here with him."

"Can anyone else vouch for you guys?"

"Sure," she said. "Buster and Kyle were playing fetch out front, and half the neighbors were complaining about Buster's barking. I was just bringing them both a snack when the police arrived. Who died, by the way?"

"Has Kyle ever mentioned the name Robert Solder?" I said.

Clemmie shook her head.

"Does he live on the island?" she said.

"No," I said. "He was here working on an anthropological excavation of a skeleton from the early eighteen-hundreds."

"The one they found at Halloween Haunts?" she said. "Or the one in the well?"

"Both."

"Maybe Solder dug up the past, and it came back to haunt him."

"That's what I think."

We both shook our heads and watched Kyle turn and face his house, his back to the officer, who was beginning to look impatient.

"I hate to ask this, but the police probably will at some point," I said. "Do you think someone might have hired Kyle to give the tree an extra chop? To make it vulnerable?"

"I doubt that," she said. "For a few reasons. One, he wasn't too happy, to begin with, that he was clearing out wetlands. Even the smallest bit of human intervention upsets the balance of nature on this island. Everyone's slicing their tiny bit back, and there's repercussions, you know?"

"I do know," I said. It's a topic of great debate on Nantucket.

"Second," she said, "Kyle's the kind to pick his own fights, but he wouldn't help someone else make trouble in this world. I know that man. Trust me. He'd look down on that kind of behavior."

Behind us, Kyle began to sing the national anthem.

"And third, look at that man. You think he had a hand in murder?" she said, shaking her head at his antics. "I'd better go bail Kyle out of this. He's going to feel really stupid."

"Need help?" I said.

Clemmie looked at my Beetle.

"You date the reporter, right?" she said.

"Peter Bailey."

"Hang around," she said. "Let Kyle give him a few quotes so you have his side for the record. In case this blows up."

"Deal," I said.

Clemmie walked over to Kyle, and I walked to my car, where I called Peter.

"Where've you been?" I said.

"Right now I'm at the gas station getting a new tire," he said. "I've had quite a day."

I smiled and let him talk, although I knew I had his day beat.

"First, Brenda Worthington showed up at the Morton house after you left," he said. "Apparently you had tea planned for this morning?"

"Oh, no. I forgot. I'm sorry," I said. "Did she talk your ear off?"

"No," he said. "She talked the ear off of Patience Cooper. I found her in The Shack, communing with the spirits."

"She broke through the gate?" I said. "It's supposed to be closed."

"I guess so," he said. "Tinker was actually the real trouble. After Brenda left, I realized he'd disappeared, but I didn't want to bother you during the excavation. I looked for him for forever, and in the end, he was on the roof of my car. Then, when I went to get him, I saw that I had a flat tire. So I put him inside and got a tow truck. You know what he did? He took a nap, right away. Can't imagine why he wanted to come with me in my car if that was all he wanted to do."

"Maybe because Brenda was able to have a chat with Patience," I said. "Cats have a sixth sense, right?"

As I was listening to Peter, I had watched Clemmie talk to the police officer, who seemed happy to have any rational conversation at this point. Up until Clemmie had begun to speak, Kyle had been singing, but he quieted down as the reality of the situation sank in.

"I need your help," I said.

"Sure," said Peter. "What's up?"

"Kyle Nelson wants to give you a statement. He's being interrogated by the police right now about Robert Solder's murder."

"Robert Solder was murdered?" said Peter.

I caught him up while I watched Kyle, who was reconciling with the officer. I could tell that Clemmie was giving Kyle an alibi for the murder. And even though the officer's back was to me, I gathered he asked the same question of Kyle that I had asked Clemmie: Had anyone asked him to cut the tree so that it could be toppled over? Kyle's vein popped up from his neck again, but Clemmie put her arm through his. He kept his temper, shook his head, and a moment later, the policeman turned around and left.

Kyle and Clemmie headed toward me. I put Peter on speaker.

"I've got a comment," said Kyle when I told him why I had called Peter. He spoke through my open window without waiting for me to get out.

"OK," said Peter.

"My comment is this," said Kyle. "Whoever killed Robert Solder, I'm sure you had your reasons. I'm not one to interfere with another man's business. When your affairs show up at my front door, however, you need to know you've messed with the wrong guy. You'd better watch out, or there will be another murder on this island."

"Got it," said Peter.

"OK, man," said Kyle, fairly calm for someone whose pulsing veins were just starting to recede.

"I'm sure the police asked you already," I said, "but where's the axe you used?"

"Left it with Old Holly," said Kyle. "Stella, I hate to say this, but you might want to talk to your cousins. Docker was bragging about having some unexpected cash on him when I saw him last night. Maybe some-one asked for their help cutting the tree."

"You think they'd do something like that?" I said, shaking my head.

"Not in a million years," said Kyle. "But murder has to be taken seriously."

"Meantime," said Clemmie, "we're twenty minutes late to have lunch with my auntie."

I took the hint and said good-bye. I realized that if I wanted to solve the mystery of how and why the tree had been left half-chopped, I would need to speak with my cousins again. I hated to admit it, but I feared what they might say. After all, they had taken on some debt recently to buy the new truck. What if they had unwittingly helped a murderer?

"Meet me at the airport for a snack?" I said to Peter as I drove away.

"See you in ten," he said.

I drove down the street to the airport restaurant, Crosswinds. They have the best dinner specials, but it was too early, and anyway I was so hungry I would eat anything. I opted for a grilled cheese and French fries, plus a chocolate shake.

"So, Brenda Worthington," I said when our food arrived. "She tried to speak to Patience?"

"Oh, she was more than talking to Patience," said Peter, popping a French fry into his mouth. "I was on my way to the car, ready to meet up with you, when I heard a thump in The Shack. I thought maybe one of the Girl Scouts was checking things out, so I headed back there before hitting the road. Sure enough, Brenda was inside. She freaked me out. When I walked in, I pushed the door back loudly, but she didn't seem to notice me. She was sort of humming while talking. I can't explain it. But then she told me she had been speaking with Patience, and I had scared her soul away."

"Did you ask what Patience was saying to her?" I said.

"Of course, I did," he said. "I'm a reporter. It's not often I get to walk in on someone chatting with a ghost. I even got a picture."

"Oh, no," I said. "Please don't tell me that she had her arm around a ghost."

"No, but you're not too far off," said Peter, pulling out his phone.

He flashed the phone to me to reveal a photo of Brenda Worthington. Topping off her usual fashion statement of slightly worn and dated leisurewear, she was wearing a Quaker bonnet.

"She thought the hat would help her connect with Patience. When I walked in, she was telling Patience about overdevelopment on the Island, but not to worry because the Quaker cemetery had not been desecrated."

"Did Patience have anything to share with her?" I said.

Peter opened his notebook.

"And I quote," he said, " 'Don't throw out the baby with the bathwater.' "

He laughed, then stopped when he noticed me staring at him.

"She mentioned a baby?" I said.

It was really odd that Brenda would mention a baby, but I found myself thinking about the diary of Mary Backus and her concern for the Coopers' offspring. I seriously doubted that Brenda had spoken to Patience, but the connection was unsettling.

"I need to visit Emily," I said about my best friend.

"Really?" said Peter, sipping the edges of a root-beer float. "I just told you that I found a woman talking to a ghost, and the next thing that comes to mind is a trip to see your best friend?"

"I think there's a connection between Robert Solder's death and the discovery of Patience Cooper and Nancy Holland. It's all connected to the story of these two friends. This feels like a murder of passion, not something that was premeditated."

"Why?" said Peter.

I knew he wasn't disagreeing with me so much as encouraging me to think through my idea.

"Yesterday we found Patience Cooper, long thought to have stolen money from her friends, but who, as it turns out, was a murder victim. Then today we confirm that her friend, Nancy, died down in the well and Solder told us all that he found a map beside her, perhaps a treasure map. A few minutes later, the map was gone, and Solder was dead. By the way, Andy doesn't want anyone to know it's missing. That's off the record."

"The map might still be down in the well," said Peter.

"I don't think so, because in a rare moment of agreement, Solder and Bellows both seemed to think it was an important find," I said. "If Solder bothered to bring up the bonnet, why not bring the item of real value with him too? Why leave the map behind?"

"And how can Emily help?"

"I'm thinking two good girlfriends can figure out what two other good girlfriends had been thinking."

"I see what you're saying, but mind if I pass on the trip to Emily's?" said Peter. "I'd like to go to the office. I have a couple of deadlines to meet."

"Are you going to print Kyle's quote?" I said.

"Not unless the police make real trouble for him," he said. "Otherwise, we might end up goading a murderer into disliking Kyle."

"I like how you're thinking, Bailey," I said.

A few minutes later, I was at my car. As I began to pull away, Peter waved his hands for me to stop. He jogged up to me.

"Forget something?" I said.

"Yup," he said.

He leaned into the car to give me a kiss. Then, in true gumshoe fashion, he headed to his car. I smiled all the way to Emily's house.

Chapter 13

Emily Hussey has been my best friend since preschool, but I hadn't seen her in three days. Her baby, the sweet Victoria, had caught a cold last week and had spread it to both of her doting parents like the plague. In fact, Emily's last Instagram post was an update on how the red patch under her nose was healing nicely. I decided she was past the chicken-soup phase, but on the way over to her house, I picked up some clam chowder from the Brotherhood. We have more choices for a good cup of clam chowder than you can begin to imagine on Nantucket, and everyone has their favorite. Emily loves the creaminess of the Brotherhood's recipe.

My dear friend was propped up in her bed when I arrived. She looked like she'd run a marathon, but Victoria slept soundly beside her, breathing easily, with the look of a cherub about her. I oohed and aahed silently over how cute she was.

"We don't have to whisper," she said. "Vicky can sleep through a tornado. Getting her to sleep is a nightmare, but once she's in dreamland, we're the luckiest parents on earth. The other day, Neal hung the new medicine cabinet—"

"The one from Pottery Barn went on sale?" I said, rising to take a look at their newest upgrade.

Emily and Neal bought a small, gray-shingled house close to the elementary school after they were married. Emily is always thinking ahead. The place was modest and somewhat cookie-cutter when they moved in, but slowly Emily has added her magic touch to make their house unique and welcoming. The medicine cabinet had been on her list for a while. The minute it went on sale, she was ready.

"It looks so good!" I said.

"Thanks. Neal was so proud to hang it up, and then in the middle of the night, after Vicky fell asleep next to us, the whole thing fell from the wall. Just fell right off. I told him to read the directions, but two years of Boy Scouts, and he thinks he could build a house if he had to. Anyway, Vicky slept through the whole thing."

"Speaking of the scouts," I said, settling into a gorgeous chintz club chair in red florals that had been a great discovery at the Hospital Thrift Shop, "I have news."

"Tell me," she said, removing the lid on her cup of chowder with a satisfied smile. "We've been so cooped up. I don't know anything that's going on."

"Put your hands over Vicky's ears," I said. "I don't want any of this to enter her dreams."

I told Emily the story of how I'd moved into the Morton house and of finding Patience Cooper's skeleton.

"Setting a good example to the girls while keeping an eye on your skeleton," said Emily with an approving nod.

"Exactly," I said. "Can you imagine us not wanting to be in a house with a skeleton at their age? Very disappointing."

Emily nodded in agreement.

When I finished telling her everything, from my discovery of Patience to the murder of Solder, Emily put her cup on the table and rubbed Victoria's back while she thought. Emily is great at seeing the big picture. It's how she works on events for her premier party-planning business. She sees the whole event in her mind as if it was finished and then makes a list of everything she needs to do to get there.

"First," she said, "I'd like to say that I wish you had picked last week to have made this discovery. The fact that you waited until I was bedridden is a betrayal of our friendship."

I smiled at her with some sympathy. It was hard for this woman of action to sit still.

"Second," she said, "I know you like the connection to this cryptic map, but I think the police have a good point that this has something personal to do with Solder. As you said, you heard Leigh fighting with him on the way down the well. You know that Bellows would love to jump in and take the lead on the excavation. And Fontbutter needs a win too. I hate to think of Agnes or Old Holly being a murderer, but you make a compelling argument for everyone. And none of those motives has anything to do with a map."

"And yet there was an important discovery this

morning, a map—a treasure map—that has gone missing. As my oldest and dearest friend, only you can brainstorm about this with me. After all, this is, at heart, a story about friends."

"Alright. We'll take the map route. Has anyone even seen it?"

"Only Leigh Paik," I said. "If we believe that no one took the map from Solder, that means he didn't bring it with him when he ascended the well. Why not bring the map up with him?"

"That doesn't sound right," she said, her curiosity about the matter appropriately sparked.

"Thank you."

"So you think someone took it when they killed Solder?"

"Honestly, I don't know. That's why I want to take a step back and review the story of the girls," I said. "Imagine if you and I were Patience and Nancy, and Jedediah washed up on Nantucket, and we both fell in love with him."

"Not an issue. Sisters before misters," said Emily.

"Exactly. The Petticoat Row ladies were like sisters to each other," I said. "Nancy and Patience grew up together, shared the same hopes and dreams. Then Patience marries Jedediah and takes her friend's money. What's that all about?"

"The heart wants what the heart wants?" said Emily.

"I mean, this was an upright member of Quaker society. Would you have ever done that to me?"

"Billy Meyers and fourth grade all over again," she said.

We both laughed.

"OK," I said, "Billy Meyers and his striped T-shirt aside."

"I still remember that shirt," she said. "Let's face it. We were in love with the shirt."

"But within two weeks we were over him," I said. "It was no fun eating lunch by ourselves, right? But Jedediah shows up in some hot shirt, on a whaling ship he joined somewhere in the South Pacific. He was new blood."

"Maybe they were tired of the schoolboys they'd grown up with," she said. "Imagine if we only had the boys we grew up with to choose from."

"And maybe a bunch of Patience and Nancy's potential suitors were on whaling voyages."

"And they're not getting any younger. And they want to get a move on."

"And then this good-looking guy shows up."

"OK," said Emily. "So here we are. You and I. Desperate."

"Lonely."

"Lonely and desperate. There's only so many nights we can hang out, embroidering, without longing for someone's warm hands down our sides."

"And Jedediah probably sensed it right away. He flirts with us. Maybe he meets you and you do that thing you do with your hair, and you guys make a date."

"And then you catch his eye because you do that black ponytail, sexy-mama-body thing where you ignore your assets because you're all caught up in your craft and your business."

"I don't do that," I said.

"Wow," said Emily. "Almost two hundred years

later, and Jedediah is still getting best friends to fight."

"So, what would we do?" I said.

"Listen," said Emily. "If we were that short on men and Jedediah really liked you, I'd get over it."

"Patience's father had recently died. By marrying Patience, Jed got a woman, a house, and a small candle-making business out back: You—Nancy—had family."

"Yeah, out by Old Holly. I might have been prettier," she said with a wink, "but you had the goods."

"Then we get to the money. How did they get caught up in the robbery of the Petticoat Ladies' funds?" I said. "I can't really believe that either of them took it, but they certainly both seemed to have died because of it. But why? They each had a comfortable life and a strong community with wonderful friends."

Emily sighed.

"You'd never rob me," she said. "I'd never rob you. That's not what best friends do. Jedediah was behind the robbery."

"I agree," I said.

We sat in contemplation for a while.

"Maybe he couldn't get through a February," I said.

Emily looked at me sympathetically. A couple of years ago, I thought I might have found my soul mate. Like Jedediah, he was a wash-ashore, someone from the mainland. Once February had hit, however, he'd left. The fact that Peter hadn't lived through a February on Nantucket yet was always on my mind. As much as I loved him, something always held me back a bit. I knew it was because we needed to get through a winter together.

"So, winter comes, and he misses his days in the South Pacific," I said. "That could be it. Patience doesn't want to leave; he does. When he finds out that Nancy has entrusted her with lots of money, he kills Patience and runs away with the goods."

"Wouldn't signing up for another whaling voyage have been a lot easier?" said Emily. "Patience could have continued to work. Quaker women were encouraged to go to school, run businesses. Aside from wearing whale-boned corsets, they were pretty progressive women."

"Greed," I said. "He had the Petticoat Row money in hand. He wanted to get off the island. He saw an opportunity and took it."

Victoria stirred. For a moment, we both froze for fear we'd ruined her nap.

"Did Solder say what was on the map?" said Emily when we were sure Victoria would not wake.

I tried to remember.

"He said there was an X near what looked like a grassy area of the island. But he didn't know where the X was, because he wasn't familiar with the geography."

"Unusual thing to embroider," said Emily.

"That's what Bellows said."

"And there was no indication of what the X signified?"

"I don't think so," I said. "I guess we assumed it was connected to the money. Solder said there was a phrase across the top: 'My Love, My Treasure.' Love and treasure in one phrase. What if the treasure represented something else? Not money?"

"Like what?" said Emily.

I looked at Victoria and thought of Mary Backus's journal entry. She mentioned the offspring of the Coopers.

"What if Patience had a baby?" I said. "I mean, if Jedediah was a killer, he had probably shown his true character beforehand. If she had a baby, she might want to protect it from Jedediah. In her diary, Mary Backus said that Nancy looked forlorn after her friend disappeared. She probably knew something bad had happened. I mean, her friend would never leave her baby behind."

"I like it," said Emily. "I mean, that's something that could drive a person down a well. And it would explain why she took the map with her. She wouldn't want it to ever get into Jedediah's hands. She wouldn't want him to find the baby."

My phone rang at that moment. I looked at the screen to see my cousin Kate's name.

"Hi," I said, but my words were ill-timed.

At that moment, Victoria turned over and in doing so was roused from her impenetrable slumber. The sound of my voice, one other than her mother's, perhaps one tinged with concern, woke her, and sent her into a flood of tears that I could have taped and played in the haunted house.

"Can you hold?" I said to Kate, not waiting for her answer before I put the phone over my chest to block the noise.

"Sorry," said Emily, lifting her baby.

In one second, it was as if I had disappeared from the room. Whatever fatigue Emily was feeling from her own illness had left her. In its place was a mother in full-on action. She rocked Victoria and said comforting words to her, while simultaneously feeling her forehead for a fever.

I rose and waved, the phone still over my chest. Emily gave me a half-hearted wave as I left the room and headed downstairs.

"Hi," I said to Kate.

"Boy, that kid has lungs," said Kate.

"I know," I said, waving to Neal as I opened his front door.

Neal waved. I thought it was funny as I left that he didn't seem to notice the volume. Then I noticed his earplugs.

"Robert Solder's body just arrived," she said.

"Did you find out anything interesting?"

"I was able to take a quick look at the file," she said. "Death by strangulation. There was a hit on the head too, but it was not deadly. The coroner believes it was inflicted by someone rather than from the deceased hitting his head during strangulation. Something about the angle."

"Anything else?" I said.

"Nothing yet, but he just got here," she said. "I'll let you know."

"Thanks so much," I said.

I hung up the phone and checked my watch. It was going on four o'clock, but already the skies were dimming. Before I knew it, the cold days of winter would be here, and I'd find out if Peter could take a quiet winter on the island. I shook off the thought. Winter hadn't eclipsed the sky yet.

At the intersection of Main Street and Pleasant Street, I saw Ted and Docker's truck slowly bumping down Main Street's cobblestones. I knew that the brothers would never take money from anyone to make a curious cut into a tree, but Kyle Nolan was right. Murder had to be taken seriously and all avenues had to be investigated.

"Hey," I called, and honked my horn.

Docker, who was driving, saw me. He slowed down so I could pull up next to him. We both lowered our windows.

"Howdy," he said. "Want one of Agnes's lemon bars? We have three left, and we're arguing over the last one."

"No, thanks," I said, looking up at their truck from my small Beetle. "Can you pull over a minute?"

Docker looked into his rearview mirror. A car was coming up behind them, so he pulled to the curb while I parked and got out.

"I spoke to Kyle and Clemmie Nelson," I said when I got to the truck.

"Why?" said Ted, his brow furrowing.

"Because I wanted to know if he had a hand in making that extra notch on the tree," I said.

"And?"

"He said he didn't, and I believe him."

"You should," said Docker. "It's a ridiculous idea."

"He also said I should ask you about some extra money you came into in the last couple of days," I said.

Ted and Docker looked at each other. I could see they were both furious that Kyle had mentioned the money and unhappy to have to talk to me about it.

"Listen," I said, "if you didn't know you were abetting a murderer, you aren't going to get in trouble. Did someone ask you to make the notch?"

"No!" said both men in unison. Ted looked angry. Docker looked horrified. Both seemed to answer from the heart.

"We have some money, but it has nothing to do with the well," said Docker. "Jeez, I wish you'd never called us into the project. If the police start snooping around, this is going to be a real headache for us."

"I'm sorry," I said, aware, once again, that my discovery of Patience Cooper had led to problems for so many. "But you can tell me. We're family. Is there something you haven't told the police?"

Again, the men looked at each other. Then Ted looked out of his window at me.

"You don't have anything to worry about," he said. "We're good. Really."

And with that, my cousins drove away. I watched with some concern as their truck rumbled down Main Street.

I had looked into the break in the tree, to decide if Robert Solder's murder was premeditated. The immediate suspects had vehemently denied having any hand in the matter, and I could not see why they would not tell the police if they had unwittingly helped. Until something about the tree made sense, I decided to leave that mystery to the police. I had other leads that interested me much more.

As I turned back to my car, I heard my name.

"Is it true that the archaeologist was murdered?" said Brenda Worthington, coming up the street toward me. "I knew it. Patience told me herself it would happen."

Chapter 14

Early yesterday morning, the top story in Nantucket had likely been the humorous anecdote of Stella Wright's broken kitchen window. I still couldn't believe that between then and now, our island's news had marched from shattered glass to a murdered man. I couldn't deny, however, that the chain of events was connected, and that I had had a hand in all of it. I'd be damned if I didn't stop these calamities before they got worse. Therefore, when Brenda Worthington told me that Patience Cooper had told her from the grave that Robert Solder would die today, I didn't walk away. Or try to have her see a specialist.

"Thank goodness she decided to speak to you," I said without batting an eye. "Were her predictions specific?"

"Not specific enough," she said. "If I'd fully understood the magnitude of what she was saying, I'd have gone straight to the police. Although I doubt they would have believed me."

She had a point.

"I believe you," I said. "When I discovered Patience's body, I felt a chill inside The Shack. Even Tinker felt it."

"That was her spirit," said Brenda. I noticed that she was quivering. It was a bit chilly out, but her body language seemed to be the result of emotion rather than the forces of nature. "Before I was interrupted by your reporter friend this morning, I connected with her. She had so many questions. I tried my best to answer them."

"Like what?" I said. "What did she want to know?"

"She asked how she died," said Brenda, tilting her head in a manner that expressed real sympathy for Patience's spirit. "I told her you might have that answer. She might try to connect with you about that at a later point."

"Huh," I said. I wondered how that would happen. Would I have to be in The Shack? Would her image pop up in the bathroom mirror at the Morton house while I was brushing my teeth? Would she knock on the door or scare me half to death? I confess my imagination got the best of me for a moment. I had the sudden worry that she'd show up in the middle of tomorrow's Girl Scouts meeting and put an end to Friday's fund-raiser for the town's neediest, once and for all.

"She also asked about her legacy," Brenda said.

"Did she tell you how she knew there was going to be a murder?" I said.

"For Quakers, death is not an end but a beginning," she said. "She told me that. And then she said to me, 'There's a map and a murder, but the two will be separate.' Does that mean anything to you?"

"Wait a minute," I said. "She mentioned a map? She actually said something about a map?"

I took a breath and decided that Brenda could have heard about the map from Agnes, Flo, or Cherry, and it might be the sort of detail to settle into her imagination and take root. I hoped her comment was no more than the result of her over-active imagination because by her logic, that meant that my theory about Patience and Nancy leading to Solder's death was wrong. If I believed in her ability to converse with the dead, of course. Which I did not.

My phone rang before I could ask Brenda anything more. Once again, it was my cousin, Kate.

"Hello?" I said, mouthing my apologies to Brenda for cutting her off.

"Leigh Paik is awake," said Kate. "I wouldn't bother you except she's been asking for you."

"Really?" I said, surprised.

"She said she needs a friend," said Kate.

"Me?" I said. "OK. Tell her I'll be there shortly."

I hung up and noticed Brenda was studying me carefully.

"Is that the woman who got caught in the well?" she said. "I hope she's doing OK."

"She'll be fine," I said.

"Can I go back to the Morton house and talk to Patience again?" she said.

"How about early tomorrow morning?" I said. "Come before I have to go to work, so I can join you. I'd like to say hello to Patience too."

"Early morning is a good time for the spirits," she said. "That would be fine."

"I'll bring something for you to wear," said Brenda, eyeing with sympathy what she seemed to view as my pitiful modern garb. "I think if you show up in jeans, with your hair all a mess like that, you will scare her. She might think you are a witch."

Brenda picked up a pebble on the ground, rubbed it in her hand, and headed down the path. I'd learned by now that there was no need for a big good-bye with Brenda. She was in her own world.

I went on to the hospital. I had spent time there not long ago, when my mother had been visiting. Before that, I had been there to visit Emily when she had given birth to Victoria. Needless to say, my feelings about the place were mixed by now.

I met Kate at reception. She looked like she was holding up without her caffeine fix, but I felt badly coming empty-handed, so I rummaged through my bag for a few Tic Tacs to give her a humble sugar fix.

"Did you find out anything else about Solder?" I said as we headed down the hall.

"They found a small thread, linen of some sort, under one of his fingernails," she said.

I stopped in my tracks.

"I knew it," I said.

"What?"

"Long story," I said, "but this is very helpful."

Why would Solder have a thread of the map under his fingernails unless he had struggled to keep it from someone? I remembered the strange way Solder's arms had been positioned in death, and decided that he had been trying to protect the map. I was on the right track, in spite of Brenda's assertion that the spirits claimed that the map and the murder were not connected.

"I'm losing it," I said to Kate, as I realized I was feeling defensive about the opinions of spirits.

Kate, thankfully, said nothing.

As we entered the ER, I noticed a police officer posted in the hall.

Kate pushed open a curtain to reveal one of the beds.

Leigh was resting in it. There was an IV in her arm and a bandage around her elbow and foot. Perhaps she'd had several visits from doctors and nurses at this point, but I was impressed by how little the movement of the curtain distracted her. Instead of looking up, she stared at her phone. I watched her finger glide up the screen and gathered that she was scrolling through her social media. Maybe the drugs had mellowed her, but there were no tears now. I've heard there are a few stages to grieving. I wondered if she was passing from one to another.

"Hi," I said.

When Leigh looked up at me, a tear sprang to her eye. I reached out and gave her a hug. I wasn't sure if she'd fall apart again, but she kept it together.

"Thanks for coming," she said. "I didn't know who to turn to."

"I'm always happy to talk," I said. "If you want me to call your family or a friend, let me know."

"I've got friends," she said. "They've been texting and Snapchatting with me. But I wanted to talk about the murder. I'm remembering a few things. I can't figure out what's useful and what sounds crazy.

I thought if I spoke to you, we might be able to figure it out."

Leigh looked up at Kate, who was still standing at the curtain, glued to the story. Realizing she was not wanted there, however, she pushed her glasses to her nose.

"Let me know when you're finished," she said, and then left.

With Kate gone, I pulled up a chair and sat by Leigh so that our heads were at the same height. This way, we could speak softly. I pulled a tissue from the box by her bedside and handed her one.

"Thanks," said Leigh.

Rather than wipe a tear, she blew her nose. The action seemed to give her strength.

"So here it is," she said. "I think I saw a ghost."

She looked at me as if expecting me to laugh or call the cops. Instead, I nodded.

"I know it's crazy," she said. "When I climbed out of the well, I happened to look into the brush, to my left. It was foggy and wet, and my eyes hadn't entirely adjusted to the light, but I really felt that there was a presence to my left. Not so much like noise of another person moving around, but just, like, a presence. So I looked, you know?"

A tear dripped down her cheek, and Leigh rubbed her hand through her hair before letting out a deep sigh. I could tell that she felt crazy having said what she'd said and frustrated that it made no sense to her.

I handed her another tissue.

She wiped her cheek.

"I think you should tell the police," I said. "Every little clue can help."

"But what if it's some sort of post-traumatic stress kind of thing?" she said.

"Do you remember what happened next?" I said.

"I unhooked my belt from the ropes, and I started to walk down the path to you guys."

"Did you see anyone then?"

"No." She shook her head empathically. "The next thing I knew, I looked up to see a tree falling toward me. I should have jumped aside, but I was so surprised, I sort of stopped and watched it happen."

"I'm sure I'd have done the same. Was the apparition you saw on the same side where the tree fell?"

"I don't know which side the tree fell from," she said.

I in no way believe in ghosts, despite the fact that several people had claimed to have seen, and even spoken to, one today—and that I, myself, had been invited to speak with one tomorrow. I had to remind myself of that point, however, at this moment in our conversation.

"There's one more thing," she said, swallowing hard. "It's about Robbie."

I tried to stay calm, but I could feel a new clue coming.

"He hadn't been himself lately. I can't explain it, but he'd seemed secretive. I thought he was holding back from me about something."

Suddenly, I felt as if Leigh might be trying to play me. Had she realized that we might have heard her on the walkie-talkie, fighting with Solder? Was she using me to create a back story she could refer to if the police's interest in her increased?

I nodded, however, as if I understood completely. After all, anyone who has ever been in a relationship that's flopped has had that moment where you know something isn't quite right.

"Do you have any idea what he was holding back on?" I said.

"No," she said. "This morning, I walked in on him in our room, and he was on the phone. He was smiling. But when he saw me come in, he quickly hung up. I asked him who he'd been talking to, and he said it was about the excavation, but I just didn't believe him. I mean, I doubt it has anything to do with someone murdering him. Right? He was smiling. He didn't look scared. He just seemed . . . deceitful."

"Right now, I think anything that could be a clue, or even lead to a clue, is important to think about. You should keep doing what you're doing. And you should tell the police."

"Why did we take this stupid job?" she said. "It's my fault. I've been telling Robbie that we needed to step into the limelight. Robbie was a genius, but he wasn't ambitious enough. He knew I'd be angry if he didn't agree to explore the well. And now he's dead because of it."

"I think they're going to kick me out of here soon," I said. "You should try to get some rest. But I do have one more question."

"What?" she said.

"What was on the map?" I said.

"A picture of the island, I think. There were a couple of X marks and a phrase across the top. I never really examined it," she said.

"Did you bring it up from the well with you?" I asked.

"No," she said. "It was with Solder. We were going to bring it up after I got the new batteries. Why?"

"I wanted to see it," I said.

"Well, I'm going back down the well tomorrow," she said. "I spoke with the Historical Association and the police. They said that as long as I'm the only one on-site, along with your officer friend, then I can. I'll take a look for it then."

"You're very brave," I said.

I gave Leigh one more hug, pulled the covers up over her, and slipped behind the curtain into the rest of the Emergency Room. The nurses at the station looked up when I appeared from behind the curtain, as if to see if I'd gathered any good intel, but I kept my word to Leigh. I smiled but said nothing. Then I headed out the door.

In the parking lot, I called Peter. The hospital is not too far from the offices of the *Inquirer & Mirror*.

"Any interest in Crab City?" I said.

I couldn't believe that murder had helped me find an interest in joining Peter at Crab City, but I needed some fresh air and a new perspective.

A few minutes later, Peter was in my car, and we were heading down the Polpis Road, wearing two *Inquirer & Mirror* sweatshirts for extra warmth.

"Have you learned anything new about Solder?" said Peter.

"You forgot to tell me that Patience told Brenda

that the map and the murder were two separate things," I said.

Peter pushed the bangs off his forehead.

"I don't recall her saying anything about a map while I was in The Shack," he said. "But it's kind of eerie that she knew about one."

"I don't believe Brenda can talk to the dead," I said, pulling onto the dirt road toward the beach.

"She's pretty convincing," said Peter.

"I'll find out tomorrow, either way," I said. "I have an appointment to meet with her."

I pulled up to the parking area by the U Mass research cottage, and Peter and I rolled up our jeans. Then, I ran ahead, feeling the cold sand beneath my feet. I could hear Peter behind me, so I sped up and headed to the edge of the water. It was freezing, but the shock to my skin was energizing. I could hear the splash of Peter's feet behind me. I knew he was enjoying the run as much as I was.

When we reached the bend in the water that lead to the cove where Peter was doing his work, he caught my hand. I turned to him and found myself in his embrace.

"This whole case confuses me," he said, with a kiss for good measure. "How is it possible that someone knocked over the tree and then killed Solder without anyone noticing? I mean you were there, and I wasn't, but it all sounds so impossible. Even if the police come up with a motive, how did someone pull it off?"

We were walking beyond Crab City's cove at this point, holding hands along the edge of the water. I realized we were generally headed in the direction of Old Holly's.

"That's funny," said Peter.

I followed his gaze and saw a canoe. It was untied, but it was caught in the weeds of the inlet and jammed behind a rock.

"Let's get in," I said. "My feet need to warm up."

We both headed for the boat. I noticed that it had originally been painted green but that a lot of the paint had peeled away over time. I don't know what we were expecting to find inside, but it was empty except for a pack of Marlboro cigarettes.

"Here's the oar," said Peter, sloshing into the weeds, his jeans getting wet.

I came up behind him as he lifted the oar and brought it back to the boat. As he stepped away, however, I noticed something else bobbing in the weeds beside it. I leaned over, confused by what it might be, and reached for it.

"Here's something I can't seem to escape this week," I said.

"What do you mean?" said Peter.

He dropped the oar in the boat and then turned around to face me.

"Is that a human bone?" he said, his eyes blinking as if to register the long, white object in my hand.

"It is," I said.

Chapter 15

Peter yanked off his sweatshirt. We knew enough to wrap up something of interest before taking it to the police. That, of course, was where we headed with the bone. And the pack of cigarettes.

Entering headquarters out on Fairgrounds Road, we made our way to Andy's desk. He was there, but not alone. I was surprised by his visitor. Agnes sat in the guest chair beside him, wringing her hands. Even more surprising was her reaction when she saw me.

"Oh, thank goodness. You've found it," she said as we approached with the bone sticking out of Peter's sweatshirt.

Andy turned around. Upon seeing the bone in Peter's possession, he jumped up to retrieve it, calling to another officer to get appropriate materials to bag both it and the pack of cigarettes.

"We found the bone beside a canoe out by the U Mass beach," I said, before he could ask us. "The cigarettes were in the boat."

"What were you doing out at the beach?" he said.

"We were on a date," I said, regretting my comment the moment I said it. I had forgotten Andy's sad voice when he had spoken to Georgianna earlier.

"How lovely," said Agnes, lightening the mood. "But you must have been chilly. Oh, I guess not." She giggled and winked at Peter.

Andy pulled over two more chairs, and we all sat.

"Agnes was just telling me about a bone that sounds just like the one you found," he said. "So let's all of us get down to business. Does anyone know whose bone it is?"

"That's what I was starting to tell you," said Agnes. "I do know."

We all looked at her expectantly. Agnes felt the top of her head for her glasses, but they weren't there. This time, they were hanging from her sweater. Once she found them, she was out of tricks, so she took a breath and faced us.

"I took it from Patience Cooper's skeleton," she said.

Now it was Andy's turn to look at me.

"Did you see Agnes take the bone?" he said.

"Not at all," said Agnes, looking pleased. "I was very stealthy. I was in and out last night before anyone could see me. I was going for a pinky bone, or something small, but the femur popped right out. It was as if Patience wanted me to take that one, of all the others. And I know it's the femur because when I got home, I googled it."

It occurred to me that the noises I'd heard last night might have included Agnes's robbery.

"I was in The Shack this morning," said Peter.

"Brenda Worthington was there, and the chain across the door was broken. I assumed she did it."

"No, I did," said Agnes.

"Brenda was there?" said Andy.

Peter and I nodded. Andy took out his notepad.

"So, Agnes, you broke the lock last night?" he said. Agnes nodded.

"With a chain cutter," she said.

"And you have a chain cutter because . . . ?" said Andy.

"Because I locked my own shed last spring and found I had lost the key when it came time to plant my bulbs," she said, as if he was a silly fool to ask.

"So you broke into The Shack and stole the femur," said Andy, not batting an eye. "And why did you take the femur?"

"I wanted to learn more about my family's history," she said. "I bought one of those 23andMe tests. I thought I'd check it out."

No one said anything. I figured Andy could handle this one. He did so by moving on. I thought he made the right choice.

"I was planning to return it right after the excavation this morning," said Agnes. "That's how the trouble began. I put it in the back seat of my car. When I was finally released from Old Holly's abysmal house, I returned to my car, but the bone was gone."

"Why didn't you tell someone right away?" said Andy.

Agnes touched her head again.

"Because I thought maybe I'd left it on the kitchen counter before I'd left," she said. "I was in quite a

hurry and was feeling very nervous this morning, as
you can imagine. I was running late to meet the girls
for breakfast. They took me to the bakery for a bite
before we had our class with Stella. Of course, when I
got home, it wasn't on the counter. So I called the
girls on the off chance that somehow it had ended
up with one of them in all of the confusion. It took
me a while to hunt down Cherry because she was at
the Marine Home Center getting thread for the cobwebs."

"They're crocheting cobwebs for Halloween
Haunts," I helpfully explained to Andy.

Peter was beside me. I thought I heard him suck in
a laugh, but Andy was in no laughing mood.

"And after the ladies didn't have the bone, you
came here?" he said.

"After I checked at the bakery," said Agnes.
"Then, of course, I came to you. We couldn't have
Patience's leg floating around town, now, could we?"

In spite of the professional distance Andy was trying to maintain, I noticed his lip twitch too. He jot-
ted down Agnes's last comments and then turned his
attention to me.

"And how do you fit into all of this?" he said.

"Peter and I found the bone in a canoe by the
U Mass beach. You might want to have a team get
down there for fingerprints, but there were no other
physical clues."

Andy made a note. I noticed Peter took out his
notepad too. I wondered if poor Agnes would find
herself in the papers. Between Kyle Nelson and
Agnes, Peter was amassing some winners.

"I made sure I left the door secured when I left

this morning," said Peter, helpfully. "I slipped the chain through the lock and tied it."

"Thanks for the info," said Andy. "And the bone."

"How did it get out there by the canoe?" said Agnes. "What a mystery."

Andy and I looked at each other but didn't say a word. I knew we were thinking the same thing. We'd both been at the water's edge near the end of Old Holly's property. It was possible that someone had taken the bone from Agnes's car and left with it via the water.

"Solder was hit with something blunt," I said.

Andy nodded.

"Mind taking Agnes to her car?" Andy said to Peter. Then he turned to Agnes with a stern look.

Agnes raised her hand.

"I know," she said. "I shouldn't have taken the bone. I'm sorry about that. I hope you don't need to arrest me, but I understand if there's a fine. I'm an upstanding citizen, and I'm prepared to face the consequences."

"I appreciate that, Agnes," said Andy. "And when I figure out the protocol, I'll be in touch. For now, I would ask that you stay on the island until further notice."

Agnes nodded seriously. Then she rose and left with Peter's hand under her elbow.

"I appreciate that you think the murder was premeditated given the serious problems Solder posed for so many of our suspects, but there was a thread found under his nail," I said. "Someone must have taken the map from him. Did you find any prints on the batteries?"

"Only Leigh's," he said.

"Suggesting that there was no elaborate plan ahead of time to kill Solder. No one was tampering with her walkie-talkie to separate the two of them," I said, hoping Andy was beginning to see this story my way.

"Or, that the murderer wore gloves," he said. "Do you believe Agnes's story about losing the bone?"

"You don't seriously think Agnes killed Solder, do you?" I said. "I have it on good authority that the hit on the head didn't kill him."

"Can you please leave your cousin Kate alone?" said Andy. "The police have their own connections. Official connections, in case you've forgotten. I'll have the forensics team confirm that the bone was the cause of the bump on the head. Someone could have removed the bone from Agnes's car."

I thought of the Candleers' admission that Agnes had joined the fray when we'd jumped in to help free Leigh. I wanted to tell Andy about it, but I'd promised her I wouldn't. Unless I had real evidence that she had a hand in the crime I would stick with that promise, but I knew we had to consider all suspects.

"What would her motive be?" I said. "She was the one who suggested the search to begin with."

"I assume Agnes's motive would have to do with Patience Cooper and Nancy Holland. You're the one who's been arguing that the murder has to do with the two girls," said Andy. "You tell me."

I looked at my feet, then the ceiling fan, then clicked the stapler on Andy's desk. Anything to avoid his look. I couldn't submit to him that Emily and I had spoken about how female relationships work and had concluded that the events didn't make sense. Nor could I explain that I was going to meet Brenda and try to reach Patience tomorrow.

"Go home," said Andy.

"None of this would be happening if I hadn't found Patience Cooper. There's no way I can let this go, so why not tell me what you know?"

"Because there's a murderer on the loose, and I don't want you to get hurt," he said.

"I've heard that before," I said.

"And I still mean it," he said.

I don't know what Andy was expecting, but I wasn't moving. I stayed in the chair until he opened a file in front of him. I thought he was going to read something to me from it, but he didn't. He took his time, reading its contents to himself. I was beginning to think he was willing to wait me out, but then he pulled out a page.

"What is it?" I said.

"You win," he said. "Since you're the one with a chummy connection to Leigh, I'll share this with you. Then you go home."

"Deal," I said.

"We had a man search Solder's room at his B and B," he said. "He found an engagement ring. Looks like Solder was planning to propose to Leigh."

My heart sank for Leigh.

"She said he seemed weird around her, especially this morning. That must have been why. Before Neal proposed to Emily, he was so crazy she thought he was taking her out to break up. Leigh jumped to the wrong conclusion."

"Yeah," said Andy, throwing the paper back into the file.

"Leigh Paik told me that she had permission to descend back down the well again tomorrow," I said.

"And it will be a strict, professionals-only outing. Plus, Fontbutter. He's savvy. With Solder gone, he was able to convince the chief that he's representing Old Holly. Personally, I think Solder had a point about inviting too many spectators," he said. "Look where it got him."

"Andy," I said, "you weren't going to keep tomorrow's plans from me, were you?"

"What you didn't know literally wouldn't hurt you," he said. "No one is allowed down the well or in the vicinity. This is a crime scene."

"At least tell me this. If Leigh's still a suspect, why are you letting her back to the crime scene?" I said.

I looked at him carefully.

"Because of the path in the woods that you, Stella, found yourself. Along with the cut in the tree, it was your discovery that cemented the possibility that this was a premeditated crime. In addition to the suspects from yesterday, we're looking for someone completely outside of those who were at the excavation. So, I will both keep an eye on her, and use her for any leads I can find. Anyway, I'm going down with her," he said.

"What kind of suspects outside of the ones on island?" I said.

"Solder was a purist," said Andy. "You saw it yourself. He rubbed a lot of people the wrong way. In the last year alone he had issues with people in Egypt,

Iran, and even the Metropolitan Museum in New York."

"And yet you still want to head down that well tomorrow," I said. "Admit it. You want to see if the map is down there after all, don't you?"

"I want to look for clues, and I need a guide to get down there," he said. "I also have questions for a suspect, which I believe I can effectively ask while at the crime scene."

"Let me come with you," I said.

"I'll take loads of pictures for you," he said.

"But we're coming at this from different angles," I said. "You might not know what to shoot. What you find down there might hold the answers to this case."

"I'm sure you can see that there are a lot more leads right here at ground level that need to be investigated first."

I disagreed, but I knew there was no use arguing. Some things were better done alone.

Chapter 16

When I left headquarters, I went to the Marine Home Center, which sells everything you might ever need, from hardware to throw pillows. I'd seen Leigh and Solder's climbing equipment. I knew it was unlikely I'd be able to replicate it, but I needed a plan to get down the well, which I now planned to do.

My strategy was to wander the hardware aisle until something caught my eye. Problem was, the store closed at five o'clock, and it was now after four. I didn't have much time to be picky.

As I passed the tool section, I grabbed a headlamp with an elastic band. I figured that would be better than using my cell phone's flashlight option. I knew that one of the Girl Scouts had left behind her bike and helmet when her parents had come to pick her up by car after we discovered Patience. The elastic band could fit over the helmet.

I also tossed a small nylon backpack into my basket. It was just big enough to hold my phone. The real challenge was still how I was going to get down the well. I remembered Cherry throwing the pebble over its side this morning, and the silence that had followed.

At the end of an aisle, I saw a bunch of ladders. I knew that sneaking onto Old Holly's property with a huge ladder over my shoulder was about as clever as calling Andy from Marine Home and telling him my grand idea to head down the well, alone, tonight. Luck, however, was on my side. Tucked behind a couple of huge metal ladders, hanging from removable display hooks, I saw a few rope ladders.

"Come on, come on," I whispered to the inventory, my eyes grazing over the stock. One advertised a five-foot length. Another ten. Neither seemed long enough. I was calculating how many sheets I'd need to tie to the bottom of the ladder for extra length when I saw a few others hidden behind a box shoved between the ladders and the display. I pushed it aside, learning, as I did, how much noise a ten-foot aluminum ladder can make, but my efforts were worth it. Down below, I was rewarded with a little blue bubble on the top of the rope ladder's packaging that said DELUXE X-TRA LONG, FOR BUILDING USE. EQUALS FIVE STORIES. Even better, the top end of the ladder had a sturdy hook, unlike the others. I imagined I could sling the hook over the side of the well, thereby saving myself from Nancy's fate.

"Stella?"

I turned to find Shelly, the Girl Scouts troop leader, walking down the aisle with a basket of acrylic paints.

"Whatcha got there?" she said.

"This?" I said, from behind the hefty bundle in my arms.

I could see misgiving written all over Shelly's face. I knew it had nothing to do with the fact that I might be on a covert mission to break into a well. No. I knew what she was thinking. She was wondering if I'd come up with a new feature for the Haunted House that would add more work to her to-do list between now and Friday. I could see that, behind her suspicious eyes, she harbored a true fear that she'd be climbing down or up two stories to attach a fake witch to the house, or something worse. She'd likely be relieved to know I would be risking life and limb at the well rather than creating any more complexities for the Halloween event.

"The broken window in my apartment spooked me," I said. "What if I had a fire? I'd need something to climb down to safety, right? Can't be too careful."

Shelly nodded, approvingly, obviously glad to be off the hook.

"Good idea," she said. "I was going to call you, by the way. With all the interest in skeletons on the island, the girls have realized they have street cred."

"In spite of the murder today?" I said. Perhaps I'd underestimated this gang.

"I called the Chief of Police, who assured me that the murder was specific to that man Solder, and not because of skeletons. The parents ended up being more of a problem, but they calmed down after I told them what the police told me. We're going to have a meeting after school tomorrow, to see how things go.

Assuming we have no more calamities, we feel we can proceed."

"I'm thrilled," I said.

"I don't think it would have happened had you not moved in to that house," said Shelly. "The island's neediest have you to thank."

"Not at all," I said, eyeing one more thing for my basket, a box of latex gloves. No way was I going to contaminate evidence. Or get splinters.

I could sense the sun was setting, that time was ticking, but I smiled, patiently, as Shelly showed me a couple of paint pots and asked my advice on which color would be best for the witch's cauldron they were making. When we finally had that business settled, I headed to the register, casually grabbing the gloves on the way. I paid and headed straight to the Morton house. My phone rang as I parked the car. Peter. I decided not to loop him into this trouble, so I let it ring, then texted him that I'd call in a few.

I headed into the house and upstairs to my room. Tinker followed me.

"How was your day?" I said to my little friend.

He purred and jumped on my bed. I noticed that having had the room to himself today, he'd made himself comfortable. There was a nice round indent on one of my pillows and another one on a sunken old club chair. He'd certainly picked the two coziest spots in the room, and I was happy he'd been contented. Haunted or not, I still liked the Morton house. The old nooks and crannies were like blank canvases I wanted to fill with stories and candles and creativity.

Right now, however, my creativity was focused on what I should wear to break into Old Holly's property and climb down his well. Dark clothing to hide myself, durable clothing for the exertion. My jacket was navy blue. I'd have preferred black, but at least it was dark, and it was short. I could be active in it. Among the belongings I'd taken with me to the Morton house were black jeans, dark sneakers, and a black hoodie. The back of the hoodie had an ad for the Rose & Crown, a great pub in town, but it was the warmest thing I had. Plus I'd won it at the bar's turkey bowl last November, so it felt like good luck.

I dumped my purchases onto the bed. Tinker hopped up, showing interest in the items. He sniffed at the ladder. I wondered what he smelled. I lifted the item to my nose, but all I got was the aroma of the thick nylon strings that wound together to make the strong rope.

I plugged my phone into the wall, to make sure I was at 100 percent before I left. I had every intention of taking many photos once I arrived at the bottom of the well. Then I went to the bathroom to freshen up.

"You're crazy," I said to my reflection.

The feeling lasted about three seconds. Instead of psyching myself out, I put on some lipstick and packed the bag.

"Keep guarding the house," I said to Tinker. "Home sweet home, right?"

Tinker meowed in agreement. As I headed downstairs, I found myself imagining what the Morton house walls would look like with a fresh coat of paint. Maybe I was trying to keep myself from overthinking my decision to break into Old Holly's property and drop down his well at night, but if so, it did the trick. By the time I closed the door behind me, I had chosen a pale blue.

Outside, the street was quiet, which was exactly what I wanted. There are a few homes on the street, and none too far apart. Houses in Nantucket's town were built fairly close together in comparison to those out by Old Holly, and as a result, anyone could see me jump in my car and head out. I looked into the front windows of the homes down the road as I pulled away, however, and felt fairly certain no one saw me.

About fifteen minutes later, I was heading toward Old Holly's driveway. For obvious reasons, I couldn't park at his house, so I searched for a place to hide the car. The fog had picked up again, as it often does at night. I could see it floating in front of my lights, low and thick, as I slowed the car to a crawl on Old Holly's quiet road. When I was close enough to the house that I could walk, I pulled onto the shoulder of the road. My car is a bright red, so it was useless to try to camouflage it. I drove the Beetle a little deeper into the brush, crossing my fingers that there would be minimal scratches as I heard twigs and branches scrape across it.

Turning off the car, I grabbed the bag and the ladder, and hopped out. In less than a minute, I was headed down Old Holly's driveway. The moon was getting full, as I'd known it would from Peter's moon watching, but clouds and fog passed it intermittently, making the path hard to follow.

A policeman was in a patrol car since the well was still a crime scene. Fortunately, he was looking at his phone, so he wasn't hard to sneak around. Once I passed the car, my dark attire began to pay off. I easily slipped into the darkness of the night.

As I made me way across the cold, dead grass, I saw only one light on in Old Holly's house, the one in the living room. I could hear that the television was on, which gave me more confidence that I could make it to the well without being caught. I knew if Old Holly was watching baseball, there could be a war outside, and he wouldn't bother to check on it. Even still, I drew my hoodie up and dipped my head down. My pace was fast, but light. In no time, I'd passed the house and was headed down the field toward the well. I was less concerned about noise now. Instead, I feared I'd stand out in the empty field if the clouds parted and Holly happened to look out of his window. I kept to the perimeter of the field for as long as I could.

About halfway down the field, I stopped. I was only about five yards from the table the police had set up this morning. It was still on the field, exactly where we'd left it. The reason I stopped was that I heard a noise. I waited a moment to see if I could determine the direction it had come from and what kind of animal had made it. As I waited, I noticed that there was no noise coming from the main house. No cheers of victory. No curses of discouragement. Nothing. I knew immediately that something was off.

The noise began again.

Footsteps. Human ones.

There was no doubt about it.

I ran the extra few yards and dove under the table. From my hiding place, I waited for what felt like an eternity. The footsteps continued, in a pattern of start and stop. Whoever was making them did not seem to be following a certain path. It seemed more like the steps of someone in search of something, but what? Me?

It occurred to me that in spite of the many items I had in my bag for the climb, I did not have anything to defend myself. If I had learned anything, it should have been that Solder would have benefited from some sort of defense. Right now, all I had was a folding table.

I silently cursed myself and looked around for a stick or anything useful. Oddly, I did find something. It was an old TV antenna, the kind used before the days of cable. I wondered how much other junk my cousins had had to haul off the property, but the slim iron rod seemed as good as anything for protection. I was reaching my hand out toward it when I heard a grunt. The voice was one I had heard before, earlier in the day. It was the sound of Old Holly when the starting pitcher had walked someone to give up a run.

Sure enough, from my hiding place, I saw Old Holly emerge from the thicket. His head hung low, and he was muttering to himself. I guess my ears aren't as strong as my sense of smell. I couldn't make out what he was saying. My eyes, however, had adjusted to the darkness. As Old Holly stepped from the brush and onto his field, I saw him clearly. I saw everything from the whiskers peeking out from the hood over his head to the heavy hiking books on his feet and the item he held in his hand. An axe.

I put my hand over my own mouth, lest I let out a

cry of surprise. The last thing I remembered from the crime scene today was the police searching for the axe, without success.

I watched until Old Holly reached his house door. Fortunately, his head stayed focused on the ground in front of him, step by step, until he stepped inside.

"You moron," he shouted at his TV with his axe in his hand. I gave him another minute or two to settle into his chair and then crept out from under the table.

After tripping over a few twigs and branches on the short path to the well, I was face-to-face with Nancy Holland's tomb. The police, I noticed, had put a tarp over the well rather than secure all of the wooden planks that had originally protected it. This was good news for me. All I had to do was loosen two of the stakes that held down the tarp and push aside one of the planks to create enough room for my body to fit.

I dropped my backpack on the ground. I was still concerned that Old Holly could notice me if I turned on my helmet light, so I proceeded in the dark. Pulling the strings open on the ladder, I began to unroll it. My adrenaline was running high. I was excited to find out what awaited me at the bottom of the well.

"Perfect," I said to myself when I adjusted the hook to fit over the edge of the well.

The ladder began to fall into the abyss. For a moment, I didn't hear anything as the two ropes and the small wooden rungs that held them together tumbled downward. After about three seconds, however, I heard a clack of wood against stone. Then another, and another. Fortunately, I could no longer hear Old Holly yelling at the television, so I knew he couldn't hear me.

I secured the strap under my helmet and put my backpack over my shoulders.

"You're crazy," I whispered to myself.

The well's wall reached the bottom of my rib cage, but in the dark, with the prospect of climbing over the rough and uneven stones, the structure seemed much higher. I leaned against it with both of my arms and hopped up, bracing the tips of my rubber-soled shoes against the wall to give me traction as I scrambled up the edge. I felt along the ladder until my hand reached the far end of the rope. Then I pushed my foot that was dangling over the well until I felt it hit the first rung.

"Now or never," I said.

With that, I hoisted the rest of my body overboard.

My first rung was a disaster. Bringing my outer leg over the edge hadn't gone as smoothly as I could have hoped. Although the hook did its job of keeping me from falling to my death, the ropes did not cooperate. I immediately swung to my right in a way that reminded me of those carnival games where you try to climb up a ropes course designed to topple you over if you don't have perfect balance.

Fear of losing my life, however, gave me magical abilities. Although I at first flailed and grabbed and spun around, my body and the ladder eventually came to a compromise. Once I'd gotten my sea legs, I turned on the light. I didn't look down, for fear that the depth would be too much to see, given my precarious position. Instead, I focused on the stones of the well and the distance between my foot and each rung as I descended.

"One. Two. Three," I said, counting my way down.

The counting was comforting.

The rubbing of my fingers against the stone wall was not, even with my gloves on.

When my foot searched for but could not find another rung, I took a deep breath. Finally, I looked below me.

The good news was that I could see the bottom of the well.

The bad news was that it was still too far below me that I could not jump without risk of breaking a bone or two. And even if I'd devised a way for a successful jump, there would be no way I could pull myself back up the ladder when I was done.

So there I was, dangling from a ladder five stories below Old Holly's well. Adding to my frustration was the scene below me. I could see poor Nancy Holland.

I knew immediately that she had had a bad ending. I didn't know much about bones aside from having viewed Patience Cooper's in The Shack. She had looked mostly like the skeleton that had hung from a hook in my biology class in college. The bones generally lined up with the image in my textbook.

Nancy's bones, however, did not match up. Her right thigh bone lay perpendicular to her hip bone, and her shin was at a right angle to it. I could see this because the dress she'd been wearing when she tossed herself over had flown up over her torso. And her shoe had flown clear across to the other side of the well. I wondered if her bonnet had stayed on or if Solder had found it lying somewhere else too.

Behind Nancy's head was a dark bloodstain. I didn't remember Solder commenting on it, but it made sense. I couldn't see the back of her head, but it was a safe guess that when her head hit the ground, it had probably cracked open. Even if she had survived the fall, she wouldn't have been able to stand.

"Ow," I said, as much about poor Nancy's legs as about my own, which were beginning to ache.

I risked taking one hand off the ladder for a second to adjust the light on my helmet. By raising the angle, I was able to get a better look around the perimeter of the well's floor. My eyes sought the map. Solder had not shared how big it was, and I had not asked Leigh. All I knew was that it had originally been in Nancy's canvas sack, and that it was not in there when Solder's body and backpack were found. Looking around the bottom of the well, I could not find it either. Nancy's dress might be covering it, but it was hard to tell.

There were some leaves and rocks and, of course, Nancy's shoe. To Solder's point, the space was impressively empty for a tomb that had only been covered by the planks. The family had done a great job of protecting Nancy from the elements. It reminded me of the equally odd burial of Patience Cooper. Neither woman had had the dignity of a proper burial, but they had remained protected for over a century.

Then I had my big idea. I remembered that I'd tossed the old TV antenna into my backpack after Old Holly had returned to his house. It occurred to me that if the antenna opened out long enough, I might just be able to poke around Nancy's dress to make sure the map wasn't there. I reached behind me to pull it out.

Once again, as I took my hand off of one side of the ladder, the ropes began to swing around in a circle. I'll describe it, so you don't need to try it out at home. Understand that it's downright tricky to reach into a backpack on a swinging ladder. Eventually, I was able to brace my back against the stone wall by spreading my feet to both edges of the ladder and poking my knees into the next rung, thereby creating two rungs' worth of space. In this awkward position, I pulled out the antenna and proceeded to rehang the backpack on my front versus on my back.

For a moment, I thought I'd really figured things out with my multi-limb balancing act, so I leaned forward, my elbows against either side of a rung a couple rows up from my knees. That's when I knew I'd pressed my luck. Once again, I was spinning in circles, now with an antenna in my hand and my headlamp highlighting every stone in circular fashion. I'd gone from feeling like I was on a ropes course to feeling like I was on a carnival ride I'd tried during college called the Gravitron, during which a seat belt and centrifugal force were the only things that kept me from flying into the park grounds. The only noise other than the knocks and bumps created by my tormented body was the whistling sound of the wind as it tore over the well.

And, of course, once I twirled one way, I then twirled the other, until finally I had a moment to fight back and regain my balance.

"Ha!" I said to the ladder.

Careful not to make any more radical movements,

I opened the antenna with my teeth and then reached out to the body below.

The stick was too short.

If I'd had about three more feet, I might have made it.

I don't know if you've ever found yourself in a similar predicament. If you have, I'd be curious to know what you decided to do. Stay? Go? Anything in the middle?

Me? At that moment I thought, hell, what do I have to lose? Fully prepared for another battle with the ladder, I slid my body downward, keeping both hands steady until my knees were at my chin. Something like a ballerina fantasy came over me. Or a trapeze artist. Whatever it was, I pulled down on the ropes with my forearms and gently reached my legs through the rung so that I was seated on the lowest rung of the ladder.

It was a miracle of coordination. It was also quite a relief to be off my feet. I'd been holding the antenna in my mouth, and now, clinging my arms around the ropes on either side of me, I took hold of the steel rod and pulled it open. I was even thinking I might be cocky enough to take my phone out of the knapsack to take a few pictures if I found the map.

I am proud of the fact that I am resourceful. A woman of action. A problem solver. The flip side, however, is the occasional overreach. Once again, the rod was too short. It took no more than a moment of trying to reach out to Nancy's dress before the ladder began to violently rock again. I hadn't thought it could get worse, but suddenly, though my back had been resting against the well's wall, I lost my grip. Next thing I knew, I was falling backward. I was aware that my helmet was doing a good job of staying on my head, that my backpack was still hanging in front of me—actually now over my face. My head had just reached back to see the floor below when I stopped falling.

It took a second or two for me to realize that as I'd tumbled backward, my feet had splayed outward and hooked around the ladder's ropes. Given the situation I was in at that moment, I know it sounds crazy to have felt so good about myself, but I really did. I rocked back and forth like a piece of meat hanging from a butcher's hook, but I was able from that vantage point to finally get a good look at Nancy. Her dress was hiked in a way that showed me much of the ground below her, and I was able to determine that the map was not there.

Now, more than ever, hanging upside down on a ladder in the middle of the night in an old abandoned well, dangling over a skeleton, I felt sure that I'd been on the right trail. Both Nancy and Patience had been murdered, and Solder's murder was the result of someone wanting to get their hands on the map.

"Son of a gun," I said.

Then, my phone pinged. There was no chance I was going to take pictures tonight, but the phone's screen shone through the nylon bag. I could read a text from Fontbutter.

Call me. We have work to do.

Chapter 17

Unable to respond to Fontbutter's text for obvious reasons, I took hold of the ropes before the ladder could fight me. With a stroke of good fortune I'll not soon forget, I found strength in my forearms to pull myself back up to a standing position. There's nothing like adrenaline to conquer all things.

By the time I reached the top of the well, I was good and tired. The first burst of adrenaline had ebbed, leaving my forearms with an ache I knew I'd be feeling tomorrow. I was grateful to feel the fresh air when my bloody knuckles made their first grasp of the well's wall. I pulled myself up and swung my leg over the edge, amazed I was still alive. Slowly, and quietly, I rolled the ladder up. It looked so innocent in my hands, but we both knew what we knew. With the bundle in my arms, I flung my other leg over the well's edge, and jumped to terra firma. I felt for a moment like a sailor returning to land. The ground seemed to sway below me, so I squatted down beside the well to compose myself.

While my thoughts were fresh, I tried to rebuild the case. This morning, Leigh had left the well to replace the walkie-talkie while Solder was focused on Nancy's body. He'd taken her bonnet and the canvas bag containing the map. He put both of these into his knapsack, left his helmet, and ascended from the well. It occurred to me now that the only reason he might have left the helmet was that he'd heard the tree crash and Leigh scream. Fearing for her safety, he had likely rushed to harness himself to the ropes and climb up. By then, all of us had entered the thick foliage in search of a path to Leigh.

It was during this window of time that someone had strangled Solder and had taken the map, embroidered on a piece of linen. Since the police had been unable to find that map on the initial suspects—namely, Fontbutter, Bellows, and Leigh—I assumed that the thief and murderer had taken off through the trees on their way to the boat. I still didn't understand what had happened with the tree, but I had to admit that it pointed to the idea that the murder had been premeditated. Had someone known the map was down there before the dig? I thought of Old Holly and Agnes. Perhaps even Bellows?

Before heading home, I had one more thing to do. I stood up, put myself in order as well as I could, and headed up the field, this time unafraid of who might see me. As I drew closer to the house, Old Holly's cries became louder, but I couldn't tell if his team was winning or losing. Even when he was excited by a play, he still sounded somewhat angry.

I knew the man was inside. Every living creature

within ten yards of the house could hear him. At my knock, however, the house became silent.

"I know you're in there," I said. "Muting the television won't work."

"Stella? What do you want?" I heard from inside.

"I want to know where you found the axe," I said.

There was silence, and then the sound of the ball game resumed.

I knocked again.

"I'll stay here all night if I have to," I said.

"Knock yourself out," he said.

"I'll call the police," I said.

"You'll save me the nickel," he said, making me wonder what sort of phone plan he was on.

At a loss, I decided it was me versus the television, so I banged and banged against the door until I won. Old Holly opened the door. In lieu of a greeting, however, he let the door hang open while he returned to his chair. I dropped the ladder at his feet, walked past him and went to his kitchen.

"What're you doing in there?" he said.

I returned, handed him a beer, and put a dollar on the table next to him for mine. Then I sat on the sofa and watched the game with him. By the seventh-inning stretch, Holly had had six beers. I know because he directed me back to the kitchen to get each of them. My patience was finally rewarded at the seventh-inning stretch.

"I found the axe, if that's what you want to know," he said. "Strangest thing. It was under the porch."

"What were you doing looking under the porch?"

"I damn well wanted to find my axe. Someone

takes my axe, I'm going to find it. The police looked everywhere, but then I remembered the porch. Low and behold, there it was."

I believed that he'd retrieved the axe from where he'd said because the knees of his pants were covered in dirt. I'd been wondering about the stains for the last two innings.

"Did you call the police?" I said.

"Haven't yet," he said, scratching his belly. "I decided before I made a fuss about my discovery that I'd make good and well sure that the old axe was responsible for the cut in the tree."

"You shouldn't have done that," I said. "If there were fingerprints, they'll now be hard to lift."

Holly scratched his head.

"I hadn't thought about that," he said.

"Or had you? If you were the one who made the hack to the tree in the first place, you've now done a good job at turning the story around."

"What do you know?" said Holly, indignantly. "I saved the police quite a bit of work. I walked right down to the tree, and I matched up my axe head with the cuts."

"One trip down to the tree and you've figured all of this out."

"I guess you aren't the only one who can solve a murder," said Old Holly, with more than a little grandiosity.

"So," I said, taking the bait, "who did it?"

"That fellow from the museum," said Old Holly.

At this point, he raised a hand for me to be quiet and turned back to the TV.

"Bellows?" I said. "Why do you think Bellows did it?"

Old Holly answered by raising the volume on his television. I had to wait until the end of the seventh inning before Old Holly turned his attention back to me.

"Because," he said, as if it had been a mere moment since we'd last spoken, "I found him creeping around my backyard tonight. He doesn't think I saw him, but I did."

There were so many things I wanted to say, but I knew I was competing with a commercial break, so I went right to the heart of it.

"What was he doing?" I said.

"Snooping around my woods," said Holly. "I was on one side. He was on the other. Dumb fool didn't even notice me. His head was to the ground. Looking for something. He probably left a clue behind and was trying to find it before the police did."

Like a map he'd hidden, I thought.

"I'm going to call the police right after the game," he said. "I've got the whole case solved. That Kyle fellow and Bellows were in on it together. Kyle used the axe to loosen the tree. Bellows did the murder. As I said, beat you!"

I was intrigued by Bellows's decision to revisit Old Holly's house tonight. That certainly didn't look too good, and I had no problem with Old Holly calling the cops on him. He evidently did not know that Kyle had an alibi, but I hoped his call wouldn't stir things up again for the gardener. I gave Old Holly a stern look.

"Tell me," I said, "how come you were the one I

saw walking around with the axe tonight? If Kyle was behind this, wouldn't he have taken the axe with him?"

"I guess he wanted to pin it on me," said Old Holly, a little defensively.

"You'll have to do better than that with the police," I said. "It was your axe. You were the only one able to 'find' it." I used finger quotes to make my point. "And, frankly, I can think of more motive for you to kill Solder than for Kyle or Bellows."

"Me?" said Old Holly. His face became as red as his baseball team's uniform. "Why would I kill that skinny little fellow?"

"Means and motive. You've contracted with a TV developer to make this into a show, and you had a scientist in charge who had no interest in letting you move ahead with your plans. With Solder's death, you now have a sexier story and no one standing in your way. I'm sure you could use the money. Who couldn't?"

"Not for murder," he said. "You're as crazy as the rest of them."

He looked genuinely outraged as he said the words, and I did feel that the man was speaking the truth. But facts are what count, so I pressed on.

"What about the fact that you were the only one who did not join us at the excavation?" I said. "Were you watching TV, or did you sneak down to the well and attack Solder from an entry none of us knew about?"

"Out," said Old Holly, pointing to his front door. "You get out of here."

"I will, but I'd think twice about calling the police on Kyle," I said. "I'm only telling you now what the police will think when you tell them you found your axe."

At this point, Old Holly began to breathe heavily. I was afraid I'd gone too far. I ran to the kitchen to get him a glass of water. After a few sips, he put the glass on the table next to him.

"Do you think Bellows found anything when he was here tonight?" I said.

Old Holly shrugged.

"Are you sure it was him?" I said.

"I am," he said. "I studied him carefully. The fog was playing tricks on me. At first, he seemed almost ghostlike. I can't explain it. Maybe the whole area was giving me the creeps, but I saw him before I heard him. It was eerie."

I nodded. How many people had felt the presence of a ghost today?

"I think that's why I lost my voice to call out to him," said Old Holly. "I just stood and watched while he circled the well, his head down."

"Did he pick up anything?" I said.

Old Holly shook his head.

"If anything, I think he tossed something into the well," he said. "He leaned over the edge a couple of times."

What had I missed by the well?

"You need to hand over the axe to the police."

"Now I don't want to," said Old Holly.

"I'll talk to Bellows," I said. "I'll see what I can find out to bolster your story."

"Talk to him in the morning," said Old Holly. "Then I promise I'll give them the axe. I like the idea of having someone else on my side."

I wasn't sure I was on his side, but I promised I would.

Old Holly sighed and looked back at his game.

"I don't like this," he said. "You all should have left well enough alone to begin with."

I left the man staring blankly at his TV. When I reached my car, my phone rang.

"I told you to call me," said Fontbutter. "I like your idea about interviewing me at the site where the other skeleton is. It's time I saw the other victim. I'm going to come by your house in the morning. We can do some establishing shots of the space near Patience Cooper's body. I can do a combination of film and digital, so I'll bring my handheld for this. It will be easy for you to use. The dig's tomorrow at ten, so I'll come at eight thirty. Also, I like the idea that you make candles."

"It's not so much an idea as a business," I said. "I have a store, the Wick and Flame, in town."

"Exactly," said Fontbutter. "I'd like you to have two dozen black candles handy when I come. When I shoot my scenes down in the well, I'm going to light them around the perimeter. You know, to create the 'old Nantucket' vibe."

"Sure," I said, always happy to sell two dozen candles in one go, "but if you're going for authenticity, you'll want white candles, not black."

"I love your trivia, but white won't give the right effect," said Fontbutter. "Let's stick with black. See you in the morning."

I said good-bye, but the line had already gone dead.

I could easily have stopped by the Wick & Flame on the way home to pick up Fontbutter's order, but I needed to work. When I'm in the zone, doing what I love best, I am at my most relaxed and sharpest at the same time. It's in those moments that I sometimes make my greatest decisions or have my biggest ideas. I had enough supplies back at the Morton house to fill the order, so I headed home to work. Driving back to the house, I decided that pillar candles in different heights might add interest to the scene Fontbutter was trying to create.

When I got home, I could see that Peter's work at securing the chain on the door to The Shack had held up, so I headed inside. I set up my makeshift workshop in the second of the three bedrooms in the Morton house. The windows were closed, but they were old, so I could hear the occasional breeze. Tonight, there was no banging outside my house whenever the wind blew. It was as if Patience and I were enjoying a respite from the murderous activities of the last two days. I melted wax and colored it a deep black with a touch of blue, small enough that, to the naked eye, the candles were black but somehow still popped with vibrancy. The candles were unscented. I assumed there would be no need for the extra ambience of scent if they were only going to be used for the film. One by one, I poured the candles and let them set, enjoying the comfort of a living space that was hospitable to my trade. The kids in the town might think I was a witch living with a skeleton this week, but my haunted house was quite cozy.

Enjoying the house as much as I did, I had brought a candle clock with me from the store for an authentic experience. When my work was done, I curled up in bed with my candle-by-the-hour set for thirty minutes. My bed was inviting, Tinker having warmed it up for me, and I treated myself to an overnight mask. Waiting for it to set, I scrolled through my social media to see what I'd missed in the last day. I was not surprised to see that many of my local friends had posted photos of The Shack, respectfully taken from the sidewalk but with comments that were filled with speculation about who was buried inside.

When my candle hit the half-hour mark and extinguished, I gasped. It was very efficient, but I found myself startled to be in the dark so suddenly. I lay in bed, Tinker snuggled against me and purring in his sleep. As my eyes began to shut, I wondered if Brenda would be able to add more to my evolving understanding about the story of Patience and Nancy in the morning.

Chapter 18

Some advice: do not fall asleep with a face mask on—especially if it's a clay mask. Although a trip down a well had led to a good night's sleep, I woke up surrounded by flakes of clay. Expelling a few that had managed to find their way into my mouth, I realized I was parched.

I rinsed my face and put on a pound of moisturizer. Tinker stretched in one delicate move that I'd be proud of in a yoga class and joined me in a perch on top of the toilet as I pulled myself together.

"This is quite a case," I said to my furry friend after gulping down some water from the faucet. "There are too many suspects. Too many motives."

Tinker's not one for unnecessary drama, which is something I like about him. He focused on the light coming through my window. I could see he was deciding whether to soak up the sunlight or paw at the dust particles that were illuminated by it.

"Hey," I said, putting on a pair of moon-shaped earrings, "eyes over here, buddy. We have work to do."

Tinker compromised. He jumped up onto the windowsill to both enjoy the sun and humor me. He looked adorable up there, so how mad could I be? I don't have a window in my own apartment's bathroom, but I could imagine enjoying a little ritual like this. I gave Tinker a pat on the head, glad that he seemed to be happy with his sojourn here. He didn't even seem to mind the ghosts and goblins on display downstairs. I only hoped that when the Girl Scouts came later today, he wouldn't object to any additional décor. My one concern was the Candleers' cobwebs. I could only imagine how beautiful they'd be to Tinker in the sunlight. Fingers crossed he'd behave.

"Who dunnit, my friend?" I said to him.

His answer was a blasé tail whisk. I was on my own.

"We have a suspect," I said. "Jameson Bellows. He fits the bill too. He was the first person on-site to acknowledge that the map was an important find. He was found sneaking about the Holland property last night as well. Why? To find something he'd left behind? To add a clue to distract the police?"

Tinker licked his paws. I stopped to watch him. He stopped to watch me. I took that as a sign he was listening.

"I still don't know how or why that tree fell, but the man had motive. He wanted the map—and maybe he took advantage of the opportunity."

I walked into my bedroom and pulled out the most innocuous clothing I had—a pair of leggings and a T-shirt. I decided these would be the simplest clothes to wear underneath the Quaker dress Brenda had promised to bring. I was looking forward to trying on the outfit. I may not have been going to the excavation this morning, but I had a busy schedule before my store opened.

Heading down to the kitchen with Tinker at my feet, I prepared breakfast for the two of us. Tinker dove into his Friskies while I buttered a piece of toast. My mind, of course, was still on murder suspects. After I put the dishes away, I checked the time, wondering where Brenda was. I had hoped she would have come and gone by now. I didn't want Fontbutter to arrive while she was in her Quaker dress. I couldn't imagine what he would think up to exploit her for his film.

I walked to the living room windows that looked out over the street. It was dead quiet. Many leaves had blown across the path to the front door during the night.

It would be tough to miss the excavation today, but I thought of another way I could keep focused on the case. A lunch break with Bellows.

I'd left Bellows's card in my car, so I headed out to grab it. It was on the floor of the passenger seat, where I'd left it yesterday. I made a couple of drafts of a text, deciding on tone and content. After a few minutes, I came up with something I felt would entice him.

> *Stella Wright here! Are you free to meet today? I have a few questions about candle making in the time of Patience Cooper that I'd love to ask you. I'm thinking of a new line of candles inspired by Nantucket's days of yore.*

I hit SEND. I felt clever having come up with a topic of conversation that had little to do with the murders. As my number-one suspect, I didn't want him to have any idea that I was on his trail. Candles seemed an innocuous topic. And a line of candles inspired by Patience might actually be really interesting, come to think of it.

I was staring at the screen, waiting for a reply, but no pings, bings, or rings followed. Since I was waiting for Fontbutter, Brenda, and now Bellows, I grabbed a decorative witch's broom by the front door to sweep the pathway for my visitors. While I did, I noticed two kids walking toward me. The school bus stops only a couple of blocks away, and I figured they were headed there. As they approached me, one nudged the other, and the two began to giggle. I waved but was surprised when they avoided my greeting and walked past me. The wind picked up at that moment. My thick, wild hair was lifted by a gust of wind. Tinker mewed from the living room window and tapped his black paw against the glass pane. A skull made of papier-mâché sat beside him, covered in fake blood. I realized I must look perfectly cast in the doorway of one the island's haunted houses.

I checked my phone again. Still no message from Bellows. Plus I noticed that Fontbutter had said he'd be over by eight, and it was now ten after. I wondered what was keeping him from the meeting he had seemed so excited about last night. Then I heard a noise out back. I put the broom back beside my front door and headed toward the sound.

"Helloooo?" I sang as I neared The Shack.

Unravelling the chain, I peered through the door. Solder and Leigh had removed their table and equipment, but the sheet still hung in front of Patience's coffin. I walked across the room and lifted the covering. The skeleton, minus her femur, was still nestled inside the stones.

Behind me, the air picked up. I turned around to find Fontbutter in the doorway.

"Great. You're here," he said. "I knocked on the kitchen door, but we must have missed each other somehow."

Unlike yesterday's pinstriped suit, the TV director was now dressed for action, more or less. He wore black jeans, a black button-down shirt, black sneakers, and a black bomber jacket. His hair and mustache were as slick as ever, but today he looked like the kind of guy who could climb down a well and emerge in one piece. Over his shoulder, he carried his familiar camera bag. In his hand he held a black-cotton duffel bag.

"How's old Patience today?" he said, looking at the skeleton. "Ready for your close-up, old gal? We'll find your good angle."

I could not help but feel protective of my skeleton. I didn't like the idea of Fontbutter taking advantage of Patience Cooper. The woman had clearly been through a lot in her day. I wondered how she'd feel about being broadcast on TV over a hundred years later.

"Are you sure you're allowed to be filming here?" I said. "While there is a murder investigation going on?"

Fontbutter dropped his duffel bag to the ground and crouched beside it.

"I'm not sure what one has to do with the other," he said, pulling a small black box from it. I was starting to see a theme here. My black candles were just his color.

"Nancy Holland and Patience Cooper were friends," I said. "We wouldn't have been exploring the well for Nancy's body had we not found Patience first."

Fontbutter paused and looked up at me. He stroked his mustache.

"It's like this. Baskin-Robbins and Dunkin' Donuts share retail space," he said, "but if someone chokes on a donut, do we boycott ice cream? I think not."

"So Patience and Nancy are like Dunkin' Donuts and Baskin-Robbins?" I said, resisting the temptation to point out the many flaws in his analogy.

"Exactly," he said, looking relieved I had caught on. "Can you hold this mirror for me?"

He stood before me, handed me a mirror, and began to comb his perfectly straight hair. Had he gotten tanner overnight?

"I'm going to have you shoot me in front of Patience," he said, now taking a small light from his bag. "But first I want to take a few still photos of the room so I have them for reference before other shoots. Can you unpack my camera?"

I put the mirror down and followed instructions. Fontbutter was engrossed in taking his photos. He began by shooting the hearth, the stones, the empty room. Then he focused in on the skeleton, taking similar photos to those that Solder and the ME had taken yesterday. I watched, impressed in spite of my-self. I could see the man's genuine enjoyment of his trade, and his excitement about the project. If I hadn't been so suspicious about how his show would turn out, I'd have been pretty excited to be involved. For now, however, my objective was to get to know the man better, to see if there was a clue that pointed to Fontbutter as the murderer.

I looked at the video camera I was holding and wondered if I'd found my opportunity.

"The light is good for outdoor shots right now," I said.

"You're right," he said.

To my delight, he headed out the door.

"Feel free to peek into the Morton house too," I said. "It's an antique itself. You might want to shoot there."

"I knew I'd like you," said Fontbutter from out-side. "You're a problem solver. That's what you are. Be right back."

"Yes, I am," I said quietly.

The moment Fontbutter left The Shack, I turned on his camera. I was not familiar with this sophisti-cated model, but I realized that the buttons were self-explanatory. In less than thirty seconds, I was flipping through videos. One was taken prior to his puddle-jumper flight from Boston to Nantucket, in which he spoke into the camera's microphone like an adventurer heading off to the wild, seeking the truth of the past. I rolled my eyes and moved on to the videos from yesterday.

I hit PLAY on the first video at Old Holly's house. It

was a short clip of Old Holly, fumbling with his clicker to find the ball game. I could imagine the opening shot, where an unsuspecting old local spends his afternoons on mundane things while the find of a lifetime is entombed in his backyard. It wasn't far from the truth, but I didn't appreciate anyone from my town being portrayed in such a way.

Next Fontbutter had filmed the walk down to the well. I remembered this video. The Candleers and I had led the way, with Flo carrying her stadium chairs. When the path to the well came in view, Fontbutter raised his camera higher and zoomed on the path. I noticed a SLO-MO button and hit it. As the frames moved one by one, I studied the perimeter of the shots, hoping to see someone who should not be there. Bellows was the only person who had been on the scene whom I could not find in the video, but I remembered he had arrived after us.

There was only one more video. I pressed PLAY. The scene started at the well, where we had gathered before Solder and Leigh had begun their descent. Leigh was attaching her ropes to the belay device, tugging on them to make sure they were safely connected. She looked up and smiled, sweetly, to the camera. At that moment, Solder walked into the frame from behind Fontbutter.

The door to The Shack opened, and I calmly looked up, hitting STOP as I did. Without a word, Fontbutter sneezed, walked directly to the table, and lifted the mirror again. His hair was still straight, but its general configuration was slightly askew.

"You didn't tell me you had a cat," he said, repositioning his locks. "I'm allergic. Unfriendly creature too, isn't he?"

Tinker has a good radar about people. His evident disapproval of Fontbutter only fueled my mistrust of the man.

He put the mirror down and set up his lights.

"Where's a good place for coffee around here?" he said.

"The Bean."

"Call them and tell them I'll be there in twenty," he said. "I'll need one regular coffee. Also, add one hazelnut with almond milk. Does your friend Southerland like anything special?"

"Regular with two sugars," I said.

"Then two regulars. No, make that three. Old Holly might want something. And don't forget the one hazelnut with almond milk."

I called The Bean and got Clemmie on the phone.

"A man named Fontbutter will be picking up the order," I said.

"What are you doing making coffee calls for someone with such a ridiculous name? You're not an intern," she said.

"Just happy to bring you business, Clemmie," I said.

I've been on both sides of the proverbial pond— both the big fish in my small hometown and an invisible one to island visitors. I found pros and cons to both sides. With Fontbutter, however, it really was only the promise of bringing business to The Bean that kept me from telling him what he could do with his coffee.

Five minutes later, I was focusing the lens of the director's camera and tightening the screw to a small tripod upon which it was secured. Fontbutter touched his moustache one last time and then nodded that he was ready.

"Action," I said, hitting the RECORD button.

"Murder in Nantucket!" he said. "My research into Nancy Holland's death has ended in murder. Robert Solder, preeminent forensics anthropologist, was found strangled today in front of the well in which he had just found the body of Nancy Holland. The story, however, starts here, at the burial site of Nancy's best friend, Patience Cooper."

For someone who didn't believe that Solder's death had anything to do with Patience and Nancy, he sure seemed to like the connection. I was about to say as much but held my tongue as Fontbutter began to tell the story of Patience Cooper. I was glad that at least he stuck to the facts of the story, although several times he added the words "evidently" and "as we understand it now." Another favorite was "Legend has it."

"As I start this investigative adventure," he said, finishing up the story, "I am most excited by one fact that was not well-known among this small community. At the northeast point of the island, there is a treasure, related to Patience Cooper and her friend, Nancy Holland. I am hopeful that as this story unfolds, we will learn more not only about these two old friends but also about their secret fortune, which is estimated at over one hundred thousand dollars."

I thought how interesting it was that Fontbutter

knew so many details of a map we'd never seen. He was either a great salesman, or he knew more than he should. But how?

He looked from the camera's lens to me and made a slicing motion across his neck. I was startled by the gruesome gesture.

"Cut," he said.

"Oh," I said, collecting myself. "How do you know about where the treasure lies and how much it's worth?"

"Showmanship," said Fontbutter with a wink.

"I was wondering. That time you heard Solder speak at a conference, did he say or do anything that could have made him any enemies?"

Fontbutter leaned toward me. Although there was no one else in the room, he looked both ways.

"I heard him on the phone to a museum in Cairo," he said. "And I have a theory."

"What is it?" I said.

Before he said another word, there was a crash at the door.

The room had been so quiet that both Fontbutter and I jumped. We looked to the door to see the silhouette of Brenda Worthington. She was sitting on the ground, her legs out and facing us, as if she had taken a few steps backward and had fallen.

"Are you OK?" I said, rushing to her aid.

"Sorry, but I must cancel," said Brenda, standing quickly. "I don't think Patience will be speaking to me any longer. So sorry."

Brenda turned and scurried across the field. I followed.

"Brenda?" I said. "Stop!"

Brenda stopped and turned.

"I had a dream last night," she said. "I was coming to tell you that Patience won't speak to me anymore. She told me she was moving to the other side. Now that her body has been found, she can rest."

Without another word, Brenda turned and continued her retreat from the Morton house. I knew she was lying. She was carrying a bag over her shoulder from which I could see the sleeve of a Quaker-style dress. If she hadn't planned to "introduce" me to Patience, why would she have brought the dress?

I returned to The Shack, wondering if Fontbutter was behind Brenda's change of heart.

"Do you know Brenda Worthington, the woman who was just here?" I said.

Fontbutter was reviewing my video job.

"This looks good," he said. "I think I'll move on to the excavation."

At that moment, my phone pinged a response from Bellows. In a stroke of good luck for me, he was heading over to the Whaling Museum in town to work on his exhibit, and could meet now.

Fontbutter had packed his bag when I looked back up.

"You didn't answer me," I said. "Do you know Brenda Worthington?"

"Was that Brenda Worthington?" said Fontbutter. "I wish I'd known. I've heard about her and her ghost tours. I tried calling her to do an interview but haven't heard back. She's local-flavor gold."

Fontbutter's answer gave me a solid understanding of why Brenda made a quick escape. Being on Fontbutter's show was probably a terrifying proposition for someone like her.

"Get in touch with Brenda today," he said as we both headed out of The Shack. "Set up an interview for tomorrow."

"Will do," I said, knowing that would be a waste of time. "By the way, what's your theory about Solder? You said you had one."

"Cairo," said Fontbutter, picking up speed as we headed across the lawn. "I thought there was something sneaky-looking about the fellow when he hung up from the phone conversation I heard him have with someone in Cairo. You know, there's some tricky business in the world of anthropology. Stolen goods, faking authenticity. You name it. Our Solder might not have been the saintly scientist everyone thought he was."

"Interesting," I said, remembering Andy's growing suspects list as Fontbutter tossed his bags into his rental car and took off.

I wondered how much I could trust Fontbutter's story as I headed into the main house. I gave Tinker a snuggle and grabbed my bag and car keys. I remembered that Leigh said she had worked in Cairo. She had said she had loved to belay down excavation sites there with a professor. Was there a connection?

When my hand reached the doorknob, I stopped, thinking now about Brenda. She had been very late for our appointment. Perhaps she had decided to wait me out and visit The Shack on her own. Fool me once, right? I dialed Peter.

"Morning," he said in a cheerful voice.

I know this man. He is cheerful, yes. But not when I've woken him. In that scenario, he would be cordial, perhaps understanding, even a bit happy someone had started thinking of him in the early hours of the day. But chipper? Never. As with Leigh and her suspicions about her own boyfriend, my radar went up.

"How are you?" I said, in an equally chipper voice to let him know I was on to him.

"I'm OK. How're you?" he said.

For the record, I'd given him a chance to come clean.

"What's going on?" I said.

"What do you mean?"

"I mean why do you sound so happy?" I said, realizing I'd need to be direct.

"I'm no happier than usual," he said.

"Oh, it is getting worse and worse. We can discuss this later. Right now, I'm heading into town to talk to Bellows. I have it on good authority that he's been back to the well, and I want to know why. I'm concerned, however, that Brenda might break into The Shack again. I don't want her in here without me. Sounds like an opportunity for a reporter, don't you think? Why don't you work in the Morton house today? It's very cozy here, and you can stake out my place. Plus, it would be nice to come home to that cheese spaghetti you promised me."

"Sweet talk, eh?" said Peter.

"Did it work?" I said, opening the door.

"Yes," said Peter. "Well, no. I'd be happy to be your man of the house, but, really, I can't leave. I've got some stuff here I have to work on. I'll tell you about it later. I promise. I've got to go, but talk later, OK?"

The line went dead.

"OK," I said.

But I was not OK. It was completely impossible for me to comprehend how Peter could be thinking about anything else. Something was off. If I'd had more time to dwell on it, I'd have headed over to his office, but Bellows was waiting. I opened the door and headed to town.

Chapter 19

I've always had a soft spot for Nantucket's Whaling Museum, in part because its oldest section was originally the 1847 Hadwen & Barney Oil and Candle Factory. In case you ever visit, which I highly recommend, there are many galleries that feature artifacts pertaining to Nantucket's whaling life and culture. The main attraction is a forty-six-foot-long spermwhale skeleton suspended from a ceiling. I prefer its other highlight, a massive lever press that was used to refine oil to make candles.

As I crossed the street, I glanced at a text from Peter on my phone.

> *Sorry. Busy here. Peace offering . . . did a deep search on Bellows. Be careful. He was arrested once for trying to break into the Seamens Bethel chapel in New Bedford. The pulpit is in the shape of a ship's bow. He was drunk and wanted to climb it. Headline was 'Thar He Blows: Historian hits cop during Seamens*

*pilgrimage.' Probably seemed funny at the time, but
is it, in retrospect?*

I flashed my membership card at the front desk,
then passed the installation of a huge glass lens,
from the island's Sankaty Head Lighthouse, that sits
at the base of the museum's stairs. I headed up to
the second-floor galleries, where I knew the special
exhibits were. Taking a left, I headed down the corridor, beneath the old town clock, which had been
restored and was now displayed higher up in the
staircase connecting the three stories of the building. At the end of the hall, I nodded to a dapper fellow made of wood. He's an old figurehead from a
whaling ship's bow, who, wearing a topcoat and always looking ready for tea, had led his ship through
the oceans. You've got to love him.

Next to him were double doors, closed. Across the
doorway was a rope from which a sign hung. It read:

PARDON OUR APPEARANCE AS WE PREPARE FOR
CAPTAIN'S LOGS AND MARITIME JOURNALS
OPENING THIS JUNE.

Here I knocked.
"One moment," Bellows said from the other side
of the door.
I jiggled the doorknob, but it was locked. I could
hear sea shanties playing on the other side of the
door. Not my favorite music, but it fit the venue.
When Bellows opened the door for me, I noticed
that his face was flushed and his sleeves were rolled

up. I thought of Peter's text. I wondered if he was someone with anger-management issues or simply a historian with a misplaced passion for the Seamen's pulpit.

"Good morning," he said, with a wild cheerfulness. "Come in. I'm mapping out some of the upcoming exhibit this morning. I received a shipment I've been waiting for of logs and diaries."

I matched his jolly greeting and joined the work in progress. On the far side of the wall, there were about four wooden crates with the words FRAGILE written across each of them. Two were open. Styrofoam pellets spilled over and onto the table upon which the crates sat. Next to them were two plastic bags that each contained oversized books with worn leather covers. I assumed they were the logbooks Bellows had requested from the places I'd heard him refer to yesterday in the library.

In addition to the books, I also noticed several sepia-toned photos laid carefully across the table. I was here to interview a potential murder suspect, but I couldn't help but be drawn to these images. One, in particular, caught my eye. It was of a woman in what looked to be a swing, dressed to the nines, with a couple of guys on either side of her. She looked rather serious, however, for someone on a swing.

"That's a gamming chair," said Bellows, following my eye. "Wonderful example from New Bedford. Nantucket has a treasure trove of logs and photos, but I've been rounding out its collection with items from other whaling centers as well."

"What's a gamming chair?" I said.

"Gamming was a diversion for a wife who went to

sea with her husband, as well as the captain and crew," he said, joining me in admiring the photo. "When whalers met at sea, the crews exchanged visits. The captain's wife was lowered from ship to whaleboat in a gamming chair and was rowed to another ship for a festive social occasion, like visiting with another captain's wife."

"Not an easy life," I said. I couldn't help but admire the women of Patience and Nancy's era. In a community that supported women's advancement, they ran businesses, invested, traveled the world, and made decisions for their communities alongside the men. Nantucket women rocked.

"Tell me about your candle idea," said Bellows.

Now that we were on his turf and talking about his specialty, Bellows seemed less stuffy and, well, downright nerdy. I thought it suited him better.

"Candles, right," I said. "I'm making clock candles with my class right now."

"Agnes and the ladies?" he said, with an air of suspicion that reminded both of us about murder and our morning spent together only yesterday.

"I was wondering if I could learn a bit more about other accessories that went along with candles," I said. "It could be interesting to have my own historical display in the store. Maybe sell a few items."

I was making this up on the fly but loving the idea, I must admit. Often the best ideas come when I walk through an unexpected door and keep an open mind. I'd never have thought that helping the Girl Scouts might lead to a new product line in my store. Bellows seemed to like the idea. His eyes brightened.

"I'd be happy to help," he said. "In fact, if you'd

like to use my name—for credibility, of course—I could design a little something for you."

"That would be great," I said, *as long as you aren't arrested for murder.*

As Bellows launched into a monologue about candle snuffers, candlesticks made from the island's lesser-known craft in silversmithing, and wick trimmers, his passion and ambition were palpable. This was a man who'd found a niche, one that gave him immeasurable pleasure, but one that did not match his obvious ambition and need for accolades.

"You can see why it is important to understand and celebrate these objects. It's also why I think that piecing together the tale of Patience and Nancy might be one of the most exciting stories we have left to document," said Bellows. "And I don't think that Fontbutter is the man to tell that story."

"You are. Of course," I said, nodding with certainty for effect, and deciding to get to the heart of my visit. "Is that why you went to the well last night?"

Bellows gave me an indignant look, but I raised my hand before he could argue.

"The police don't know," I said. "But a little birdie did tell me. It was a bold move. Especially with a murderer on the loose. They might think you look suspicious. That maybe you killed Solder in order to take over his work."

"You think that I killed Solder?" said Bellows. "That's insane."

"You had the opportunity to kill him," I said. "You could have strangled him before the rest of us arrived on the scene. With Solder out of the way, you could take possession of the two skeletons and solve

the historical mystery. It would add a little shine to
your reputation, wouldn't it?"

Bellows's whole body seemed to perspire. He sat
on a bench along the wall and rubbed his head until
his hair was as messy as Old Holly's backyard. He
looked like a man who wanted a drink.

"This is preposterous," he said.

"Then what did you do at the well last night?" I
said.

Bellows crossed the room with purpose, but when
he reached the wall, all he did was straighten an
empty frame that hung there. I waited, assuming he
was thinking about how to answer me. Finally, he
turned around.

"I do have an agenda," he said. "I will admit that.
But I didn't kill Solder. And I would never, ever, jeop-
ardize the authenticity of an excavation. As you said,
I want to take over the excavation now that Solder is
dead. That's all. Fontbutter is not the man to peel
back the layers of the story."

"But you are," I said. "And if you are in charge,
Fontbutter will also have to put you in his production. You might land a leading role in his movie. I
imagine that might help your career quite a bit too?"

"Yes, but I did not kill the man."

I kept a cool eye on my suspect and said nothing.

Bellows stood and crossed over to one of the logbooks.

"Did you throw something down the well last
night?"

"No," he said, looking like he might faint.

"I can't help you if you don't tell me the truth," I
said.

He picked something up from behind one of the crates. He held it up for me to see. It was a long piece of linen.

"The map?" I said, shocked to have found the missing piece of evidence.

Bellows, however, shook his head.

"Not the real map," he said. "I heard that there were no photos of the map, and that Ms. Paik hadn't studied it carefully. Then I overheard Officer Southerland say that it was missing. I told you I'd never compromise the integrity of my work, but I'll confess I was tempted to do so. I found this linen embroidery of Nantucket Island that was made around the same time. It was in the storage facility of artifacts out by Bartlett's Farm."

"You stole it from the warehouse?" I said.

Bellows looked at me frantically. He didn't look like a guy who might strike me, but I could see a man who was willing to do crazy things, like break into a church to see its pulpit or steal a map to embellish a story.

"And you figured if they found a map, they'd need you to solve the mystery of Patience Cooper and Nancy Holland," I said.

He nodded.

"I didn't do it, though," he said. "I couldn't. As much as I wanted to. And I'm so glad I didn't because look what I received today."

I walked over to a logbook he'd opened. The pages were filled with beautiful drawings of whaleboats and whale fins. I knew about these books. The images looked like colorful doodles, but the imagery had practical purposes. In days before Excel spreadsheets and laptops, the captain could quickly count his whales' tails to determine how many of the creatures had been caught, and where.

"See here," said Bellows. "This book is from the *Aurelia*. The ship made its voyage through the Pacific in eighteen thirty-seven. Look at this."

He pointed to an entry in beautiful, flowing script. Honestly, it was so artfully written that I had a hard time making out the words for a few moments. When the letters came together, however, my mouth dropped.

"Jedediah Cooper?" I said, looking at the name the *Aurelia*'s captain had added to his entry.

Bellows nodded.

"Agnes's family legend is missing some details," he said.

He walked across the room and unwrapped another journal. This book was leather-bound, with the name *Poponscott* embossed across its cover.

"I was able to do some digging of my own to find which ship Jedediah Cooper arrived on. Says here that he came to the island on the *Poponscott* after having been picked up in Hawaii. It lists the *Aurelia* as his last ship.

"I called a colleague who has access to the *Aurelia* log. Jedediah is listed as part of the crew. He was kicked off of the ship, however, something he likely didn't tell the captain of the *Poponscott*. The *Aurelia* log says he was dismissed for ungentlemanly conduct with the captain's daughter. This captain had brought his family with him. Looks like Jedediah smelled money and tried to woo the daughter. And look at this."

Bellows took out his phone and opened it to a picture. It was of an old newspaper clipping. I had to hand it to the man—he was good at what he did. I wasn't sure where he'd located the article, but I was shocked by its contents.

"Jedediah Cooper had a wife before Patience?"

I read on. The story told of Mrs. Alysia Smythson Cooper, who had been attacked and robbed while coming home with the town's collection for a new church steeple.

"Sound familiar?" he said.

I nodded.

"Jedediah Cooper sounds like a serial killer," I said. "The captain was wise to have kicked him off of his ship. And Nantucket was, unluckily, the place where he landed. He married Patience for her money, but he must have imagined a much more lavish life when he heard about the Petticoat Row ladies' plans to invest in a whaling ship. It was easy money. By knocking off Patience, he could take the money and run—until he found his next victim."

"But it still leaves unanswered questions about Nancy's map," he said.

Bellows and I nodded. I considered his story. He'd filled in a lot of the holes about Nancy and Patience. I was starting to get a real picture of the man who had conned them both.

"Who left Nantucket with Jedediah?" I said.

"A very good question," he said.

I'd arrived feeling that I'd found Solder's killer, but now I was not so sure. Bellows had been able to build a fascinating story without ownership of the skeletons. He was quite remarkable.

I looked at the time. Leigh would be descending the well in an hour. Soon, Old Holly would be handing the axe over to Andy.

"Let me know if you find out anything more," I said to Bellows. "I think you're on to something."

I left Bellows and headed back down the corridor, aware of the eyes from the portraits of old sea captains hanging on the walls. Old Holly's story about seeing Bellows had been true, but for a reason we had not begun to imagine last night.

On the other hand, although Bellows had not gone through with his idea to throw a piece of linen into the well, I couldn't completely check him off my list of suspects for one key reason: There was no way he could have overheard Andy talking about the missing map. He'd been very clear about the fact that he didn't want to create a craze for treasure hunting. So how did he know the map was missing?

My suspect was still a suspect. I knew Andy would feel the same when Old Holly told him about last night. I knew the police would question Bellows. I felt, however, that I'd known the right questions to ask and had come away with a much better understanding of the mystery at the bottom of Solder's murder.

Chapter 20

In order to get from the museum to the Wick & Flame, I took the path that led past The Bean. When I turned the corner, I was surprised to see Emily out of the house.

"I had to get out," she said, waving to me. "Neal's covering for me for ten minutes so I can get a muffin."

"How are you doing?" I said, opening the door to The Bean for her.

"Slowly but surely," she said as we headed to the counter. "Morning, Clemmie. Can I have a cappuccino?"

"You need tea with honey," said Clemmie, taking one look at my friend.

"She's right," I said to Emily. Her eyes were still deeply ringed.

"Ugh," said Emily. "Fine."

"I'll take the cappuccino," I said.

We found a back table and took a seat. We waited

for our names to be called, but instead Clemmie came from behind the counter and served us personally. Then she grabbed a chair and joined us. Immediately, I told Clemmie and Emily about the likelihood that Jedediah had been a serial killer.

"It must have been so much easier to be a serial killer in the old days," said Clemmie. "Jump on a ship and no one knows who, what, or when."

"I knew he was behind this," said Emily.

I nodded; my coffee cup raised.

"Any new suspects for the murder of the scientist?" Emily said.

"I thought I'd narrowed in on someone, but now I'm not so sure. The police have cast a wide net, but I'm still focused on the historian, the producer, and Old Holly."

"You know, you can learn a lot about a person from the kind of coffee they order," said Clemmie.

"What does Bellows order?" said Emily.

"The guy who is visiting at the Historical Association?" said Clemmie. "He's fussy. One day black coffee, the next a lot of milk."

She nodded with authority, but I wasn't sure how to add that to my suspect profile.

"What are you thinking?" Emily said to me.

"I'm reshuffling all I know about my suspects," I said. "I think I forgot to mention Leigh."

"Who's that?" said Clemmie.

"Solder's girlfriend."

"Can't help you there. I didn't serve Solder or his girlfriend. And I don't know about the producer. One the one hand, he's thoughtful because he orders for others. On the other hand, he ordered a hazelnut for himself, which I find is usually a favorite of prima donnas."

Emily laughed. Neal, who is the opposite of a prima donna, was obsessed with hazelnut. I knew, however, that she'd tease him about it tonight.

"I bet Leigh did it," said Emily. "Isn't it always the husband or wife?"

"I hope she didn't do it," I said. "They had a fight as they were going down the well that we all heard. She told me it was because he had been acting really weird lately, and she was convinced he was hiding something from her. She thought he was cheating, or something worse. She said he'd been acting strange. Turns out, however, he was acting fishy because he'd bought her an engagement ring."

"Oh, man, that's going to hurt," said Clemmie. "Really bad decision. She could be flashing a ring this morning, but instead she killed the guy."

"Is it possible that Solder was going to propose but was also acting fishy about something else?" said Emily. "Maybe something was going on with him, and someone killed him for it."

"The police think so," I said. "Actually, Fontbutter thinks so, too. I know he's a suspect, so I take it with a grain of salt, but he thought Solder had some shady dealings in Cairo."

"That opens up the suspect list," said Clemmie.

"Clemmie has a point," said Emily.

"But I went down the well at Old Holly's last night, and there was no map. I maintain this is the key clue to solving the crime. I am more convinced than ever that the motive for murder has to do with the discovery of Patience and Nancy."

"Excuse me?" said Emily, choking on her muffin.

"You went down a well?" said Clemmie, shaking her head. "At night? Alone? You go, girl."

"I did," I said. "I won't be able to comfortably lift my arms for a couple of days due to their soreness, but I saw for myself that the map was missing."

"So what does that have to do with cutting the tree?" said Clemmie. "No one knew Solder was going to find a valuable map."

"I still don't know. Also, anyone could have made the cut," I said. "Even Old Holly. The axe that was used was under his porch. The confusing and frustrating point is that two of my key suspects couldn't have pushed over the tree. They were with us by the table. Only Leigh might have been able to push the tree and then claim she was trapped."

"Hey," another barista called out to Clemmie.

We looked to the counter to see that the line was growing.

Clemmie stood.

"Let me know if I can help," she said.

"Me too," said Emily, rising as well. "I'd better get back to Neal."

"You have four days to recover," I said. "I'm still hoping to see you at Halloween Haunts."

"I thought it was canceled," she said.

"We're going to see how it goes today," I said. "The Girl Scouts are meeting there after school. I'm going to make sure they leave excited about it. We're not going to drop the ball for the town's neediest. No way."

"Good for you," said Clemmie.

Fortunately, it was a busy day at the Wick & Flame, so I couldn't dwell too much on the fact that I was missing the excavation at Old Holly's, or wonder what news Peter wanted to tell me. In addition to selling out my Tinker Specials once more, I decided to keep busy by making more of my candle clocks. Customers enjoyed the live exhibit, and I even sold a couple.

At about two, when I was beginning the get antsy about what had happened at the well and my impending date with the Girl Scouts, I got a phone call.

"Hello?" I said, not sure who belonged to the number on my screen.

"Hi," said Leigh. "I got your number from Kate. Just thought I'd reach out to a friendly voice after this morning."

"I'm so glad you did," I said. "How did it go today?"

"Well, I did it," she said. "I climbed back down the well, in honor of Robbie and to be the professional I know I am. It was my first solo. Andy came with me, which was so nice."

"I think it took a lot of courage to go back there," I said, realizing she'd had no idea Andy was keeping an eye on her. Well done, Andy.

"I made sure my walkie-talkie worked this time," she said with what sounded like a choke in her throat.

"Did Fontbutter drive you crazy? I know he showed up," I said, trying to change the subject to some mutual commiseration.

"Actually, he was fine," she said. "Andy wouldn't

let him come down, but he gave me your candles. I lit them and took a picture. It was beautiful."

"Are you free for a drink this evening? We should celebrate."

"I'd love to," she said. "The police have asked me to stay for at least twenty-four more hours because of their investigation, but I can't wait to leave Nantucket. I have a funeral to plan, you know."

"I know. But tonight, take a break if you can. Red or white?" I said.

"Both?" she said with a chuckle.

"The Girl Scouts will be gone by five. Come then," I said.

When we hung up, I thought about the police's request that Leigh stay on island for twenty-four more hours. That meant that Leigh was still on their list. I called Andy, but he did not answer, so I left him a message to get in touch.

A moment later, I was rewarded, as promised, with at text from Leigh that contained her photo of the bottom of the well. Fontbutter had been right about choosing black candles. The popped against the pale stones and flickered with mystery. I couldn't help it, but suddenly I hoped I'd get a credit in his show.

It's unusual for me to feel this way, but when I turned my sign to CLOSED, I was excited to head out the door. I went straight to the liquor store. A lot of anchor stores have closed on Main Street since I was a kid, but an important one remains: Murray's Beverage Store. I popped in, grabbed three bottles of wine—a white, a red, and a rosé. Remembering there was very little at the Morton house, I grabbed three more. I also picked up a couple of pre-made cheese plates. I bought more than I needed for some wine with Leigh, but they were on special. And, let's face it, I'm a sucker for cheese.

I knew there was real hope for Halloween Haunts when I pulled up to my newfound home. Opening the car door, I once again heard the shrieks and laughter of the girls. I was glad I'd risked being the town witch if that was what it took. Tinker seemed quite pleased too. Before I'd even opened the front door, he sprang onto the windowsill to greet me, wearing a tiny witch's hat that someone had made.

"Greetings, Witch Scouts," I said when I entered.

"Mwahahaha," screamed the girls in unison.

Their cackles were music to my ears.

I dropped the wine in the kitchen and was delighted to see that screens had been put in the living room to create a path that would be part of the haunted-house section of the event. The girls were planning to start the haunted part of the visit in the living room and then continue it through the kitchen and up the back stairs to two of the bedrooms that opened into each other from the back. The tour would end in the third room, where I had set up my workspace last night. I'd be sure to clean it out for them.

"Come see our spider webs," Cherry called to me.

I was happy to hear her voice. That meant that Agnes and Flo were by her side.

Making my way back through the maze, I heard their voices in the dining room, which had been designated for younger visitors. There would be craft tables set up to make necklaces, sand sculptures, and beaded Halloween jewelry, along with some face painting. When I entered the room, I saw that the craft tables had been set up. Two Girl Scouts stood on ladders, while Cherry, Agnes, and Flo called out orders about how and where to hang their truly gorgeous spider webs.

"I told you we could do better than that gauzy stuff," said Flo as both Shelly and I entered from different sides of the room.

"You weren't lying," I said.

I couldn't imagine how long they'd worked to make so many cobwebs, but their inventory seemed endless. Fortunately, the ceilings in these old houses were quite low, so the Girl Scouts could reach the beams from a small ladder. Every corner glistened with their threads, and they even extended up toward an old chandelier.

"Ms. Stella?"

Three scouts came bounding into the room, holding their cellphones.

"Your candles look so pretty!" said young Jane, the most boisterous imp. She flashed a picture of my candles in the well, a similar version to the picture Leigh had sent to me.

The picture was on Fontbutter's Instagram account. I noticed he did not give me credit for the candles. I guess Clemmie had been right about hazelnut coffee drinkers.

"Why are you following this account?" I said to the scout.

"He followed us, so we follow him," she said.

I now remembered that Fontbutter had originally learned about the stories of Nancy and Patience through the Girl Scouts' feed.

"We've been posting great photos for Halloween

Haunts," said the girl, touching her screen and handing her phone to me. "Check it out."

Indeed, the girls had done a great job at recording the development of Halloween Haunts. There were photos of meetings, decorations they'd made, images of the house as we turned it from a run-down and forgotten home into one of the town's best attractions. There was even a photo of Tinker, nestled between photos of the Candleers' cobwebs, and a couple of images about the discovery of Nancy at the well.

Outside, I heard a horn honk. On cue, the girls began to gather their belongings and head out the door, each knowing that their parent's arrival was imminent. I handed the phone back to the young Girl Scout, thinking something was not quite right about the photos, but not sure why. They were innocuous enough.

I couldn't shake the feeling, however, that something in general was not right. I looked about the house, and could think of nothing out of place. The girls had returned, Halloween Haunts was back on track, Shelly looked pleased, and the Candleers were on a roll.

"Can we stay and finish the living room now that the screens are up?" said Flo.

"Not without the girls to help," said Shelly. "It's their project."

"Pish posh," said Agnes. "We're going to drape them over the edges of the screens. They don't need to be here for that."

I looked at them, bright-eyed and ready to keep working.

"Can you make an exception, Shelly?"

Shelly seemed to catch on that the work was as good for our Candleers as it was for her scouts. She nodded, and the ladies got to work.

I walked to the window to watch the girls pile into their parents' cars, some alone, others with friends. Tinker hopped next to me. He whisked his tail and curled up for a nap.

"Quite a crowd," I said, still experiencing that nagging feeling. "Do you ladies want some wine? I have red, white, and rosé."

"Red is good for the heart," said Flo.

"Then let's start with red," I said.

I went to the kitchen and opened the bottle of red. I'd just passed around the glasses when there was a knock on the door.

I opened the door to find Leigh, on time.

"I'm so glad you made it," I said.

"Hi, sweetie," said Cherry. "Be careful. We've got cobwebs everywhere!"

"I'm so glad you invited me," said Leigh, looking around the house. "This looks amazing. And that red wine looks delicious!"

"Join us!" said Flo.

"Come on back to the kitchen," I said, leading her through the maze the girls had made today.

"You have a really nice town," said Leigh.

I turned around and handed Leigh her glass. She was seated at the kitchen table, looking tired. Her canvas bag was overflowing with the day's tools, and gear sat atop the table next to her.

"I know you are living through your worst nightmare," I said. "I'm glad our town can be here for you."

"Cheers!" she said.

As I took a sip from my glass, my eyes fell upon Leigh's bag. Specifically, I noticed a coffee cup from The Bean, shoved into a side pocket. It was safe to assume that the drink had been given to her by Fontbutter, as part of his contribution to the morning. What I found interesting, however, was a marking on its side: HN.

"The coffee at The Bean is delicious, isn't it?" I said. "I've never tried the hazelnut."

"Hazelnut is the only flavor I drink," said Leigh. "It's my weakness."

"Like me and cheese," I said, my throat beginning to tighten.

"This is an amazing spread," Leigh said, reaching for a piece of cheddar.

Her confession about her love for hazelnut coffee made my heart sink.

The thing was, no one had been drinking coffee when we were at the well yesterday. In spite of that, Fontbutter had known without consulting her that I should order a hazelnut for Leigh today. Worse, his request had been the only flavored order I'd made. I could think of no other way he'd know Leigh's weakness but that he had already known her before the excavation, and known her well.

I thought again about Fontbutter's videos. Specifically, my mind went to the clip featuring Leigh before she descended the well. I remembered her smile, and Solder coming into view. I had assumed she was smiling at Solder, but now I wondered if she had been smiling at Fontbutter.

It was my turn to take a really big sip of my wine.

I put down my glass as the Candleers chatted audibly in the living room next to us about whether they needed more cobwebs. Their presence gave me the courage to press on.

"How long have you known Fontbutter?" I asked.

Leigh lowered her glass. I knew I'd asked a valid question from the fear I could see in her eyes.

"It's not what you think," she said.

"Then what is it?" I said.

"I met Fontbutter at the conference in Boston," she said. "That's all."

"And then you met again yesterday."

"If you think this has something to do with Robbie's death, you couldn't be further from the truth."

At that moment there was a knock on my door.

"I'll get it!" said Cherry.

"What's the news?" said Agnes, coming into the kitchen with Flo and Cherry.

Andy followed behind them. He noticed that Leigh was in the room and nodded. His expression was serious, all-business.

"Good job today," he said to Leigh.

"Thanks," she said. She looked at me desperately. I was tempted to tell Andy about the coffee, but did that prove she was a killer?

"I heard you were hanging cobwebs here, Agnes," said Andy. "The fingerprints came back on the bone You'll be relieved to know that we were able to pick up a partial print of someone else."

"Andy Southerland, I've known you since you weren't even my own height," said Agnes. "The fact that you could have thought me capable of such violence even for an instant is something that's going to take me quite a while to recover from."

"Who else handled the bone?" I said, hoping against hope that Andy didn't say Kyle Nelson or my cousins, Ted and Docker.

"I'd like a whack at them," said Agnes.

"Cool your knickers," said Flo.

"Well, who?" I said.

"Brenda Worthington," said Andy. "We have her prints on file from a few years ago. She tried to block the demolition of an old house. It seems that Brenda hit Solder over the head."

"But, she wasn't at the dig," said Cherry.

"Apparently she was. Do any of you know where she is?" said Andy. "We haven't been able to find her."

Chapter 21

My head was spinning, but I kept my cool.

"I haven't seen Brenda since this morning," I said. "She told me she had lost interest in communicating with Patience Cooper. That she no longer wanted to visit The Shack. She left quickly and said she might try her luck with Nancy instead."

"I didn't see her at the well," said Andy.

"Who's Brenda Worthington?" asked Leigh, her eyes beginning to brim with tears.

Flo sat down beside her, and I could hear her tell Leigh about Brenda's tours.

"Let's check out The Shack," I said. "I had a thought when I left this morning that maybe Brenda wanted to be there without me. But why?"

"I don't know," said Andy, "but let's check. You all stay here."

"OK," said Cherry, refilling everyone's glass.

"Are you kidding?" said Agnes. "I'm coming."

"Sit," said Flo. "Leigh is upset. Let Andy and Stella do their job. We'll do ours."

I opened the back door, still wondering if I'd let my imagination run wild about Leigh and Fontbutter. I took a breath, told myself to get it together, and headed to The Shack with Andy.

"You OK?" said Andy, probably noticing my frustration.

"I'm fine. How're you doing? How's Georgianna? I haven't seen her lately."

"I guess you didn't hear," he said. "We broke up a couple of days ago."

I stopped dead in my tracks and looked at Andy in the twilight. He stopped as well but didn't make eye contact.

"I guess I got so caught up with Patience and Nancy that I haven't thought about much else. What happened?"

"She thought that I was holding back," he said.

"I'm so sorry," I said.

"Let's go see if a killer is in The Shack," he said. "We can talk about relationship problems later."

As we reached The Shack, Andy raised a hand and motioned for me to stand on the protected side of the door. He put his hand on his holster and leaned against the wall.

"Brenda Worthington?" he said. "This is Andy Southerland. If you are inside, please signal your presence."

Silence.

"Brenda," he said. "I'm here on official business. If you are inside, you need to let me know."

"Brenda?" I said. "It's Stella. Andy needs to talk to you. I'm here too."

We waited a few more moments, but there was no sound.

"I'm coming in," said Andy. "If you are inside, raise your hands in the air."

Andy motioned for me to stay put and headed inside.

"All clear," he said, a moment later.

I turned on my phone's flashlight and joined him.

"Do you think she's at Old Holly's?" I said.

"I already called the police officer on guard," he said. "He hasn't seen anyone."

"Well, I wouldn't rely on him," I said, remembering how easily Bellows and I had passed him on our own visits to the well. "I have a feeling his night vision isn't the best."

"How would you know that?" said Andy.

I'm pretty good by now at keeping a straight face with Andy, but I turned off my flashlight to be on the safe side. There was no need for him to know I'd been down the well last night. We now stood in the dark. I wasn't sure where to go next. I was also aware that Andy was leaning against the wall of The Shack and not really moving.

"Any reason why?" I said.

"Why what?"

"Why Georgianna thought you were holding back?"

"Did it seem like I was holding back?" he said, putting his hands in his pockets.

"I think you're always holding back a little," I said, feeling a lump in my throat I hadn't expected. I hated to see Andy sad.

"Maybe I shouldn't hold back so much," he said.

"Maybe you shouldn't."

"Maybe you shouldn't either."

"Wait," I said. "Why? Did Peter say anything to you? He was acting very strangely when we spoke this morning."

Andy chuckled. His jaw shifted, and I knew he was done talking.

"What the hell," he said. "I've got to go find Brenda."

And then he was gone.

"That was very romantic," said a ghostly woman's voice.

I aspire to be brave, but this wasn't my finest moment. I ran to the doorway, ready to run back to the house, fly up the stairs, and jump right under my bed; except I realized after I'd crossed the threshold that it was not Patience who had spoken to me. I stepped back inside.

"Brenda?" I whispered, then turned my flashlight on again.

From the chimney space, I saw two feet drop to the ground. Brenda knelt and crawled out to join me.

"I climbed up as far as I could when I heard you coming," she said. "I almost fell out when Andy looked up the chimney, but thankfully it's dark up there and I was too far up for him to see me."

"That was very ingenious," I said. "But the police are looking for you. Brenda. And they're going to find you, one way or another. Even if you escape here now, they'll find you."

"Why are they looking for me?" she said.

Brenda was dressed in normal clothing, but the

look in her eyes was wild. If someone had told me she was possessed, I might have believed them.

"Why do you think they're looking for you?" I said, wondering if an open-ended question might help us cut right to a confession.

"I don't know anymore," she said, wrapping her arms tightly around her body.

"They found the bone," I said.

Brenda dropped her head into her hands.

"I don't know how I've gotten caught up in everything," she said. "I was only trying to help protect Patience and Nancy. Now I've killed a man."

"You killed Robert Solder?" I said.

"I didn't strangle him," she said, looking up at me. "I heard he was strangled. But I went to the dig yesterday, and now the anthropologist is dead."

"Oh, Brenda," I said. "What did you do?"

"I went to the well after Peter found me in The Shack," she said. "By the way, I'm glad he found Tinker. I wouldn't have let him out of the house if I'd thought there was any risk of him running away. I just needed some time to get a head start. I didn't want Peter to see me heading to Old Holly's. Oh, and I feel badly about the tire, too. I took the bus as far as the Miacomet Road and walked the rest of the way."

"Why?"

"I felt compelled to go. I wanted to protect Nancy. And when I arrived, I saw the bone in Agnes's car. She is a thief! I thought maybe Patience had sent me there to find the bone. I knew straightaway it was Patience's femur, because it had been missing from

The Shack, so I took it out of the car. I intended to return it here."

"But instead of returning the bone, you headed into the forest," I said. "Why?"

"I heard Solder mention a map on the walkie-talkie. None of you were looking," she said. "And I realized if I headed into the brush from the side of the property, I might be able to catch a glimpse of what was going on from behind the well. Sure enough, I did. But then the tree fell over."

"Did you push the tree over?" I said.

"No," she said. "But as I reached a small clearing, I heard the tree fall behind me. After a minute or two, I saw Solder come up from the well. He looked confused. He was holding the bag, and I figured the map was in it. I stepped out from the clearing and asked him, very politely, for the map. Very quietly, he told me to stay calm. That everything would be OK. I whispered back to him that I would take good care of it, but he kept backing away from me. Before I knew it, I'd hit him on the head with the femur. So, you know, I couldn't bring it back here. When he fell down, I took the map, but nothing else. I'm not a thief. I only wanted to protect Patience."

"Where's the map?" I said.

"I don't have it with me," she said. "It's hidden, and I won't give it to anyone."

One look at Brenda and I could see I wasn't going to get anywhere fast.

"What did you do after you took the map?" I said.

"I ran through the path to the water," she said. "I knew there was an old canoe there. Some kids in the area hang out there to smoke. Their parents think they're out getting exercise, but they're just going for a smoke. I saw them once when I was at the Field Station. I told them off, but I knew they hid cigarettes in the old canoe."

I remembered the cigarette butts. Her story lined up.

"Why haven't you handed over the map?" I said. "This might have something to do with Solder's death."

"I think it might," said Brenda, beginning to shake again. "I would have turned it over, but I've been afraid for my life. That night, I found a note under my door. The author said they'd seen me take the map, and that if I didn't leave information about where the treasure was hidden, the person would turn me in for murder—or worse. I've been terrified."

"You've been blackmailed?" I said.

Brenda nodded.

"By whom?" I said.

"I don't know," she said. "I left the information on the board outside The Hub, as directed. But it was dark, and I was afraid."

"Brenda," I said, an idea beginning to form. "What information about the map did you share?"

"I said the treasure was in the northeast part of the island," she said, "but it's not, really."

Fontbutter.

"Brenda," I said, "lay low. I've got to go."

Chapter 22

I ran back to the Morton house and entered the kitchen through the back door. Inside, Cherry was opening the rosé.

"You should have bought more red," she said. "It's not good to mix."

"I didn't know I'd be having a party," I said. "Leigh, where's Fontbutter tonight?"

"How would I know?" she said.

"There's no time for that," I said. "Where is he?"

Cherry stopped pouring. The Candleers looked at Leigh, their goodwill fading fast.

Leigh dropped her head.

"Whatever you might think," she said, "I loved Robbie. I was going to let him down easy. As for Hugh, I don't know where he is."

"Fontbutter's name is Hugh?" said Flo.

"You and Fontbutter?" said Cherry. The ladies looked very disappointed in her choice of man.

"You were the one who told Fontbutter about our discovery of Patience and our plans to look for

Nancy, weren't you?" I said. "He didn't find out from a Girl Scouts feed."

Leigh nodded.

"But Hugh has nothing to do with Solder's death," said Leigh. "What motive would he have?"

"You and Solder had the find of the century," I said. "I don't think Fontbutter would have stopped at anything to get the exclusive scoop. Add a map that might be worth a fortune to the story, and you have motive."

Leigh put her hand over her mouth.

"If you're right," she said, "he's used me."

"Fontbutter's B. and B is on Cliff Road, right?" I said. It was a guess, but many of the B & Bs are around there.

Leigh nodded.

"The Cliff Lodge Bed and Breakfast," she said.

"See you in a few," I said, glad I hadn't finished that glass of wine.

I was in my car and down the road before anyone could stop me.

As I reached Cliff Road, I made out the shadow of a man in the mist. I slowed down and opened the window.

"Hop in," I said to Fontbutter.

"I bin' to Rose'n Crown," he said, his step faltering. "Good pub."

"The best," I said. "Hop in."

"No thang you."

"I know about Brenda and the map," I said. "It's over."

Fontbutter didn't miss a beat. He took off at what was probably his full speed, but his feet took him in

an S-shape as he forged ahead. I watched him dive
into the darkness, into a small pathway between two
houses. I pulled the car over to the shoulder of the
road and parked. My car couldn't fit through the
hedges, but I could.

I didn't have to go far. About ten paces into
the hedged pathway, I tripped over something an-
gled across the ground.

"Ow," said Fontbutter, who was lying next to me
on his stomach.

I didn't have any real fear that Fontbutter would
be able to escape me again, but to be sure, I crawled
over to his splayed body and sat on his back.

"That feels nice," he said.

"I know you killed Solder," I said. "And I know
you're planning to frame Brenda Worthington."

"The ghost lady?" he said. "You're crazy. She
couldn't kill a fly. I still can't believe she hit him on
the head, though. She could have killed him right
then'n there."

"Do you admit you've been blackmailing Brenda?"
I said.

"Whatever," he said. "It's jus' business. Nothing
personal."

"A man is dead," I said.

"I think I can't breathe," he said. "Would you
mind getting off of my back?"

I decided we'd had enough death on Nantucket. I
slid off of him. Fontbutter rolled over and leaned up
against the hedge. Before speaking again, he hiccupped.

"Sexy move," he said, pulling a leaf from his mustache, which reached up on one side and down on

the other, giving him the look of that theatrical comedy-tragedy mask.

"Murderer," I said, taking my phone from my pocket to call Andy.

In a surprise rush of dexterity, Fontbutter pulled the phone from my hands.

"I didn't kill anyone," he said. "I didn't even steal the map. I don't want anything underhanded to stain my work."

"You didn't steal it, but you had no qualms about torturing Brenda to get information about it," I said.

"Face it," he said. "It's much cleaner that way. You could say I hit the jackpot. You can't say I'm a killer."

I sat very still as I realized I had nothing to defend myself. Fontbutter said nothing for a moment. Beside him was a whiskey bottle, half full. If I could grab it from him, I knew I could use it as protection if he got violent. Unfortunately, it was too far away for me to make an easy grab. Fontbutter would likely beat me to it.

I was trying to figure out if I could take him on, mano a mano, when he reached into his jacket pocket. I flinched, which made me want to kick myself. There was no need for him to know how scared I was.

I'm not sure what I expected Fontbutter to pull from his jacket, but I was surprised when I saw it was a shot glass. He raised it to me, as if making a toast, and picked up the whiskey bottle. I was relieved that he was more interested in drinking from it than using it to assault me.

"Want to know about Brenda?" he said.

I nodded.

He poured and handed me the glass.

"Then you'll have to drink up," he said. "I don't like drinking alone. For every shot you do, I'll tell you sumfin' interesting."

He poured, hiccupped, and handed me the glass.

I downed it. I don't have the highest tolerance, but there was no way I was going to pass up the opportunity to learn more.

"First," he said, after I handed back the empty glass to him. "All I did was see the Worthington lady smack Solder and take the map," he raised a finger for emphasis, "but as I said," he raised it higher, "I didn't kill him. Want another?"

I nodded. He poured and waited to continue until I handed back the glass and he took another shot for himself.

"I may be slick and good at my job, but murder's not my thing," he said. "I jus' wanna good show. The last two have been terrible. But don' tell anyone I said so. Anyway, if I killed Solder, Leigh would never speak to me again. I like her. A lot."

His speech ended with him putting his finger against his lips.

I sat back against the adjacent hedge, feeling warmer from my shots, and thought about Fontbutter's admission.

"You saw Brenda leave with the map?" I said.

He poured, and I drank.

When I finished, he nodded.

"She was in her Quaker getup," he said.

I realized who the ghost was that everyone had seen.

"I tried to go after her right away, to get the map,

but she was fast, and I was afraid I'd get lost," he said. "As I headed back to the well, I heard a thud. It was a strange noise."

"I think I'll take another shot," I said, horrified to relive the gruesome story.

Fontbutter took one for himself, then passed one to me. I'd had four shots now, and I felt quite light-headed.

"When I returned to the well," he said. "Solder was on the ground with the rope around his neck. I was suddenly glad I hadn't taken the map. It wouldn't have been a good idea to be found with the map on me. That's for sure."

I wasn't feeling all that friendly toward the man, but I gave him a thumbs-up.

We shared another drink.

"Did you see the murderer?" I said.

Fontbutter rubbed his face.

"I couldn't see for sure because of the fog," he said. "But I think it was Bellows."

"Why didn't you tell the police?" I said.

"In due time," he said. "It's important to build the story. I was going to find the treasure first, then solve the murder. I thought I might need to interview Bellows and get some help on Nancy's story. Can't have him in jail yet."

"You are despicable," I said.

"I know," he said.

"Have you found the treasure?" I said.

"Not yet," he said. "I've looked damn near everywhere, too. Somebody probably dug it up a hundred years ago."

Or Brenda is cleverer than you know and sent you

to the wrong place, I thought, remembering her pride in sharing that fact with me. I was drunk, but I didn't say that part out loud.

My ears had started to ring a bit, so I wasn't sure of myself at first, but there was a sound at the end of the pathway. I realized that footsteps were heading our way. Fontbutter and I both turned to see who was out there.

In silhouette, I saw the outline of a woman with a large, overflowing tote bag. She was walking quickly, her head down.

"Shelly, baby," cried Fontbutter.

The woman stopped and shrieked.

"In here," he said.

"Fonty?" said a voice that was absolutely Shelly's. "What happened to you?"

She stayed in the entry of the path. I realized she could not see me behind Fontbutter.

"You left for the little boys' room and never came back," she said. "I've been waiting about twenty minutes."

"I knew there was something I forgotten," said Fontbutter. "'n you wanted to know about someth'n."

"The map," she said. "Where was the X on the map? You said northeast on your Instagram post, but where, exactly?"

"Mizz Shelly," said Fontbutter, "I have the feeling that you invited me out tonight to find out about this map. And not for my moustache. I feel used."

As the two of them worked out her intentions, I thought about Shelly in a new light. She had been the person who had been so interested in using the

Morton house. She was the one who had asked me to call John Pierre.

Unfortunately, however, it was now my turn to hiccup.

"Who's with you?" said Shelly, nervously.

"Shelly wants a part in the show," said Fontbutter. "She thinks I'm not on to her, but I am. I's happ'nd before. She was coming on to me, but I love Leigh. So . . . but I snuck out from the bathroom. I'm 'n honorable lover."

"Who's with you?" Shelly said again, now quite loudly, as if her volume could drown out Fontbutter.

"Hi, Shelly," I said.

"Stella?" she said. "Is that you? I'm getting out of here. You two are crazy. You'd better watch out, Stella. Don't assume Peter will put up with you. There's a lot of other women on this island who think he's a catch."

"What?" I said, but Shelly was gone.

Fontbutter started to laugh. He handed me another drink.

"No, thanks," I said. "I think we've had enough. Hand me my phone."

"Sure," he said. "But your policeman can't arrest me. No evidence of anything. Brenda can't even identify me. And you're drunk. Can't believe a word you say."

Fontbutter rolled onto his hands and knees, and after a few false moves, he gained his balance.

"Gotta go," he said. "You going to be OK?"

"Yup."

"Listen, I will tell you one more thing."

"What?" I said to his raised finger.

"You're fired," he said, turning the finger on me. "You are the worst employee I've ev'r had."

"I quit," I said.

"I still say," he said as he walked away from me and down the path, "you should be looking into Bellows. If it wasn't me, or you, or the old broads, or Brenda, it's got to be Bellows. Leigh would never have hurt Solder. I was just a confusing fling to her. But she helped me land the best picture I'll ever make."

"Again," I said. "You are despicable."

Chapter 23

I know when I need help. This was one of those times.

I dialed Peter. No answer. I couldn't imagine anything more important than Robert Solder's murder for a reporter. The hermit crabs certainly didn't hold a candle to this.

I toyed with dialing Andy, but Fontbutter had had a point. Finding me loopy and loitering by a hedge didn't bode well for my credibility. Right now, I didn't want anything stopping me. I was ready to solve the case of the missing map and Patience Cooper's murder. Hopefully Solder's too.

I opened and scrolled through my contacts, looking for someone to call. I wished Emily was feeling better, but then I hit a name I knew I could trust. I pressed it and waited.

"Hello, lady," Clemmie said after two rings.

"Did you mean it when you said you'd help me?" I said.

"Are you drunk?"

"I'm sobering up fast, but I can't drive," I said. "And I need to follow up on some leads sooner than later."

"I'll be right there," she said.

I liked that twenty minutes later, Clemmie did not ask why I was on Cliff Road, my car parked neatly, but the rest of me still a bit trashed. She just opened the door and tucked me in. Even better, she handed me a coffee.

"Black, no sugar," she said. "Where to?"

"Shelly Montague's house," I said. "It's a few streets down, off Cliff. Make a right."

"I know her," said Clemmie, pulling out of her spot. "She's a half-and-half lady."

I wondered what that meant in terms of her potential to kill.

"Why Shelly?" said Clemmie.

"I'm not sure yet," I said, feeling the coffee doing its trick. "Here's what I know. Brenda Worthington stole the bone from Agnes's car and hit Solder on the head with it because she wanted the map. She thought if he had it, the spirits wouldn't rest. She didn't want anyone going down the well or bothering these old bodies. She really believes in this stuff."

"Oh, my lord," said Clemmie. "She killed the man?"

"Turn here," I said. "No! Wait. It's two more streets."

"You're going to get us killed," she said. "Drink that coffee. Then call your policeman and tell him to arrest Brenda."

"Why does everyone keep calling him my policeman?" I said. "And Brenda didn't kill him. Fontbutter said he saw her hit him but not strangle him. She hit him and took the map. Then Fontbutter blackmailed her to give him information."

"We still don't know who killed Solder?"

"First things first. Turn here!"

Clemmie stepped on the brakes and turned left.

"Over there," I said, remembering the front door from our first Girl Scouts meeting to discuss Halloween Haunts. I joined the meeting to give the girls the exciting news that John Pierre Morton had loaned us his house.

Clemmie turned off her lights but kept the car running.

"I'll be right back," I said.

"Hurry up," she said. "This is creepy."

I ran across Shelly's front lawn and up to her door. The lights were out, but I knocked.

I knocked again and saw the curtain of the front window part. A moment later, she opened her front door.

"What do you want?" said Shelly. "I won't tell Peter, if that's what you're worried about."

"I have one question," I said, sticking my foot across her threshold so she couldn't close the door on me, "How did the chain in front of The Shack get unlocked to begin with? After all those years. Did you know Patience was there?"

"I don't know what you're talking about," she said.

"Why were you so interested in the Morton house for Halloween Haunts?" I said.

"Because it's a great house," she said, calmly.

"Shelly, a man was killed," I said.

"What does that have to do with me?"

"I don't know," I said. "What does it have to do with you?"

From behind Shelly, a soft voice cried out.

"Mommy?"

Shelly looked behind her and up the stairs.

"I've got to go," she said.

I kept my foot where it was.

"Why did you want to use the Morton house?" I said. "If you don't answer me, I'll make sure you answer the police."

Shelly looked back up the stairs.

"Coming, honey," she said.

She turned back to me impatiently.

"Fine," she said. "The other day, I was cleaning, going through old boxes that have been passed around my family forever. I came across one diary written by someone named Mary Backus. I was going to donate it to the Historical Association, but something caught my eye. The diary mentioned a man with some old-fashioned name who was looking for a treasure map in his house. There was an address, and when I heard you talking about John Pierre Morton's house I realized it was the same place."

"And you decided you could poke around for treasure while you led the Girl Scouts?" I said. "I feel like that goes against troop rules."

Shelly rolled her eyes.

"It didn't matter anyway," she said. "The treasure was down Old Holly's well, right? I tried to ask that producer about it tonight, but I give up. I'm not meant to be rich. I'm just stuck with a good-for-nothing ex-husband."

"Give me the diary," I said.

Shelly grumbled and shut the door, barely missing my foot.

A moment later, she peeked through the curtain to make sure I was gone.

I waved.

The door opened again. Shelly shoved a book into my hand and slammed the door.

I walked back to Clemmie's car, feeling good.

"Do you have a Ziploc baggie?" I said when I got back into her car.

"You think I drive around with Ziploc baggies?" said Clemmie. "What is that?"

"Hopefully more clues," I said, "but we need to keep moving."

"Where to now?"

I opened my phone and looked up "Nantucket Lore & Legends." I dialed Brenda.

No answer.

I sent her a text.

I need to see the map.

She did not respond.

"The Morton house," I said to Clemmie.

"I'm not going to look at that skeleton," she said. "I hate skeletons."

"I'll only be a minute," I said.

"You told me you needed help," she said, driving to the house. "So far, all I am is a chauffeur for a drunk lady. I want some action."

"If all goes well, you'll have more action than you can imagine," I said.

"Good," she said, heading across Main Street. "But no skeletons."

"Got it," I said.

I started to read the diary while Clemmie drove. The cover was similar to the one Agnes had photocopied for me, but it did not have initials on it. I surmised from the dates and stories that I was reading another diary of Mary Backus, written at the same time as the one Agnes had given me.

A few minutes later, we reached the Morton house. The lights were out. I took it the Candleers had left. Then I saw movement through a window on the second floor, from the room I'd used as my workshop. It wasn't Tinker.

"Gotcha," I said.

"Who?" said Clemmie.

"Be right back," I said.

I jumped out of the car and shot up the stairs. At the landing, I turned on the hall lights.

As I suspected, Brenda peeked around the doorway.

"Don't be scared," she said.

"I need to see the map," I said. "The only place it can be is with you. That's the safest place, isn't it? Don't worry. I won't take it from you. I just need to see it."

Brenda looked me squarely in the eyes. She reached into her blouse and pulled out the map. I took a few pictures of it with my phone. As I did, I noticed that the stitching seemed hesitant in certain places. As if the X had been sewn in several times, in different areas, before landing in its final place.

"Are you sure there isn't anything else you want to tell me?" I said, handing the map to her.

"Like what?" she said, retreating into the room.

"Like the tree?" I said. "Old Holly found the axe under his porch."

"How did you know?" she said, sitting on the rocker.

"You said you scurried around Old Holly's property after you left Peter in The Shack," I said. "I sat up on Old Holly's roof the other day. It would have been a maze to get to that well any other way except the path my cousins and Kyle had made. The only way you could have snuck back there without any of us noticing was if you'd been there before. You knew the lay of the land."

Brenda looked at her hands.

"I was protecting the dead," she said. "I went to chop the tree down before your excavation, after the men cleared the path. I was hoping when you arrived the next morning and could not get through, you'd all come to your senses and leave poor Nancy alone. But I couldn't get the tree down, so I hid the axe under the porch and left. When I overheard you talking about the map, I knew I'd been summoned by the spirits. As I passed the tree, I gave it one more push. This time it toppled down. I had no idea that the woman would get hit. I didn't know she was there. I wasn't trying to kill anyone."

Brenda burst into tears.

"Lock the front door behind me," I said. "I'll be back in a few."

Leaving the Morton house through the kitchen door, I hopped across the backyard to The Shack. Once inside, I turned on my phone's flashlight. This time, I was not interested in history. I needed a tool.

I searched the ground until I found the spade I'd used to take down the Cooper's Candles sign—the spade that had been my tool when I started the entire chain of events.

Armed, I jumped back into Clemmie's car. My senses were strong again, my inebriation no longer an issue.

"What's next?" said Clemmie.

I opened the photo of the map and showed it to her.

"We find the X," I said.

Easier said than done. I had no idea what I was looking at.

"I hope it's a lot of money," Clemmie said. "If we find it, can we keep it?"

She started the car.

"Where are you going?" I said.

"To Hummock Pond," she said. "The X is out by Ram's Pasture."

"How do you know?" I said.

"Kyle and I go there for picnics," she said. "There's a clearing back there that we love. Just where that X is. It's a spot that's not for tourists. We love it."

I was happy I'd called Clemmie, the wife of a man who knew the island's flora and fauna, its nooks and crannies. I had a feeling we were about to find ourselves a treasure, one that, in turn, would hopefully help us capture a murderer.

Twenty minutes later, we were bouncing down a dirt road that my Beetle would have flat-out died on. As we were nearing the beach on a dirt road, Clemmie suddenly pulled left and headed over a field.

"We don't do this during the day," she said. "We walk. Even Kyle has no interest in getting hassled for being the only pickup in the middle of an empty field. But I've always wanted to do this. He's going to be so jealous."

"Are we almost there?" I said, balancing myself against the dashboard.

"Hang in there," she said. "You dragged me all around. Now it's my turn."

With one more turn, we found ourselves in an enclosed field.

"What a rare find," I said, jumping out of the truck.

"You can bring Peter," she said. "We won't mind. Kyle found it once when he was doing a job."

Clemmie turned on her phone's flashlight.

"Where to?" she said.

I looked at the map again.

The X was in a circle of trees like the one we were in. It was truly a miracle that the land had not been touched. I held the map in the same direction we were in, hoping that Patience had taken geography into account. The X was in the upper-right corner of the field.

"Come on," I said.

Clutching my spade, we ran across the field. In the area the map had indicated, we began to look around for something, anything.

"How long ago was that map made?" she said after a few futile minutes.

"Over a hundred years ago," I said.

"Let me call Kyle," she said. "He'll know."

I kicked around the ground while Clemmie told

Kyle about the map and about where we were. When she hung up, she marched into the brush.

"Where are you going?" I said.

"The plants grow," she said. "The circle was probably bigger back then. Kyle said to walk in about five feet. That's where the original X probably pointed to."

"Genius," I said, taking a similar path a few feet away. I never needed the spade.

A few feet into my search, my foot hit something. I looked down to see a pile of wood. I flashed my phone onto the unusual configuration and realized that each piece of wood was about three inches wide and two feet long; they were fastened together into a frame with a flat, rotting bottom. I thought it might be an old box when I noticed two other, curved pieces of wood below it.

I was looking at the remains of what could only be described as a cradle. One of the rockers had fallen off. The bottom was cracked and rotting, but it was an old cradle, without a doubt.

I sat by the relic and opened Mary Backus's diary. A few minutes later, I had the answers to the story of Patience Cooper and Nancy Holland.

"Why are you sitting here? I'm looking everywhere. I can't find a thing," said Clemmie, sitting down beside me. "Look at this! It looks like a cradle."

"Shelly didn't understand Mary's diary," I said. "She didn't understand the treasure. Emily and I had the right idea the other day. Patience had a baby boy. She gave him to her friend Nancy to protect him from Jedediah. They moved the child from place to place so that his father couldn't find him. Each took turns caring for him. And they passed the map back and forth, each time with a different location about where the baby was. That explains why there were pinpricks on the cloth."

"How did Mary know about a baby if it was such a secret?"

"Because Mary was Jedediah's lover," I said. "This was her real diary, with all the good stuff. The diary I found at the library had the same dates as the entries here, but a completely different story—one that would cover her tracks in case anyone ever became suspicious about her and Jedediah."

"What a witch," said Clemmie.

"Mary was the one who left Nantucket with Jedediah. In the first diary I read, she wrote about her excitement about an upcoming visit to her cousin in Louisiana. In the diary I read tonight, she wrote that she was sad for her parents that she would never make it there. They'd never know that she was heading to sea with her one true love."

"Oh, boy," said Clemmie. "Bad choice."

"She was no saint," I said. "She and Jedediah killed Patience and buried her in The Shack, where we found her. Then he went to get the baby, his treasure, from Nancy. She must have killed herself, with the map, to save the child from discovery. Jedediah got the money, but at least he left without the child."

"She was a good friend," said Clemmie.

"The best," I said, missing Emily. I was so happy Victoria had come into my friend's life, but now I decided to do a better job helping her and Neal.

"I hope someone found the baby," said Clemmie.

I looked back into the cradle, happy that, for a change, there was no skeleton with my discovery.

Clemmie and I both looked across the field. There was movement ahead, but I couldn't see what it was. Clemmie saw it too and grabbed my spade.

"Stella?" I heard Andy say.

"Andy?" I said as his form emerged from the darkness. "What are you doing here?"

"Kyle Nolan called me," he said, finding us. "Clemmie, your husband is worried about you. Right now, I have my officers looking for Brenda Wentworth. Please don't tell me you're wasting my time."

"We figured out the mystery of Patience Cooper and Nancy Holland. And we found the treasure. It was a baby." I showed him the photo of the map and the cradle. "The husband married and killed women for money; he jumped from ship to ship between marriages, which is how he got away with his life of crime. Then he had a baby with Patience. She realized she married a monster, so she hid the child. She and her friend shared in the baby's care and passed secret information about his whereabouts in domestic linens Jedediah would never look at. Finally, he took the money from the Petticoat Row ladies, killed his wife to cover his tracks, and took off with his lover."

"How did you get this photo?" he said.

"That's all you care about from that story?" said Clemmie.

"I got it from Brenda."

"I knew it," he said. "Were you hiding her?"

"No!" I said, "But I've got to go. I promised Clemmie I'd show her a good time tonight. I am having a little party in about an hour. I highly recommend that you come on by. In fact, I'll deliver Brenda. Ready, Clemmie?"

"Kyle is really missing out," she said. "Can he come?"

"See you in an hour?" I said to Andy.

"What are you up to?" he said.

"You worry too much," I said. "I promise you will have a great night if you come."

"It's my job to worry," Andy called out as Clemmie and I took off across the field.

Chapter 24

"We're catching a thief, right?" said Clemmie as we climbed into her truck. "We're not really having a party. I'm not dressed for a party."

"Why can't we have a party and catch a thief?" I said.

"I don't know what to wear to that kind of event," she said, driving us across the field and back onto the dirt road.

I called Peter. Thankfully, he answered.

"Drop everything," I said. "I don't care what it is. I have an emergency need for as many hermit crabs as you can gather and get to the Morton house in the next twenty minutes."

"I'm your man," he said and hung up.

Love that guy.

"By the way, I still think it was Brenda," Clemmie said. "I'm with Andy. Are we going to tie her up and then have a party? Throw hermit crabs on her? That's sick, Stella. I expected more from you."

"Brenda's not guilty," I said. "Fontbutter gave her

an alibi. He confessed that he saw Brenda run off with the map after hitting Solder. I remember that the police arrested Brenda once for trying to stop someone from tearing down an old house. If you look at her actions, they all point to one thing: protecting the past. First, she tried to sabotage the path my cousins and Kyle had made. It was cold, dark, and windy that night, and she could not quite pull it off, so she gave up and hid the axe under Old Holly's porch. She wasn't worried about anyone finding it, because she hadn't succeeded. The next day, however, she finds out from Peter that there's going to be a Netflix special, and she loses it. She heads back to Old Holly's, where things only get worse. She sees Agnes has stolen Patience's bone and rescues it, so to speak. Then she hears us talking about the map. By the time she succeeds in knocking over the tree, her mission knows no bounds. She hits Solder with the femur, takes the map, and hightails it out of there, escaping by the canoe."

"So Brenda is going to be a guest at your party?" said Clemmie.

"I'm not worried about Brenda," I said. "But, sure, she's invited."

"Who else?" said Clemmie.

"Our suspects," I said.

"Kyle's got to come to this," she said. "He's going to divorce me if he misses this party."

"OK," I said. "Our suspects, and Kyle. And Peter."

"And Andy," she said.

"Hopefully."

"And who are our suspects?"

"Leigh, Bellows, and Fontbutter."

"Why them?" she said.

"Because they have weaknesses in their stories," I said.

"What are these weaknesses?"

"Leigh could have knocked over the tree, strangled Solder, and then pretended she was stuck. She says she would never kill Solder, but we only have her word for it. "

"It's her," said Clemmie. "I always thought it was her. Didn't I tell you at The Bean?"

"It could also be Fontbutter," I said. "He could have killed Solder when he returned from chasing Brenda. With Solder gone, no one could vouch that Brenda had taken the map. And then he could take over the show with Leigh, as he has."

"I never thought about that," she said. "He was smart to tell the truth about Brenda. Then no one thinks he's lying. A lie of omission is what they call it. I watch *NCIS*."

"And then there's Bellows. Why did he return to the scene of the crime? Of all of our suspects, he's the only one who has a history of violence. He fought with an officer in New Bedford in order to get access to what he considers his own realm of historical artifacts. If you ask me, he and Brenda have a little too much in common that's not healthy."

"Do you know which one of them did it?"

"I think I do, but I'm not going to take any chances," I said.

"How about the candle ladies?" asked Clemmie. "Can we invite them?"

"Sure," I said. "They can handle themselves."

"And definitely Shelley," said Clemmie with a laugh. "I'd like to see the look on her face."

"And Emily," I said. "She'll never forgive me if she's not there."

At this point, we were pulling up to the Morton house.

"Party, party, party" said Clemmie. "What is this going to be? Like one of those murder-mystery parties?"

"Sort of," I said. "I need you to set up my wine and cheese. I'll invite everyone."

"I'm on it," she said. "Kyle can bring me a dress. And some extra wine. And Perrier for you. Stella Wright has already sobered up once tonight."

"Thanks," I said.

While Clemmie hustled inside, I typed up a text I planned to send to everyone on my list:

> *Good news. I've found the map. I'm having a few people over for drinks in a half hour. Get over here so we can put our heads together and figure out where the treasure is before the police come and take it. Time is ticking.*

Within five minutes, every person on the list responded that they would be over shortly.

My guest list settled, I got to work on my party.

"Brenda?" I said, when I entered the house.

I ran upstairs.

"You still here?" I said. "I need your help."

The light went on in the bedroom, and Brenda stepped out.

"We're going to catch the murderer," I said. "Do you trust me?"

"I'm not sure," she said.

"What do you have to lose?"

"Well, there's—"

"All I need you to do is collect the candle clocks that are in my workroom and bring them downstairs. Put them everywhere."

"Like the olden days," she said, immediately interested.

"Unplug every lamp, and unscrew every light bulb too," I said.

"I'm on it," Brenda called up to me.

When she disappeared, I grabbed all of the Candleers' spider webs from the second floor. My arms loaded, I went downstairs and out the kitchen door toward The Shack.

Outside, I noticed how bright the moon was. I guessed it was almost full. I crossed the field, excited to set my trap.

Balancing my spider webs on one hip, I pulled at the chain with my free hand. Without a moment to spare, I ran across the room to the hearth. Patience's grave was still covered by a sheet. As I remembered, it dropped about a foot over the edge of the hearth so that some of the hearth's opening was slightly hidden.

"Perfect," I said to myself.

"What is?" said Peter.

"Oh my God, you scared me," I said.

He came into the room carrying a dripping wet bag. Fortunately, the room was dark enough that no one would notice the drops of water, but a wet bag wouldn't do for the plan I had in mind.

"Take your T-shirt off," I said.

"OK," said Peter, "but this is not at all what I was expecting when you called me about hermit crabs. I thought you were working on the murder case."

"I am," I said, taking his shirt and drying the crabs in it. "Here. Hold these a second."

"I'm both fascinated and disappointed," said Peter. "I'm not going to lie."

I laughed, in spite of the fact that I was racing against time to catch a killer.

Lifting the spider webs, I headed to the hearth. Once inside, I turned on my light and searched for stones that were loose in a couple of places. Carefully, I began to tuck the strong but delicate web into the stones.

"Hand me the crabs," I said.

I stuck my arm out of the hearth and felt Peter's T-shirt in my hands. The crabs were squirming around, as I'd hoped they would. When I stood back up, I placed his shirt above the netting and finished tacking the web to the circumference of the chimney. When I'd finished, I had a heavy package resting upon the circumference of the spider web, which was attached at all sides. Above, there were yards more of the spider web.

"OK," I said. "Let's go to a party."

"I have no shirt," he said.

"I noticed," I said, tearing myself away from The Shack and heading back up to the house.

"Hello," said Clemmie when we entered the kitchen. "Look at you two. Kyle, look at these two."

Clemmie had changed. She was wearing a dress. Red. Sequined. Awesome. Her blue tresses were up in a high bun too. Fabulous. Kyle came into the room in a green, silk dress shirt and jacket.

"Kyle, give Peter your shirt," she said. "You can pull off a jacket with no shirt."

"Yes, I can," said Kyle, following his wife's orders.

"Nice shirt," Peter said to Kyle.

"Thanks," he said. "I got it on Amazon. It's a good thread count. I'll send you the link."

"Thanks, man."

"No problem," said Kyle.

"Stella, put some lipstick on," said Clemmie, handing me a tube of bright pink lipstick. "You'll feel much more prepared to catch a killer."

"I can't argue with that," I said, dabbing some on.

"The cheese is plated, and the wine is airing," she said.

Turns out, even while catching a thief, my appreciation for cheese is strong. I took a few cubes of cheddar as Clemmie left the kitchen with generously flowing platters.

"Are you going to tell me what's happening?" said Peter.

"I think it will work best if no one knows," I said. "Everyone? Grab a match, and let's light these candles."

In no time, the house was lit only by candles. I made a few adjustments to the height of my candle clocks, so that they were all burning at the same level, and finished just in time for the first knock at my door.

"What do you want us to do?" said Clemmie.

"All you have to do is drink wine and eat cheese," I said. "The killer will reveal himself without our having to do a thing."

I opened the door to Fontbutter.

"Gorgeous," he said, sober and washed. "Truce?"

"Truce," I said. "Now hand me your phone. No pictures tonight."

Fontbutter looked annoyed but complied.

The Candleers arrived next, and I took their phones, too. I was pleased they liked my décor. I had an ulterior motive for my party, but I had to admit the place looked good. Once again, I found myself thinking about how much I loved the Morton house. I would be sad to leave it.

It took all of about five minutes for the party to assemble. Once everyone's phone was collected, we all gathered in the dining room. I let the guests mingle for another twenty minutes, allowing their anticipation to grow. When the time was right, I lifted a spoon and clinked it against my glass to get everyone's attention.

"Thanks, everyone, for coming," I said. "I have a confession to make."

"You killed Solder?" said Old Holly.

"No," I said, ignoring his bad joke. "My confession is that this is really a surprise party."

"You didn't find the map?" said Bellows. I'd noticed he'd been perspiring more than usual since he'd arrived.

"No, I did," I said.

There was an audible sigh of relief from everyone in the room.

"Where was it?" said Leigh.

Clemmie circled the room and poured more wine into everyone's glasses as I continued.

"Brenda kindly helped me with the map," I said. "But that's only the beginning of the story."

I held up the diary of Mary Backus.

"I came upon a diary earlier tonight that gave me the whole story."

"You mean it was all in her book?" said Shelly. "What did I miss?"

"Turns out, I found more than the map," I said. "I found the Petticoat Row treasure."

I watched everyone's face as I spoke those words. Bellows and Fontbutter looked like they could have sprung from their chairs to grab the book from me.

"The treasure is more valuable than Mr. Bellows even suggested. We found coins, silver, and other valuables that the women had collected.

"Where is it?" said Fontbutter.

"At the moment, Patience is guarding it," I said.

"Nice," said Flo.

"Meanwhile, the police are about to arrest someone for the murder."

Again, I scanned the room. My eyes rested on one person among the group who looked ready to bolt at my words. I decided to go with my gut and turn on the heat.

"Earlier today, I told the police I'd heard about an art dealer in Cairo who'd had shady dealings with Solder. They followed up and said that as a result of my information, they'd found their man."

"Who?" said Agnes, rising indignantly from her chair.

"I don't know," I said, "but I have it on good authority that they are on their way to make an arrest now. Once we have word that he's in custody, we can all take a look at the loot and celebrate."

Everyone applauded.

"This is thrilling news," said Cherry. "I love that we're going to have a private showing."

Most people in the room raised their glass in agreement.

Like clockwork, at that exact moment, all of my candles extinguished themselves.

In a flash, the party was left in pitch black.

"Where are our phones?" said Agnes as everyone voiced their confusion about the darkness. "I need a flashlight. I can't see a thing."

"Can we turn on a light?" said Fontbutter.

"I'm trying," said Leigh. "They won't go on."

"Quiet, everyone," Brenda suddenly said. "The spirits are calling us."

I couldn't have planned Brenda's act any better. The room quieted down, and we sat in the dark. I sipped my Perrier.

I heard Bellows take a long drag on his inhaler.

Fontbutter sneezed.

"You and your cat," he said.

"Patience? Is that you?" Brenda said.

I heard one of the tables the Girl Scouts had set up for crafts begin to shake.

"Shhhhh," she said.

"What the hell is going on?" said Old Holly from one side of the darkness.

"Shut up, Gil," said Agnes, from the other side.

In the midst of the chaos, I made my way across the room and out the door before anyone's eyes adjusted to the pitch black. Quietly, I slipped out the kitchen door, and I ran across the yard under the dark night sky and straight into the even darker Shack.

There I crouched, in the corner of the cold room.

"Come on," I said, growing a little nervous.

I waited.

Then I was rewarded.

A dark figure came into The Shack and headed straight to the hearth. I watched the silhouette feel about Patience's burial place. Having no luck, I saw him duck into the hearth. After a moment, I heard a horrible, terrified scream.

A ghostly apparition, covered from head to toe in the Candleers' cobwebs, flew out of building and across the yard. Tinker ran in circles around it. Finally, the apparition fell to the ground.

"Help me," he said, choking in his shroud.

"Not until you confess," I said.

"I'm being attacked," he said through the white threads. "Patience has me."

"She wants you to confess," I said.

"I did it," he said. "I did it! I killed Solder. Patience, leave me be. Someone help me."

"What is going on here?" said Andy, rounding the house and joining me in the backyard.

"Here's your killer," I said.

Andy walked over to the huddled mass. The figure had crabs crawling all over its spider webbed shroud and was shaking.

As I suspected, there was only one person who had known he'd have to bolt after my announcement that the police had followed up on a lead about a man in Cairo. Only one person would have known the story was false, and that the police would turn to the person who had fabricated the tale. That person would also need cash, and quick, to fund a life on the lam. My description of the treasure I had made up would have been just what he needed.

"Fontbutter," said Andy, pulling the cobwebs off our man.

Chapter 25

Friday night, I circled the craft room at Halloween Haunts. Inspired by Clemmie's party wardrobe, I felt fabulous in a black sequined number I'd ordered online. I enjoyed being the hostess of the party, but I knew that this would be my last night as the lady of the Morton house. I was excited to go home to my own apartment, with a brand-new window, but I knew I'd miss the place.

In my arms, I held Victoria, the beautiful if sniffly baby. True to my word, I promised Emily that I would help out more with babysitting. Emily was delighted. She and Neal were currently making their way through the haunted maze, something they certainly could not have enjoyed with a baby strapped to them.

I waved to a Girl Scout who was manning the bead table.

"Turns out they fumigated the skeleton room. No toxins," I heard a mom say as I passed through the dining room and into the backyard, which we'd decorated with skull-shaped lights.

"Bah," said Baby Victoria, in what seemed like a direct response to the woman. I wondered if the babe had spoken her first words but decided not to let Emily know. She'd never forgive herself.

The backyard had become party central, with everyone wanting to visit Patience before Bellows packed her up and took her to the Historical Association for safekeeping. I popped my head inside The Shack and waved to Leigh, who was surrounded by youngsters as she told them the story of Patience Cooper and explained to them which bone was which. The room, by the way, had not been fumigated.

"Hey," said my cousin Ted.

I turned around to find him standing with Docker.

"How's our favorite cousin?"

"I could be better," I said. "I'm still concerned about this issue of a financial windfall. What's going on with you two?"

Ted looked at Docker, who looked at me.

"If we tell you," Docker said, "you can't tell our mother, OK? She worries."

"Should I worry?" I said.

"No," said Ted with a smile. "We're buying a new truck. Our third."

"We took out a loan," said Docker. "We were afraid it wouldn't come through because we only recently bought our second. But then we got the good news. We were waiting for the right time to tell Mom, though."

"That's amazing," I said, hugging my cousins over Baby Victoria's head.

"If you ever need a loan," said Ted, "we'd be happy to help you figure it out."

"Thanks, but I don't need a loan," I said. "The Wick and Flame is doing well. Knock on wood."

"Not that I want you to leave my place, but maybe you want a mortgage?" said Chris, joining us and looking up at the Morton house.

I admired the house with him.

"Thank you, Stella," said Emily, arriving at my side and taking Victoria back into her loving arms. "It's so great not to feel sick anymore. I'm still catching up on everything I missed. It's hard to imagine that Fontbutter was caught right here, on this lawn."

"How did you know it would be him?" said Ted.

"Fontbutter told me once that his secret was showmanship, but he had a bad poker face. This time, his ambition and greed got the better of him."

"I can't believe Andy let you do that," said Emily.

"He didn't," I said. "And I couldn't tell him my plan. I think it would have been entrapment if he'd known."

"I thought the murderer was going to be Bellows," said Clemmie, joining us with Agnes. "Stella said he knew the map was missing way before anyone else did."

I pointed across the lawn to Brenda Worthington, who was out on bail for assaulting Solder and stealing evidence at a crime scene. She stood next to Jameson Bellows. The two were in deep, animated dialogue with many of the Girl Scouts. They led the first group inside The Shack to see Patience and to explain the positive power of history and spirits, neither of which, I heard them say, should be feared. As the Historical Association's new curator, Bellows had taken possession of the two skeletons and had decided Patience could hang around during Halloween Haunts.

As it turned out, the one mystery I had not known to solve was the blossoming friendship between Brenda and Bellows. It did explain, however, how he'd found out the map was missing. Brenda had kept her treasure map and her blackmail woes hidden from Bellows, but she had let it slip that the map had disappeared from the crime scene. Seems in spite of his love for history, his love for Brenda enabled him to believe that Patience had told her so.

"Where's Leigh," said Agnes.

"She sent me a text today," I said. "She's in New York. She's going to stay there a while and finish the work Solder was starting at the Metropolitan Museum. She really did love him."

"Poor girl," said Agnes.

"So, back to this house," said Chris.

"What about it?" I said.

"You're in love with it," he said with a laugh.

"I really am," I said.

"Maybe it's time to get yourself a real home, Stella," said Emily. "What have you got to lose? If you wait, someone like Shelly will come along and snatch it up. She's had her eye on the place, right?"

"Only because she thought it was filled with treasure," I said.

"I think this place is a real treasure," said Chris. "I could help you make a lot of improvements."

Could I buy a house?

"Hi, gorgeous," said Peter. "Can I talk to you?"

"I'm all yours and in sequins," I said.

"You're killing me," he said, pulling me close to him and taking me to the side of the lawn.

"What would be the three adjectives you would use to describe this house?" I said. "Outside of being the best Halloween Haunt."

"One: creaky," he said. "Two: moldy? Three: creaky. Why?"

"No reason," I said. "What's up?"

"I need your permission to do something," he said.

"Should I get a drink?"

He handed me one.

"Oh, boy," I said. "Does this have to do with why you were so happy the other day?"

Peter's hair fell in front of his eyes, He smiled and looked at the ground.

"The thing is, I have an opportunity to work on a story for a new magazine," he said. "Long format. Investigative."

"Sounds like your dream job," I said, cautiously.

"It's short term. Not a forever thing. They've been calling me for a couple of weeks," he said. "At first I said no. Then they convinced me to at least send them my résumé."

"I guess I've been wondering what you're up to lately," I said. "I knew that something had caught your attention. It's not every day that you are too busy to follow a murder investigation."

"When it comes to murder," he said, "you've

spoiled me. I know I can wait for you to figure it out and hand me the story."

"For future reference," I said, "it's much more fun to figure it out together."

"You know I would have," he said, "but I was brushing up my résumé this time around. The thing is, if I take the job, I'll be in Iceland for two months."

"Iceland," I said, sipping my drink. Gulping it, to be honest. I had not expected Iceland.

"But I'll only go if it's OK with you," he said.

"Of course, it's OK with me," I said. "This is your dream. We'll make it work."

"I'm sorry to bring it up here," he said, "but they called today and said I need to get back to them tonight. They found someone else to hire if I wasn't going to take the job."

"You've got to go," I said.

"I'm glad you said that and, no pressure, but I was wondering," he said. "Do you want to come?"

A laugh that sounded like a firecracker shot out of me.

"I'd love to," I said. "Who wouldn't? It's Iceland for two months. That's a once in a lifetime thing, right?"

"Yes!" he said, hugging me tightly, my feet rising off the ground.

As he did, I looked at everyone gathered at the party. I was shocked by the overwhelming feeling that took hold of me, but I couldn't fight it. When Peter put me down, I knew completely that I couldn't in good faith go with him. As much as I loved him, I wasn't ready to chuck my store and my life for him.

"Oh boy," I said.

"What?"

"If I don't go with you, is it over between us?" I said, shutting my eyes tightly.

"Are you crazy?" he said. "Well, yes, you are. But in a good way. What I mean is, I'll be back if you don't want to come. I don't want to force you into anything."

"Then," I said, still surprised by my words but sure they were the right ones. "I'm going to sit this one out."

"I'll bring you fermented shark and sheep's head and all the delicacies Iceland has to offer," he said. "Thank you, thank you, for supporting me."

"Same to you," I said. "Can you excuse me?"

I walked around the corner of the house and made my own phone call.

"John Pierre?" I said. "Do you have any interest in selling the house?"

"More than you could ever imagine," he said.

"Let's talk tomorrow."

I hung up and sat on the stoop of what might soon be my kitchen stairs. Looking up at the sky, I imagined the clouds that would roll by me from my chaise in the days and weeks to come. I decided right then to buy a diary in the morning. I had kept one in college, but since my business had taken off, I'd had no time to keep up with the practice. After a week of living in Patience Cooper's shoes, I decided to start again. I could see how these private musings and collections of ideas painted stories of individuals and the worlds in which they lived in a way that was unique.

I waved across the lawn to Cherry, Agnes, and Flo, who were wearing matching witch's hats. To my surprise, Old Holly came up to Agnes and handed her a cupcake he'd purchased from the Girl Scouts' outdoor snack table.

"You OK?" said Andy, sitting beside me. "I heard about Peter."

"Think he'll come back?" I said.

"Sure," said Andy. "He's crazy about you."

He put his arm around my shoulder and gave me a knock on my head.

"What's not to love?" he said.

Stella's Favorite Clam Chowder

The secret? Quahog clams which are found along the shores of the Cape and islands!

Try this recipe from
Nantucket Sampler of Recipes from The Homestead
And learn more about the Homestead of Nantucket at www.thehomesteadofnantucket.com/

Ingredients
4–5 thin slices fat salty pork
1 onion
3–4 medium-sized potatoes
1 quart dry quahogs
2 level teaspoons flour
1 quart milk
1 quart water
1 tablespoon butter
Salt and pepper

Directions
Fry pork and remove from kettle.
Fry finely chopped onions and potatoes in the fat until they are golden brown.
Add hot water (1 quart or 3 pints).
Cook 10–15 minutes.

Wash the quahogs, removing the dark part from the stomachs. Chop or grind the quahogs quite fine. Cook with above for 15 minutes. Do not use any quahog water.

Add flour thickening stirred with milk, butter, and seasoning.

This will serve 7 or 8 people.

By Linda Backus
Based on material featured in *Nantucket Sampler of Recipes from The Homestead*, third revised edition, published by The Homestead of Nantucket, 1992.

From Cherry Waddle's Diary

Today's To-Dos . . .

DNA kit. Who am I really related to?
Buy milk, butter, quahogs.
Drop off fresh chowder for Emily. She was look-
    ing pale at Halloween Haunts.
Propose fundraiser idea for Offshore Animal
    Hospital. Flo can help.
Create Instagram post on candle clocks to show
    off my pumpkin candle.

~~Candle Clocks Rock~~ – too cute
~~Telling Time the Old Fashioned Way~~ – makes me
sound ancient

Why Candle Clocks?
You can read a book by candlelight before bed
and not have to worry about a fire later. Set is for an
hour and it will go out on its own!
You can impress your friends – even catch a killer!
– by having all the lights go out at the same time. Ad-
vise making a dramatic announcement right before
the candles extinguish.

ADVICE: Don't use a candle clock if time is of the
essence. They should be called candle timers, not
clocks. Learnt the hard way and missed Stella's final
class.

And, dear Diary, I'm heading to the opening of
Bellows' exhibit tonight. I'm glad he decided to in-

clude so much about Nantucket's captain's wives and the amazing lives they led, from staying home and running this island to heading out to sea with their men. Nantucket women made their mark. Brava!

Acknowledgments

I love puzzling out Stella's mysteries along with her. She is a great character with whom to spend my days. Many thanks, as always, to Christina Hogrebe, Norma Perez-Hernandez, Larissa Ackerman, and Michelle Addo for supporting Stella and the Nantucket Candle Maker Mysteries by making sure that the books find their readers. I am also grateful to Michael Bergmann and Jonathan Putnam, who always, bravely, read my work at early stages and give me the honest truth about what's working—and what's not.

For the writing of *15 Minutes of Flame*, I would especially like to thank Michael R. Harrison, Obed Macy Director of Research and Collections at the Nantucket Historical Association, who kindly answered so many of the questions I had about a bygone world I was trying to recapture. Nantucket is truly a town of generous neighbors, and I am also grateful to Jeanine Borthwick for introducing me to Kristin Campbell and the Homestead of Nantucket, a unique housing alternative for Nantucket's seniors. They kindly shared the clam chowder recipe that was originally featured in their very own cookbook.

Like Stella, I couldn't do anything without my friends and family, so I am sending my everlasting gratitude to them. We had a full house in Nantucket when I was writing *15 Minutes of Flame*, and I appreciate everyone's enthusiastic interest as I developed the story . . . My parents, Rini and Tom Shanahan, are great readers, site scouts, and now salesmen for my book (their friends are the best!). And Steve, Tommy, Carly, and Bandit are the cozy to my mysteries. I love you all so much.